THINGS WORTH BURYING

THINGS
WORTH
BURYING

MATT MAYR

Baraka
Books

Montréal

ISBN 978-1-77186-204-2 pbk; 978-1-77186-219-6 epub; 978-1-77186-220-2 pdf

Cover by Richard Carreau
Book Design by Folio infographie
Editing by Nick Fonda and Robin Philpot
Proofreading by David Warriner

Legal Deposit, 2nd quarter 2020
Bibliothèque et Archives nationales du Québec
Library and Archives Canada

Published by Baraka Books of Montreal

Printed and bound in Quebec

Trade Distribution & Returns

Canada – UTP Distribution: UTPdistribution.com
United States – Independent Publishers Group: IPGbook.com

We acknowledge the support from the Société de développement des entreprises culturelles (SODEC) and the Government of Quebec tax credit for book publishing administered by SODEC.

For my father, who taught me how to be a man.

"During the first part of your life, you only become
aware of happiness once you have lost it. Then an age
comes, a second one, in which you already know,
at the moment when you begin to experience true happiness,
that you are, at the end of the day, going to lose it."

– Michel Houellebecq – *The Possibility of an Island*

FALL

1

A hunter from the south reported the camp. It had stood for fifty years but an outsider believed it didn't belong. He didn't think that maybe it was he who didn't belong. But that's how they are, these southerners. Ignorant to the way things work. They roll into town for a week to hunt our moose and bear and think they know a thing or two. They buy a hat from a tourist joint and think they understand. But I'll tell you this: they don't understand a goddamn thing.

The hunter reported it to the MNR, who referred him to the OPP, and the cop, who was new in town and didn't know his asshole from his elbow, needed me to take him out there. The sun was low, and I wanted to be home with my family, but the rookie cop said it was urgent, so I led him. The trees were an ink-black shadow, wide on the horizon, and the orange-blue sky was as beautiful as it gets. That time between night and day, when the failing light drums up colours out of nothing.

I turned on my headlights, but quickly turned them off preferring to drive by the natural light as long as possible. The cop didn't get the message and lit up my rear-view like a bonfire. I got an eye full of spots and felt like hammering the brakes so he'd rear-end me. My truck sat nice and high and had a steel bumper; it would've caved in the hood of his cruiser, would've made the trip just about worth it.

The gravel road twisted and turned through a fifteen-year-old cutover. The new growth was mostly alder and poplar. They grew like weeds, and a road like this could become over-grown in a few years. That's all it was out here—old cutovers and new ones, untouched timber and new growth, and the roads that connected it all. When I was a kid I memorized them by the yellow kilometre markers stuck into the ground in the deep ditches. Twenty-one—Thompson Road; Thirty-five—Lampson Road. Dozens of roads named after road-builders and foremen. Roads named after lakes and geological oddities. Roads that had numbers and letters, like the pool had run dry. After the logging companies were finished, they became access points for fishermen and hunters. Places where no soul has ever laid a boot print. The real end of the line.

I stepped out of the truck, and the crisp late-October air smelled of rotting leaves. I hadn't seen the cabin in years, and even in the evening light I could see that things hadn't changed. The rusted-out Chevy was parked beside the woodpile where my father had left it, weeds and saplings growing through holes in the fenders and where the bumper met the body. A nylon clothesline hung between two spruce trees. The shithouse was intact. The cabin was fifteen by thirty feet, built from plywood and two by fours. The walls were insulated, and at one time the roof had proper shingles. Now, there was a rotting blue tarp draped over the roof to keep the water out.

If my father were alive, he'd have been standing in the door-way, a glass of whiskey in his hand. He had a nose for weakness, and would've told the cop to go fuck himself. Instead, it was just me and a cop who appeared no older than twenty-two, his brand-new uniform looking like it had never been washed. Rushed into the job like all the other cops who aren't from around here, who see only crimes in the abundance of small liberties being taken. They don't understand that people have lived a certain way their whole lives and want to be left alone. They are tourists, passing through.

"Your father's cabin?"

"My grandfather's."

The rookie cleared his throat and walked over to the cabin. He was confident beyond his years. He had a piece of paper in his hand and held it out like a judge. "I have an order from the Ministry of Natural Resources that this cabin is to be cleared out and dismantled. You've got thirty days."

There were other papers stapled to the door. "You didn't see any of these?"

"I haven't been here in years. Doesn't the ministry handle this type of thing?"

"The ministry is stretched wide and thin with hunting season. So we're assisting." He looked in the window, nearly pressing his nose to the glass. "Thirty days to clear it out and dismantle it."

"You said it was urgent. Thirty days doesn't sound urgent."

"Urgent enough. This has gone on long enough."

I shrugged. "It's not my problem. You want to come back and torch it, be my guest. That's how you guys do things, isn't it?"

"If a cabin isn't taken down by the owner, we do have an obligation to burn it."

"Do what you have to."

The cop stared at me. His eyes held no emotion. He looked at the pastel sky to the west. "Rain is coming. What time you got?"

"Almost seven."

He opened the trunk of his cruiser and returned with bolt cutters, a blow torch and a jerry can of gasoline. "Grab the water out of the back, will you. I don't plan on coming out here again."

"It'll be dark soon."

"Easier to see the hotspots when it's done. It's your choice: come back and dismantle it like the order says, or we burn it now. I can make it your problem, willful disobedience, something along those lines, but I'd rather not. Your family occupied it for over fifty years. I'm sure you spent your share of time here, which makes you culpable. Or, two and a half hours now, and that's the end of it."

I never met a cop I liked, or one opposed to bending the law to serve an immediate need. They had no vision, no creativity. The result of a lack of budget or a lack of intelligence, or both.

But if the cabin didn't come down now I'd be out here again, and that was the last thing I wanted.

"Burn it," I said.

The rook smiled. He snipped the lock and pushed the door. The rusted hinges gave a tired squeak. "Procedure. Need to make sure there are no combustibles. Anything in here you want?"

"Not a goddamn thing."

I stood on the porch while he looked through the cabin. It had fallen apart since my father's death. I'd meant to clear it out but never got around to it, figured there wasn't anything worth keeping. Clumps of old mattress and rotted books. The floor sagged in the middle of the room. My grandfather's whiskey glass, the one with the pewter deer, sat on a shelf above the table.

The cop came out carrying an axe and a hammer, a few other tools. He left the glass. "These are worth saving. Looks like the mice got to the place pretty good."

He circled the cabin, splashing gasoline on the walls. He lit the blow torch and circled again, touching it to the base of the wall every few feet, and in less than a minute, the cabin that my grandfather had built in 1964, and had spent much of his life in, was an inferno.

I watched the flames curl and dance, the heat's intensity making my face hot and tight, while the fire's glow eclipsed dusk's failing light, and its violent, scorching roar drowned out all other sounds. A hot breeze seemed to rise from deep within the flames, like the fire was its own weather system. But there was comfort in its purpose: to destroy something that had once been beautiful, because there was no beauty now, just a sorry structure and an old man's wasted life. Piss on it.

The blue tarp bubbled and popped; the building leaned. The orange flames reached high, and the cabin collapsed in a shower of molten sparks. I watched until it was a smouldering pile.

When it was done, we pushed around the charred debris, and doused the remaining embers. Then the rain started. The rook was right about the timing.

He approached me through the haze of water-logged smoke. "I'd appreciate an escort back into town. I had the GPS marking my tracks out here, but the signal is sketchy, and these roads all look the same."

I turned onto the main road at kilometre thirty-three. Left went into town, right led further into the bush. The cop's head-lights never drifted more than fifty feet from my bumper. He didn't want to lose me. He was smarter than I thought. This vast rugged land, beautiful from a distance, from inside your vehicle, was an altogether different beast once the engine stopped and the sun went down. Death, out here, was measured in minutes and in small errors. At least the cop seemed to recognize that.

2

I sat at the kitchen table with a beer and watched Sarah at the sink. Her blond hair was up in a bun, a few strands brushing her neck and shoulders. She was growing it long again, the way she used to wear it back in high school, and the thought of her at eighteen gave me a twinge in my pants. Not that she wasn't beautiful now, she was. Her huge green eyes and fair skin, her tight figure, the best in town. But back then she could stop traffic. Honest to God.

"It's late. Did a machine break down again?"

"No, something else."

She turned her head, her hands in the soapy water.

"I took a cop out to my grandfather's cabin."

"And?"

"He torched it."

"You okay?"

"Fine."

"Well, you knew it was going to happen sooner or later."

I looked at her black yoga pants and bare feet. She'd been working out. She saw me looking at her and smiled, tossing a crumpled napkin at me. "Forget it," she said. "I'm tired."

She came over with a steaming plate of chicken and rice, and took a good long swig of my beer. She sat in the chair, pulling her knees to her chest.

"How's Anna?"

"I let her wait up until nine, and then put her to bed. Told her you'd see her in the morning."

"I miss her, Sarah."

"I know, but these late nights. You know what she's like if she doesn't get her rest."

"It would've been nice if you kept her up."

"Joe, it's nearly eleven. You want to see Anna, come home at a reasonable time."

"You know I don't have a choice. We're running a skeleton crew."

"Work isn't everything."

"What do you think Paul would say to that?"

I felt her eyes on me. She was concerned. She wanted to *talk*. "Do you want to talk about it?"

"No."

"You can say it doesn't bother you, but I know you and—"

"Goddammit Sarah, I said I didn't want to talk about it."

"Suit yourself." She stared out the window.

I put my hand on her knee. The tight, breathable fabric slick under my fingers. I thought of her sitting there without her clothes on, wearing nothing but the red lace panties I'd bought her last Christmas. I imagined the edge of her panties, curving around her ass to where the material thinned and puffed between her legs.

"I'm sorry; I didn't mean that. It's not about the cabin, but how he handled it."

"It's crown land."

"I know it's crown land. I know you can't build anywhere you want to. But the camp has been there longer than that cop's been alive. And he's been in town, what, two weeks? The prick has no regard."

"So what do you want him to do? He can't ignore it."

"But there's a way to do things, and a way not to do them. You don't start turning things upside down the moment you arrive. And he *can* ignore it, because every CO has."

"No cops until now?"

"No."

"He's just doing his job."

"This isn't the city. People respect each other here."

"How do you know he's from the city?"

"Because I know."

"And what does that mean, people respect each other here? Doing things your way?"

I didn't answer. I ate quietly. I loved Sarah, but I never knew if it was enough. She was strong, but she despised boredom. She would take an opposite view just to keep things interesting because she was smarter than me, and I struggled to separate this from her true beliefs. Sarah always teased that when she married me, she took the best that was available. But I had wanted her the moment I laid eyes on her. She was confident. She was pretty in a way that was better than the town. She was well-read and knew about the world. I fumbled in her presence. When she showed me the slightest interest the summer before grade twelve I spent every dime I made on her.

I always knew I'd never leave town. I'd work in the bush like my father and grandfather before him, and if I was going to stay, I wanted Sarah. But living here was a reminder that we could never be more than the accomplishments of our parents, and Sarah wanted more than that. She was writing again, talked about taking classes. There was nothing like that in town, which meant her going away somewhere. And of course there was Anna.

"Anna had soccer today. I talked to the coach about moving her up to forward like you said."

"And?"

"He said she's seven, and that she has lots of time to try other positions."

"It doesn't matter if she's seven. It's habit, she'll fade back there. She needs to be in the action if she's going to improve."

"On Saturday you can tell him yourself. You're still coming?"

"Wouldn't miss it. I told Paul this weekend is off limits."

Sarah finished my beer and grabbed us two more. I remembered my grandfather's whiskey glass on the shelf. He had never owned many things, only a few items of reasonable quality that had lasted a lifetime. "Do we still have that bottle of Canadian Club we got from your mother?"

"As far as I know."

"Still untouched?"

"Unless you're drinking whiskey, and I know that's not it. You're going out there again." She looked at me. "It's fine, I understand. One final drink for the send-off. Do what you need to do, but don't let it get to you. You don't owe your dad anything, never forget that. It's us that need you now, Anna and me." She put her hand on mine, dry from our hard water. She kissed me on the cheek, flashed her big eyes at me. "I'm going to check on Anna, and then I'm going to wait for you in our room."

I watched her walk away. A beer bottle hung loosely from her hand. She was as beautiful as she ever was, so beautiful it hurt to think about it. I'd felt the same way about her since the day I married her—happy that she was mine to hold and touch, but waiting for the day she woke up to the rest of the world.

I have a memory, clear as any other. Funny thing about my childhood, I can't remember much of it. I used to believe it was from the excesses of my youth, the drinking and the fighting, but I've come to understand it as a mental block, a curtain that keeps me from accessing parts of my past. Sarah thought I should see a shrink about it. I told her that would be the day, like I didn't believe in that crap. The truth was I didn't want to see what was on the other side of the curtain.

During the mid-nineties, the population of Black River went from five thousand to fifteen hundred as the mines closed and forestry dried up. The winter I turned nine was the heart of the town's glory years, but my father found himself on pogey because he drank and had a temper and pissed off management one too many times. We scrimped that whole year. We couldn't afford fresh meat or produce. We ate baloney sandwiches and frozen peas instead.

My father had a bull tag, but hadn't shot his moose by December fifteenth, the end of hunting season. On Boxing Day he loaded his truck and said he was going for a drive. When he came home that night, there were flecks of blood on the cuffs of his wool hunting pants. He told me we were heading out first thing in the morning, then he ate supper and went to bed.

On the drive out I already knew what he'd done, but was afraid to ask. We snow-mobiled to the kill site and he told me that sometimes a man has to do things for the survival of his family, that what the law said about killing an animal out of season had nothing to do with right or wrong, and was just a set of numbers decided by a bunch of guys who lived in Toronto and didn't know anything about us. He told me that if he got caught, the ministry would take his guns, truck, and snow machine, and fine him an amount of money he didn't have. He told me that I was man enough to help him carry the animal out, and that a person can only rely on his family when the chips were down.

We butchered the moose in the bush, the snow dyed red around us. We made it to the truck as the sun was setting. It began to snow, lightly at first, then in great billowy gusts. My father said this was a good sign—the snow would cover our tracks to the kill. But the blood, guts, hide, and bones would be found by wolves; no amount of snow could hide them. This I already knew.

On the drive home we took the turn off to my grandfather's hunting camp. He was retired by then, and like many of the men around here he'd worked in the bush. He'd driven a skidder, cut by hand before that, that's how long ago. Built many of these roads.

His hair was long and gray, and he had about a week's worth of beard on his face. He was in good shape, lean and hard, and had the stare of a man who knows his place, and yours too.

I'll never forget the dry heat of the woodstove, the hiss of the old Coleman lantern. His clothes hung from a trestle above the stove. Water dripped from the bottom of his pants.

"Bottle on the table, glass on the shelf," he said to my father. He was cooking his supper. He made me tea with lemon and honey. "Just like the Russians drink," he quipped in a German accent.

The room was simple and tidy. There was a steel-framed bed in the far corner, a canvas tarp draped over the springs and a down sleeping bag folded at the foot. Beside the bed was an oak dresser, and on top was the bolt from his .303 Lee Enfield, removed to let the moisture evaporate from the barrel. The rifle was leaning against the dresser, gun-oil dark. It was an old rifle from the First World War. The stock was shortened and oiled and had a scope. An accurate and reliable gun.

Beside the woodstove was the only upholstered chair in the cabin, a comfy-looking Edwardian deal that sat low to the ground. There was a paperback novel on the seat. A large birch stump, gray with age, was in front of the chair with an axe buried into it. When it wasn't used for making kindling, it was a footrest.

On the opposite wall was a small bookshelf and a few dozen books, all of them used or borrowed from the library. The only window was above a plywood counter in the small kitchen area where my grandfather cooked on a two-burner camp stove. A few pots and pans hung from a crossbeam. There were two lanterns, but only one was lit, and cast sharp shadows about the room.

They didn't talk much. They drank while my grandfather ate his dinner. It was how it always went with them: a bottle of whiskey and things unsaid.

My grandfather had a house in town, but the hunting camp was where he wanted to be. He would spend days out there alone, weeks, living in the bush like some coureur des bois while his family was left to fend for themselves. My father recalled this absenteeism with contempt, even as he did it himself, to his own family. As a boy I recognized his hypocrisy, and it made me hate him. My father said that my grandfather was reliving the old days when he'd first arrived in Canada, the simple life of the bush camp shantyman. He said that my grandfather's heart was out there, but failed to provide reasons for his own absences. If my grandfather went to escape the world, my father went to make sense of his own. Me, I never gave a shit about the place.

My father said, "I heard the ministry's been out here, giving you a hard time."

My grandfather shrugged. "I've seen it before. I've had all kinds try to tell me one thing or another—how to live my life, how not to live it. One time the priest came out, drove his Volkswagen Rabbit the whole way. I don't know how he got it in and I don't care. He told me that my family needed me. You believe that? The balls on that prick. But your mother was happier when I wasn't around, she told me as much, and I never liked being at home, bored me to death. He said I needed to live a life that was closer to my family, closer to God. Look around, I said to him, look at the wilderness. This is as close to God as you're ever going to get. See the thing is, son, is that I've been here longer than any of them, and I have a right to this land more than anyone can say otherwise. And I don't care about their laws. You got your moose, good for you. Never let them tell you what you can and can't do. Now drink up boy, and get a move on. I aim to be out before the sun rises."

On the way out, my father left half the moose, his offering. He was also drunk as a lord. He didn't talk during the drive home, and I could feel his anger, the simmering rage I knew so well as a kid. Always there, on the cusp, paralyzing.

I grew up thinking it was normal to hate anything that didn't fit into your mould of acceptability. That what was different was to be despised. The day Anna was born I resolved to never be the worst of what my father was. There were good aspects, sure, but I couldn't remember them if I tried.

3

I watched from the landing. The green skidder crawled over stumps and downed trees, its huge tires and traction chains making short work of the main skid trail. Water from the morning's rainfall ran in a shallow creek in the trail's right track, down the steep hill. The skidder's operator, Dan Lacroix, looked to his right, careful to avoid the monstrous bog hole where two weeks ago Frenchie had buried his John Deere to the top of its tires. We'd needed an excavator, Dan's Timberjack, and a half-day to get it out, and Paul hadn't called Frenchie since. Four men and three machines. Time was money.

This was Dan's final turn of logs for the day, and I made sure to be here when he finished. I was parked between piles of pulp-logs and the log loader, which was loading a haul truck, its clam-like grapple moving logs like they were sticks. There was a backlog of wood, and I'd made sure to have the haul trucks going all night.

Dan manoeuvred his load beside the smallest pile, lowered the skidder's blade, and turned off the machine. He jumped out of the cab holding his lunch box and thermos and walked to his beaten-up truck at the far end of the landing. I waited for him to organize his things. I watched the day's light wane behind a distant line of black spruce.

I pulled up close to Dan and rolled down the window. "Back to town?"

Dan leaned on the hood of his mud-covered truck, squinting at the noisy machinery before he turned and looked at me.

"Put in a solid twelve today and not much more to come out back there."

"I know. It's all at the road. You guys are making short work of this patch."

Dan lit a smoke. He was unshaven and looked tired. He was a hard worker and I liked him.

I said, "We have this backlog here to clear out, and then we're moving up Laurie Lake way. We're only laying it out now because we just got the contract with that new mill in Quebec. It's taking them a while to get their shit together. Feller-bunchers won't be working until the end of next week, so we won't need you until Monday."

"Next Monday?"

"No, the one after. I know it's a week off, but there's not too much I can do about it. Terry's going to pull the rest of the logs out of the bush here. He's been off since last week; I gotta give him some hours too."

Dan took a long drag on his cigarette, running his thumb across his stubble. I saw where his eldest daughter had etched a smiley face in the thickest part of the dust behind the gas tank of his truck. She was the same age as Anna. They played soccer together. "I understand," he said. "But it's getting tight, Joe, real tight."

"It's been tough all around, but things will pick up with the new mill, contracts are starting to roll in. We should have the whole crew going full steam in a month or two."

"That's great, but a month or two ain't much use when I need the work now."

"I know you do. And I got ten other guys in the same boat. I'm doing my best to spread the work around, but right now there just isn't enough."

"And next Monday, how many days then?"

"Three for sure, maybe five. It depends."

"Lots of things depending these days."

This job was Dan's livelihood. Tonight he'd go home to his wife and explain there wouldn't be any money for a while. They had a new baby, just bought a house. I took this into account.

I put my truck into gear, inched forward slowly. "I'll call you next week with the details. Anything comes up sooner, you're first on my list. You're one of my best guys out here, Dan."

I drove into the vast, clear-cut landscape. The equipment and log piles disappeared in my rear-view mirror, and the scenery turned green and full as the road left the cut and headed into old growth. I remembered the bottle of whiskey behind the seat, and took the turn off to my grandfather's hunting camp, following the grown-in road. I parked outside the wreck of the cabin wondering if I'd made a mistake, but I'd been thinking about him all day, my father too.

Hard liquor, like bush work, runs in my family. I hadn't drunk whiskey since Anna was born. Sarah had seen to that. She didn't mind the beer because it didn't turn me into a madman. But with whiskey, I was merciless. So I gave in, and I never missed it. Today was an exception. It was the way my family finalized things. The only way to send it off proper.

The hunting camp was nothing more than a smudge, its black charred remains flattened to the ground, and in the middle, standing like a miniature steam train, the cast-iron woodstove. Pots and pans were strewn about. A metal chair lay on its side. The frame and springs of the old bed were in the far corner, and looked, in their scorched blackness, almost usable.

I uncapped the bottle of Canadian Club and took a good long swig. I poured most of it on the ruins of the cabin, then let the remaining liquid trickle down my throat. I winged the bottle at the rusted pickup, aiming for the driver's side window, but hitting the front fender instead with a loud thud.

Burning the cabin was about enforcing some futile law. Its purpose was to put you in your place. The wreckage would never leave the bush. The remnants would be left to rust and degrade, but the structure was gone, as though all they wanted was to destroy the roof over your head, prove that the vast crown land belonged to them and not you. They wanted to take away your sense of security. This was the attitude that my father and grandfather had rallied against their whole lives. The unseen turn of the Toronto machine. Listen close, my father would say, and you can hear their arrogance blowing across the land, threatening your livelihood. To them, we're nothing but a pile of moose shit scraped off a boot. Remember this when they come to you smiling, full of promises, asking for your vote.

4

Anna ran down the field in a flash of red socks, black cleats, and blond hair. She took the ball into the offensive zone, cut into the middle, and headed for the goal. She drove straight through two defenders, and let go a shot that soared into the top of the net.

I cheered and clapped, yelled her name. I was a hopelessly proud father. She smiled triumphantly.

"You see that, Sarah. Just like I said, she was dying back there."

Sarah gave me a look. To her it was just a game, and she reproached me for pushing Anna from a young age. But there was potential in Anna, real potential. Sarah didn't see how it was all connected, that the way Anna handled things on the field would relate to everything else in her life. I wanted her to have that edge, that desire to realize something extraordinary. This had to be ingrained at a young age, or else never captured. I knew from experience.

There were parents all along the sidelines. At the far end I recognized the cop from the other day. He was wearing a baseball cap, plaid shirt, and denim jacket, and if I didn't know any better I'd have sworn he was local. I wondered if he was here with his family, though I thought he was too young to have a family. I walked over to him.

"Officer Taylor," I said.

He had a couple days' stubble on his cheeks, and looked older than when I'd met him. This time I guessed his age at around twenty-seven, a few years younger than me. He shook my hand but was unsure. He'd forgotten my name.

"Joe Adler."

He attempted a smile. "Yes, I remember."

"Your kid playing?"

He pointed at a young boy on the periphery who was running around kind of aimlessly. "That's him there, number four. You?'

"That's my little girl up at forward, number ten."

"The girl who just scored? She can run."

I shrugged. "She's doing okay."

"My boy's never played before," he said. "We just kind of threw him into this when we moved here." He looked away from me, embarrassed by his son's ability.

"I'm sure he'll get the hang of it. So where are you from?"

"Mississauga."

"I guess this is a big change for you."

"It sure is." He laughed and for a moment he let his guard down and I saw who he was. I recognized the resentment in his eyes. He thought he knew me and this town because he'd spent a bit of time here, and because it was small. Cops think they're quick studies, have some special ability to read people and situations. But the truth is that they're no different than anybody else—they have instincts and gut feelings, and experience that shapes them. They've just learned how to act confident in the face of confusion, while the rest of us wear it on our sleeves.

And Officer Taylor, I knew why he was here, everybody did. The OPP gave bonus pay to cops willing to work in the remote north. The ones who came were always young, straight out of school, and never stayed longer than a couple of years. They'd put in their time, then leave for greener pastures. Their yards were disasters, their community involvement nil. They were like geese heading south, made a lot of noise and left only shit piles in their wake.

"What do you think of the town so far?" I asked.

"No complaints." He spoke without looking at me. He was aloof, an unforgivable trait in a small town, because it is inevitable that our paths would cross again and again. Officer Taylor hadn't yet realized that. I thought that maybe it was time someone told him.

Anna was carrying the ball up field. She looked untouchable. She made me proud.

"So I take it you've done it before?"

"What?"

"Burned a cabin. You looked like you've done it before. Did they ship you in special? Burn all the camps north of Superior? Never been cops involved until now, and the first one that comes along lights it up like it's just another day. Not that the cabin was important to me, but it's the principle of the thing. Just a word of advice, for what it's worth. You shouldn't start turning things on their ear before you've introduced yourself. I've seen a lot of you come through, and it's always the same story. You've got some time to put in here, try to tread a bit more lightly. Otherwise you'll find people can be non-compliant when they want to be. It will help to have the town on your side, and not against you." I smiled, and reached out my hand. "It's nothing personal, just the way it is."

Officer Taylor didn't shake my hand. He stared at me with those detached cop's eyes. Eyes like nothing in the world could get to him. But he was young and inexperienced and very far from home.

"Maybe that's why they sent me up here. The hunting camp was illegal. There's nothing more to be said. People can't break the law and expect to get away with it. I let one thing go, and word will get around. This town needs to know I mean business. I'm not here to make friends; I'm here to do a job."

"This isn't some park in the city," I said. "This is crown land, and the camp's been there since before you were born. What are you trying to prove?"

"I'm just doing my job. Let your friends know that, Joe Adler. You have a nice day." He walked away from me, and I knew he wouldn't forget me. He'd be pulling my record on his next shift.

I went back to Sarah. She could tell something was wrong. "Who was that?"

"The cop."

"What did you say to him?"

I shrugged. "It doesn't matter."

I watched Anna on the field. She had a way out there that was enchanting, more fluid and instinctual than the other kids. I was right when I'd told the coach to play her up front. All that ability just waiting for release. I called things out; I righted wrongs. I never knew if this came from a sense of justice, or from some other, less honourable place. If it stemmed from love or hate, or a stubbornness to stay a course once it had started. Sarah squeezed my arm. She knew me better than anybody. "Hey," she said. "Promise me you'll leave it alone."

I nodded, but I couldn't shake it. "I promise," I said, and I really meant it.

When I was twelve I had this notion that I wanted to be a cop. My father, home on a Sunday afternoon because it was pouring rain, drunk in front of the television, put an end to the idea right quick. Grinning, nearly snarling, he said: cops are nothing but yes-men with guns. They don't have a brain of their own, need to be told what to do. Mouth-breathers, all of them. He said all this while lying on the couch with his head turned and a beer in his hand. That what you want for yourself? You want to toe the party line, take it in the ass for thirty-five years, praying for retirement? Is that a life? See how happy you are then. Besides, he said, you're an Adler, it's in your blood to defy those pricks at every turn. Because the minute you surrender what you know in your heart is your God-given right, you will know that there is no hope for you or this family. And if you don't know it, I'll be there to tell you so. You can believe that. It's in your blood, Joe, nothing can change that.

He goaded me like this until the tears ran down my cheeks, and then he started in on that. I knew what he was doing. He wanted me to leave so that he could drink in peace, but I refused. I sat there, digesting his shit, waiting for him to come around. He always did.

5

I loaded five rounds into the magazine and walked to where the gravel road ended in a small round-about. I stood there quietly, looking and listening for some sign. It was cold and wind-still; a dusting of frost covered the ground and slash piles by the edge of the road. A shallow puddle was frozen to the bottom, and beyond the tree line the rising sun penetrated the fog hovering over a small pond, looking like steam.

I followed a skid trail covered in knee-high grass down to the pond. I walked in the middle, careful to avoid deep ruts forged by the tires of heavy machinery when the trees were harvested. With each step, frost clung to my boots and the knees of my wool pants. Soon my pants would be soaked through, but in a couple of hours the mid-morning sun would take away the chill, and the dampness too.

On the shoreline were old moose tracks hardened like clay moulds. I found a nice stump among the tag alders surrounded by tall yellow grass with a good view to the water. I took off my orange vest and laid my rain gear on the stump to keep my arse dry. I scanned the shore looking for movement, listening for the snap and crash of a heavy animal.

As the sun rose higher, the fog thinned, and streamers of light reflected the humidity, creating pockets of colour here and there. Each time I came out here I searched for a moment of absolute stillness, my entire world what my senses could process. A quiet so loud it was like a rush of white noise. The only place I was ever able to live in the moment.

Paul Henri poured himself a whiskey. He looked at me, and I raised my hand. What the hell, one wouldn't do me any harm.

"That cop is an uncompromising son of a bitch."

Paul laughed. "You sound just like your father."

"Yes, he would've said something like that."

"Except he'd be drunk by the time he said it. You get to that point without a drop. I'd hate to be on your bad side."

"Maybe that's why I don't touch the stuff."

Paul stood beside his woodstove sipping his whiskey. "He's been making the rounds, making himself known. Came into the office the other day saying he don't like our haul trucks parked on the side of the highway across from the coffee shop. I asked him if he was kidding and he said it was a warning. Never mind it's the only place in town to get a coffee. Never mind it's an hour to the next town. I talked to a few guys. He's stepping on toes everywhere he goes. Wants to make a name for himself. What the hell you going to do? He'll get his in the end, is what I subscribe to."

I saw dried blood around Paul's wrists and hands. He'd washed most it off, but the remnants were there. "You get one today?" I asked.

"Yesterday evening, back at a creek. Took me all day today to haul it out. Had to cut trail, saw the quarters in half. I'm not as young as I used to be."

"I was out this morning. Nothing but old tracks. Bull?"

"A big one. He's hanging out back."

"Good weather for it. You can leave those quarters for four, five days in this cold. Don't have to worry about the shit flies laying eggs. You carry him out yourself?"

Paul nodded.

"I could've helped you."

"Not on your day off. I need you in the bush, and I need you rested. You're my eyes and ears out there."

I smiled. "Shouldn't you be trying to secure contracts instead of hunting?"

"Listen to him. One compliment and he thinks he's the boss."

I put my hand to my chest, feigning hurt.

"That's why I asked you to come over. Not that I don't like your company, but I do my drinking alone. The mill in Quebec will be up and running sooner than I thought. I need you to get the Laurie Lake cut going tomorrow. We'll meet at the shop at five to go over a few last-minute details. Next week, I'm going to Quebec. There are a few more mills out there I'm meeting with. You meet these operators in person it's a whole different game. Telephone call means jack shit. I want them to know we can provide anything they need. Timber, pulp, chips, whatever. We're in the wood business and I don't care how we do it. I'll need you to run things here, in the field. You'll be the point man. I wanted to tell you to your face, because I want to be clear about the situation. We all know it's been a tough year, but it's worse than that. Without the contract with this new mill we're dead in the water. That's why things need to run smooth. No hiccups, no delays, no quality issues. You got a man not pulling his weight, I want him gone tomorrow. It's your call while I'm away. You'll carry the big stick. Just deliver the wood on time. If we can deliver above and beyond, they'll want to work with us again. I want Northern Timber to be the first company they call when there's an order to fill."

I nodded. "I got it."

"Good. You want to see my bull?"

We went out to the encroachment behind his garage to look at his moose. He recounted his story of the hunt, how he'd been working the bull all morning, calling him in. "He was a big boy. Got mighty pissed when he came down to the creek and no piece of tail."

The quarters were hanging from a two-by-four nailed between sturdy poplar trees. They were huge even cut in half. It would've been a hard day's work to pull that animal out of the bush. Paul was in his fifties, but he was stocky and strong. Never been inside a gym, had that farm-boy strength that the lifestyle demands.

The hides were all skinned off and in a heap in the back of his pickup. "I'll take those to the reserve on my way out of town," he said. "The Ojibwa use them to make moccasins and mitts, sell them to the tourists that come through in the summer."

"You keeping those antlers?" The head was sitting on a stump. It was a fifty-inch rack at least, two shovels on either side, a real beauty. The eyes were cloudy and the tongue was hanging out the side of the mouth. It was a massive head. It would've been a feat just to carry that head out of the bush.

"Couldn't be bothered to clean it out. It would be a crime to leave it, though. I don't leave anything behind but the guts. Heart and liver, they're the first things I eat. If the Ojibwa don't want it, I'm sure someone in town will. Nice set, that one."

The sun was beginning its descent, and the temperature was falling. It would be below zero tonight. I looked at the clouds forming in the west and knew that snow was coming, the first of the year. The air smelled like winter. Paul was carrying wood inside his house. He knew the snow was coming too. His wood pile stretched from the fence line deep into the encroachment, enough wood for two winters. I grabbed an armload and followed him inside.

"You ever think about those people? The world they come from?"

He shrugged. "The cop, you mean? They don't know. Here, you got a problem, you work through it, find the means to settle it. You solve it with your bare hands. Life out there is automatic. People don't know who they are anymore."

The bare trees were jagged black lines on the horizon. The crisp breeze touched my face; I felt winter approaching in my bones. I took a piss outside Paul's garage, and then stood there, watching the sun go down. I wanted it to snow the way it did when I was a kid. The snow and the cold, the ice. The smoke from the chimneys that hovered low in the morning. There was something primordial about it. I loved winter like a child.

6

I was at the shop at ten to five and Paul was already there, had it all laid out. We needed machines and men in the field. We needed a mechanic at the shop to work on the skidders. Suddenly there was money to spend. I made calls, got things moving. We were starting in a new area, and the first thing to do was build the road.

I called Dan Lacroix at six in the morning, and he was eager for the work. Said he'd be at the shop within the hour. I sensed the relief from the other end of the line. I heard his new baby crying.

I'd already flagged the backline of the cut and the road in. In road building, you look for the path of least resistance that does the least amount of damage, and avoids waterways. Crossing a creek is a headache. You need culverts and permits; you expose yourself to the bureaucracy. If you have to cross a river, you find another way in.

It was late fall and the ground wasn't frozen yet. The new road would harden up with the cold weather, and once the snow fell and the dozer went through, it would be as firm as concrete. We had five months until the spring thaw, and at the end of it we'd be just about finished.

Most of my guys could operate different machines; I required this of them. A flexible operator gave me options. I could move guys around while keeping the machines right where they were. I could take a guy with a particular skill and move him somewhere, and someone else could come in and fill his spot and a machine would never be idle. A machine sitting idle is like money burning. Generally, I disliked owner-operators, and resorted to them only when our internal capacities were full up. The exception was truck drivers. Nearly all of our truckers owned their own rigs.

Dan Lacroix could only drive a skidder, but he was a hard worker and I liked him. I wanted to see him do well. I'd made it a point to get him trained on the excavator before the road was pushed through, but there were still a few logs to pull out of the old area, and it was a one-man job. This would've been Terry Pike's job, but I needed him running the feller-buncher cutting right of way. This was why Dan was by himself.

I spent Monday making calls and arranging things, and Tuesday I was at the designated landing area by five-thirty, waiting for the guys to show up. It was pitch black outside, and I looked at the cut map by the light in my truck, drinking my third cup of coffee. The cut was straightforward, nothing too ominous about it. It wasn't like the last area that had a big chunk of Canadian Shield exposed and was chock full of cliffs and steep ledges where machines could flip and roll and get stuck. The winter, too, would make things easier. I was hopeful that the contract with the mill in Quebec would turn things around. There were good men who needed work, and deserved better.

Terry Pike was a Newfie; there were plenty in town. Most came over in the eighties when the fishing industry tanked. Hard-working men looking for decent paychecks. Labourers, all of them. Newfies came over in groups. Two brothers, then the cousins. Then brothers in law and second cousins. Jobs guaranteed by word of mouth. If a man is a hard worker, chances are his brother is too. And a hard worker will never vouch for someone who isn't a hard worker, family or not. This I know. They found jobs in mining, but that work isn't for everyone, and a lot of them came to work in the bush. I knew a man—Charlie McCove—worked in the mine for twenty-five years, a foreman. One day, he just up and quit and came asking Paul for a job. Paul said, sure I can give you a job, but you aren't going to be making what you made in the mine. I gotta start you out on the bottom like everyone else. It was a fifty percent pay cut, but Charlie didn't care. He was happy to be out of the mine. The darkness, he said to me once, the fucking darkness all the time. I work graveyards for a month in the winter, I never see the sun, never see my kids. What kind of a way to live is that? Charlie was a Newfie too, came from a long line of fishermen. The ocean on a summer day, the crystalline sun. I could understand his sentiment. The miners all said the job took ten years off your life.

But bush work has its own challenges. A heavy equipment mechanic works on an engine in minus forty with his bare hands. That's minus forty without wind chill. So he works for ten minutes and warms his hands for two, the metal tools sticking to his hands, burning like they were on fire. Something so cold it feels like it's burning; that's the cold we get up here. I never heard of wind chill until I watched the news in a hotel room in Toronto.

The bunchers went in first, a two-man operation. The feller-buncher cut the trees, and the skidder pulled them out. The road would go from the landing area, through a stretch of untouched timber, to the block of trees that was to be harvested. Once the buncher cut the right of way, the excavator and bulldozer followed and did the work of grubbing and building brush mat. The process was exact and deliberate. Mistakes meant big costs for the company, and it was my job to make sure there weren't any.

I watched Terry Pike cut a right of way with the feller-buncher. He had thirty years of experience and was a marvel to watch. He could clear a kilometre of road over flat ground in less than a day. The saw blade ripped through the trees like they were toothpicks. Zing, zing, zing! Three, four, five trees in the accumulators before he turned and deposited them for the skidder. It was something to see, the speed at which the bush could be cut down, metres of it within seconds. The harvesting of trees always brought about mixed feelings in me. The pride of a job well done versus my love of the environment. I watched the forest canopy as the trees were felled, the crash of them overpowered by the groan of engines. Great swaths of sky becoming visible, green for ashen gray. Cutting could be depressing on an overcast day.

I drove to the old cut to see how Dan was making out. I ate my lunch parked beside his truck at the landing. The remaining logs were at the back of the main skid trail, and I waited for him to come out. I leaned back, closed my eyes.

An hour later and Dan hadn't shown. I walked down the skid trail and the soft ground was churned up, black mud seeping from depressions where thin layers of ice had been broken through. It smelled of dark earth and water. The closer I got to the end of the trail, the more I noticed the glaring silence. Dan's skidder wasn't running. An operator shuts off his machine to eat, refuel, or if the engine is kaput. I hoped it wasn't the latter.

The skid trail opened up at a final, circular clearing. The rolling ground, steep in places, was stripped bare, criss-crossed with skid trails that led back to the main trail. Stumps and slash piles of brush. Mountain maple blowing in the breeze. Sporadic trees, mostly small birch, left standing like wounded soldiers.

I saw the skidder in a steep gully near the edge of the cut, and it didn't look right. At a hundred yards I saw its tires pointing unnaturally to the sky and steel stump pan exposed, and realized it was on its roof.

The machine was at the bottom of a steep grade; it looked like it had rolled a few times. I looked uphill and saw a pile of clothes tossed on the ground. They'd flown out of the cab when it rolled over. Dan's extra clothes, his hard hat, and packsack. I imagined for a moment that he wasn't inside, that he'd gotten out and was sitting on a stump having a smoke, thanking his lucky stars. But when I got closer, I saw his body lying inside the cab on the roof of the skidder. Water had seeped inside and pooled reddish brown around his head and torso, his face submerged in the water. I turned him over and he was stiff. There was a wound just above his hairline and a fire extinguisher lying beside him. His face was white, mouth open. Water and dirt were inside his mouth. I checked his pulse, and it was gone. His face and neck were freezing cold. Dead since morning, I figured. There was nothing I could do for him. I took off my coat and laid it across his body.

I looked inside the overturned skidder's cab. The seatbelt wasn't engaged; Dan wasn't wearing it. There was a load of logs in the grapple, wedged between a stump and the overturned skidder. It looked like he'd been side-hilling, hit a stump and the momentum of the load rolled the machine. It had rolled and flung Dan around the cab and somewhere in there his hard hat flew off and the fire extinguisher nailed him in the head. It should have been secured underneath the seat but it wasn't. We'd had them checked that week; he should've secured it in place but he hadn't. The wound didn't look fatal but it was enough to knock him out while the water pooled inside the cab. He probably drowned before he had a chance to come to. There was fuel and oil mixed with the blood and water around the body. I smelled diesel and thought how I'd have to get another machine out here to right the skidder. I thought about this even as the shock of his death sunk in.

I walked back to the landing at a good clip and called the shop from the radio in my truck. Paul got on the line and asked if he was dead for sure, then said he was on his way.

I knew Dan's wife a little. I told Paul I wanted to be the one to tell her.

Some operators never wear their seatbelt, claiming that if the machine rolls they can bail out rather than take their chances getting bounced around the cab. They leave the door open in case. This was against company policy, and I never agreed with it. But some guys still did it, mostly the old-school guys. One thing I've learned is that you can't control what a person does when you're not around, especially if they've been doing things the same way for thirty years.

Paul's truck came up the hill with the paddy wagon in tow. Officer Taylor was driving. No way would a cruiser make it out here. There would be an investigation, which meant the coroner, MOL, and Paul and I recounting what we think happened.

We led the rook out to Dan Lacroix's body. We watched him poke around, connecting things in his mind. He asked me what happened, and I told him what I thought. He asked if our employees usually don't wear their seatbelts, and Paul answered that one. He gave me a look like he wanted to slug the cop.

"We have to get his body out," I said. "Can't leave it overnight, the wolves will get to it."

The cop shook his head. "I can't release the body until the coroner comes out here. What about next of kin? Does he have a family?"

"He's got a wife and two little girls. If you don't mind I'd like to tell her. Better she hears it from somebody she knows."

Officer Taylor nodded. There was no place for our disagreement out here today. "Okay," he said solemnly, "you notify the wife." He looked at Paul. "You stay here until the coroner makes it out. I'll radio it in and meet him at the road."

Paul nodded. He told me he'd take care of the skidder. It was all very calm and unhurried.

7

I stood on Jenny Lacroix's porch and told her that her husband was dead. I became the face of her husband's death. I was the messenger, the company man.

She was in the doorway of her new home with the baby in her arms, and no way to take care of either. She didn't cry, just looked at me square and asked where Dan was. We'd only met a few times. She was saving her grief for after I left. She was a strong woman.

"He's in the bush," I said. "Paul's with him. The police will be here soon. I wanted you to hear it from somebody you knew."

I asked if she had someone in town she could call, and she said there was her sister. I waited in the living room for her sister to arrive while Jenny made coffee. Company was coming and the decent thing was to make a pot of coffee. She was doing what came natural because it was all she could do. She asked if I would hold the baby. She stood in the kitchen with her back to me, shoulders trembling as she looked out the window. The coffee maker sizzled and hissed. The baby cooed, she looked just like Dan.

I lay in bed with Sarah, thinking about Dan Lacroix. Her hand moved on my chest. The news had troubled her greatly.

Several years back I had a scare. I was winching a load and the cable snapped. I hadn't noticed it was frayed. The cable snapped, and whipped inside the cab and nearly took my head clean off. The wire mesh front screen bulged out four inches.

Missed me by centimetres. It was the only cable skidder Paul ever owned, an old-timer he bought for a song and not at all conducive to our type of harvesting. Shortly after that Paul sent it to retirement. Sometimes you can take all the precautions in the world, and things still go wrong. In that case there's nobody to blame but the man upstairs. But there's always something you can do. Things happen in a moment of distraction. Dan knew to secure the fire extinguisher. He knew to wear his seatbelt. Maybe he took it off to reach something and forgot to put it back on. Maybe the bracket for the extinguisher was broken and he couldn't strap it down properly. Either one would've saved his life, which was the worst of it, because it made his death senseless.

"What if it was you?" Sarah asked in the middle of the night, shaking me awake. She was sitting up in bed, trembling. "I keep thinking about Dan, wondering what I'd do if it was you and not him. I know that's selfish of me. Poor Jenny without a husband now, two kids and no way to provide for them, but all I can think is what if it was us."

I looked at the clock; it was two-thirty. "It won't be me because I don't work on machines anymore. I'm a foreman now. I drive around and tell the guys what to do. I'm in my truck all day."

"But things happen. You're hands-on Joe, not one to sit around and watch for very long. I know this about you. So tell me what happens when it's you. What happens to Anna and me?"

I was half-asleep, had to be up in two hours. I just wanted her to be quiet. "Things can happen in any job, Sarah. For Christ's sake I could die driving to the grocery store. What happened to Dan could've been prevented a bunch of ways. It was his carelessness that killed him. Don't you say a word about it, but it's true. I would never be so careless."

"But you don't have just any job, do you? You have to work a dangerous job just like all the other men around here. Goddamn you Joe, you don't care about us." She was hysterical now, crying. I could see that she hadn't slept all night, had just been lying there getting more and more upset until she finally woke me up in a frenzy.

"What else am I supposed to do? You act like this is all some big surprise, when you've known the deal all along. Your dad was a miner, you know how it is. You grew up here."

"I should've known something like this would happen. I hate this fucking town."

"Something like what? A man died on the job. A man that I was responsible for. It doesn't change anything for us. This is where we grew up. You're not making any sense."

"You were drinking whiskey the other day. I could smell it on you."

"Just one with Paul. I didn't want to be rude. And what does that have to do with anything?"

"You're an idiot if you don't see the relevance."

"Well then I guess I'm an idiot."

"Why did you marry me?"

"What?"

"Why did you marry me?"

"Because I love you."

"No you don't. Maybe you did then but you don't now. I'm your trophy. That's all I am and that's all I've ever been to you."

My head was spinning. All I could think was that the accident had really gotten to her. She was unpredictable in this state. I needed to defuse the situation before it got any worse. "I need to sleep, Sarah. Lots going on tomorrow. Let's talk about this in the morning."

She just shook her head like we'd had this conversation a billion times and it always led to the same conclusion. But the thing was that we hadn't. Had I known how she really felt, all the things she'd bottled up inside for all those years, I would have stayed up to talk her through it, to right the ship. But instead I closed my eyes and was asleep in less than a minute. I didn't see that something powerful had built up inside her, and that the death of Dan Lacroix had let it loose. I didn't see that my greatest fear regarding Sarah might actually come to pass.

8

Hunkered. That's the best way to describe the houses in Black River. Small three-bedroom homes with big backyards, shallow basements, and vinyl siding. I remember when the siding guy came through town one spring when the town was booming and people had money to spend. There were three options to choose from: pale yellow, pale blue or gull-wing gray. Ours was gull-wing gray. Shortly after my father had it installed I shot a hole in it with my pellet gun. Actually it was my friend Pat Dermody, but I never told my father that. I would've had him beat it out of me before I rolled over on a friend.

The church was packed with people spilling into the aisles, crowded near the entrance vestibule. Old suits and work clothes. Greasy hats in hands. People had jobs to go to, but the important thing was to show up.

The priest spoke, solemnly at first, then loud and forcefully as though trying to convince the congregation that the resurrection of Dan Lacroix was occurring at that very moment. I couldn't hear his words for the noise inside the church, the sound of a few hundred shifting and sighing bodies, but I knew what he was saying. I had grown up Catholic, and the pattern was always the same. Sorrow followed by acceptance and hope and finally, celebration.

When the service was over, the funeral procession left the gravel parking lot and headed past the hunkered family homes of Allison Avenue, the street I'd grown up on. I felt the need to go because I was his foreman, the one who found his body.

It was ten-thirty in the morning on a beautiful, crisp, wind-still day. Sun and frost and the promise of winter. The cemetery was a kilometre out of town, down an industrial road. There was no parking lot, and the vehicles lined up along the steep gravel shoulder. Just past the cemetery was a sign that said: Private Logging Road, Use at Own Risk!

We gathered around the plot and I saw that it was mostly family. Jenny Lacroix was holding her baby while her other daughter Gracie held the hand of Jenny's sister. They were all wearing black. A wall of black descending in height from Jenny to Gracie. This was something I'd never seen before: a child wearing black at a funeral. It didn't seem right, like it was being forced upon her. Gracie was the same age as Anna. She wouldn't fully understand. It would take days and weeks and years for her to realize that her father was truly gone and never coming home again.

The baby squirmed in Jenny's arms, and this was who I felt for most, the child who would never know her father. She would grow up wondering what kind of man he was, if she had inherited any of his traits. She would think about the moment of his death and the nature of his work. But I knew that Jenny Lacroix would idolize the father to the children. A framed picture in the living room like a soldier lost in battle. Because this is where we grew up, and she knew the deal.

The pall bearers carried the casket from the hearse. The road was freshly graded, and they had to step over a big lip of churned gravel, their shoes sinking into the soft, dark dirt. I knew them all. They were Dan's friends, and some of them worked for Paul. I nodded at Terry Pike. He was close to the Lacroixs and had gotten Dan on with Paul. I wondered if he felt the way I did. Terry bringing him in, me sending him to his death. It was ridiculous of course to think like this. There were a million turning points in Dan's life that had led to the moment when the skidder rolled over and crushed the life out of him. He had been careless. But I had liked Dan, and if I pushed him beyond his ability it was because I wanted him to succeed. There's a saying out here: first one to complain is the first one laid off, and Dan with his family and new house had learned it quick.

The priest began and I held my girls' hands. I gave Anna's a little squeeze and she squeezed it back. She was studying the face of her friend Gracie Lacroix. I had done my best to explain things to her, and where I'd faltered Sarah filled in the blanks. Gracie's daddy has gone to heaven to be with people who love him. Sarah was Catholic too; sometimes it helped.

We never discussed what was said the other night, and I knew she was keeping things from me. She didn't want to talk about it, so I didn't bring it up. It's remarkable how long you can share a space with a person and still avoid something between you that is burdensome. Sarah could keep quiet for days; it was one of her true gifts. She'd let it build up until there was no more containing it, and then you'd better watch out. I knew better than to press her. Better to let the slow burn wear off and stay out of her way. We all have our ways of dealing with grief.

The priest finished, and the casket was lowered into the ground. Jenny Lacroix brought her hand to her mouth as she held back her tears. Standing there with her daughters, she wanted to be strong for them. I imagined where she cried when they were asleep. Maybe on the porch in the middle of the night, wishing the cold could take away her pain. She was the wife of a logger and she never pretended to be anything more than that, and she had seemed happy with that. I envied Dan for what he'd had and what he'd lost, and I thought to myself: now this is a woman.

A shovelful of dirt was laid on the casket. I looked Jenny in the eye as I shook her hand, and saw the distance in her, like she was looking through me or past me. I wanted to tell her that I was sorry for her loss, but it occurred to me that anything I said would be tired or unoriginal or unconvincing, and so I just shook her hand and put my hand on her shoulder and looked her in the eye and hoped it was enough.

As we were leaving the cemetery I saw a group of men from Northern Timber standing near the gate. Terry Pike waved me over.

"We're going to the hotel tonight. Have a few drinks for Dan." He looked at Sarah who was standing with Anna beside my truck, gave her a nod. "I understand if you can't make it," he said.

I told him I'd try, and then we headed home.

9

"There's this writing program in Toronto." She said it kind of absently from the side of the bed. She was attacking me with the news when she knew I was weakest, unable to challenge her. My head throbbed; I squeezed my eyes shut. I opened my mouth and it was a barrel of ashes, my throat like a hot glue gun. I whispered, can you get me some water, and saw that she was already holding it.

"Give me a minute," I said, stalling. I knew she'd been considering it for a while because it was well-rehearsed. She came at me with a well-rehearsed line and argument and there was nothing I could say. If she had any doubt, it washed away when I came home late and slept on the couch.

I arrived at the hotel bar after my shift, and the Northern Timber boys were already there. Terry Pike was in fine form, and it was five-thirty. He hadn't shown up to work but I didn't mention it. Dan was his friend, and Terry had a right to mourn. He had twenty years on me in the bush and that counted for something too.

They were playing Great Big Sea. There were lots of Newfies in town, though Dan was born and raised in Black River like I was. His parents had emigrated from somewhere in Northern Quebec when the mine opened. His father couldn't speak a word of English, a hard-nosed Frenchman if I've ever known one.

I ordered a beer, and Terry Pike approached me. His breath was rank, his beer sloshed over the rim of his glass, onto his hairy wrist. "The missus let you out eh?" he said too loudly. People had heard.

I knew that anything I said would lead nowhere good, but I've never backed down from a challenge in my life. Doesn't matter the state of the other man, especially in a bar filled with people who take orders from you in the field.

"What's that, Terry? Too fucking drunk to come into work today?"

His face crumpled. Whatever good spirits he'd built up since the funeral, I'd crushed with a sentence. He glanced around the bar that had grown mostly silent, and a smile slowly came across his face. He looked me in the eye and even though he'd recovered gracefully, I knew he would not forget that, ever.

"Ah shit, Joe. I didn't mean anything by it. Just never see you out anymore is all." He waved the waitress over. "Two Jameson. You're up for a shot, aren't you?" He was grinning now, and this was how he'd get me back. Get me shitfaced and send me home, straight into Sarah's wrath.

I took a long swig of beer. I felt Terry's big hand squeezing my shoulder. He was like one of those friends who tries to crush your hand whenever you see him, only Terry wasn't my friend. "Sure Terry, but just the one."

We did one and it immediately led to two more, and the next thing I knew I was ordering my fifth pint and requesting a song. We were standing beside the bar in our work boots and work pants, the sawdust and the mud falling onto the carpet getting kicked around and mixed with beer and Irish whiskey and ground into the fibres of the carpet. Fisherman's Blues came on, and it was the song I had asked for. The dusty CD case now lay upon the bar like a cracked coaster. We were drunk and we sang. The violin and mandolin started up and we hooted and hollered. It was an east coast song yet we all loved it because the east coasters here had made it popular, and we'd grown up with it. There were Frenchmen too, and Portuguese from the Azores, and Finns who were used to the cold and working outside, and Germans who had been kicked around after the war, not really wanted anywhere (and who could blame the world for not wanting them?) That was my grandfather, Lucas Adler. He'd wanted to go to America but they weren't taking Krauts in 1950, so he came to Canada and found work in the smallest, coldest, farthest place he could find, hoping that his work ethic would speak for itself and he wouldn't be just another fucking Jerry.

We sang and it occurred to me that we didn't have any songs of our own because the town wasn't very old. Sixty years and that's about it. So our culture had been imported from all over the world, rooted in hard work and hard drinking and bar songs that grabbed everyone the same way. And just as a veneer of culture was beginning to form, the town began to die. Like an abandoned garden, the short roots and sprouts of life left to wither. And here we were, the sad remains of that culture, or what was left of it, mourning one of our own, a soul that had been lost to the wilderness, the austerity, like we could afford to lose another soul.

The song finished, and Terry bought me another shot. I knew I should get home, but I didn't want to face Sarah.

Terry looked at me, the sweat glistening on his forehead. "He's got a newborn baby at home, you know." He took me by the shoulders. "I don't blame you for that, any of it. I look across the bar and I see the look on your face, and I don't blame you. There was promise in him, I saw it too. It's why I got him on. Now I visit his wife and I can barely look at her. One fucking year it took for his life to be taken. I been on for thirty and I'd trade places with him in a heartbeat."

He bowed his head, and I thought he was going to cry, so I put his shot in front of him and we did them.

"It's just that patch, Joe. It was too much for him."

"He wasn't wearing his seatbelt, Terry."

"I know; Paul told me. It was me who trained him, so I guess that falls on me. I told you I don't blame you, and I don't. You've got a job to do, harder than anyone else's because you got to make the tough decisions about who stays and who goes, and who goes where. But I can't wrap my head around it. It should've been me out there, not him. It should've been me." He looked at me, eyes glassy and angry. He was shaking. Everything repressed and he wanted to let me have it. He clenched his fist and his rocky jaw was tense and sticking out, and I thought he might take a swing at me.

"It was a straightforward job, and I needed you on the buncher. That's it Terry, there's nothing else to say, It's just one of those things."

"One of those things." He glared at me. "You tell that to his wife."

He started to say something else and I put my hand on his shoulder, gave him a look like I meant it. "Maybe you should go home."

He ordered himself another shot. "Don't worry about me. I'll tell you when I've had enough."

"And tomorrow? I need you on the buncher."

"I'll be there before all of you. Fucking count on it."

I left Terry at the bar, and as I walked out the door I saw the guys crowd around him. I wondered what they said about me when I wasn't around. I was younger than many of them, which made a good starting place for their resentment. And now a death on my watch. That was enough to make me a pariah. I knew how Terry operated; I'd heard his shit before. If the company had a union he'd be its boss, preaching about fair wages and fair hours and working conditions and how the fuck could Paul have us working that patch just the two of us. Never mind that Northern Timber was one of the few reliable employ-ers in town. Never mind that Paul paid better than market rate and hired the best men and did his best to keep them. None of that mattered to a guy like Terry Pike. Some people are just for inciting the masses, getting the blood boiling. And now Terry wanted to bury me. I could see that plain as day. All of his I don't blame you talk meant the opposite was true. He would say that I was too young and too inexperienced, tell anyone who'd listen. He'd said it to Paul years ago when Paul handed me the position, and Paul looked him square in the eye and said: but Joe's got a friggin' brain between his ears, Terry. When's the last time you ever thought on your feet, in a pinch? Terry hadn't liked that. Especially when he thought he was in line for the job, and it was me giving him his marching orders. All Paul said to me was: cut out the drinking, and don't make a fool of me.

I left my truck parked on the shoulder across from the hotel bar, and it was just like the old days. I bummed a smoke off a group of teenagers by the back exit. I hadn't smoked a cigarette in years, and it tasted good. I had half a mind to head back into the bar and buy a round, but I had to be at the landing area for sun-up, and that would be hard enough with my brain swimming as it was. I hung around outside the bar, smoking my cigarette, and then I walked home.

"How long is it?" I asked.

"You were drinking last night."

She looked more like a mother than she ever had. More than during those first months of late nights and no sleep and round the clock feeding. She wore an old gray cardigan, and her hair was in an untidy bun. She was tired, the wrinkles around her eyes dark and pronounced in the sunlight streaking through the window. But they were clear and powerful, her eyes, had fuck you written all over them.

"It wasn't that bad. How long is the program?"

"Your truck's not here. You stink like whiskey. It's bad enough from where I'm sitting."

"What time is it?"

"Eight o'clock."

"Jesus fucking Christ I have to go." I leapt and ran for the bathroom, and the sour taste of whiskey and head-splitting pain hit me hard. I barely made it to the toilet before I started to retch. It was all dry heaves. Not a single, satisfying puke. I leaned on the side of the tub with my head between my legs.

She stood by the doorway shaking her head. "Maybe you should take the day off."

"Can't."

"You can't go in like this."

"I've gone in worse. I just need a coffee. Did you make coffee?"

"Unbelievable. Did you even hear what I said? I want to do this, Joe. I need to do this."

"What about Anna? Who's gonna take her to school, pick her up?"

"My mother."

"You already talked to her? How could you do that without talking to me first?"

"When? You're up early, home late. I only see you at dinner, and we can't talk then because of Anna, and then it's the television and your beer and hockey. I have to make decisions. I can't wait for you to be home, or for you to be sober."

"That's not fair. It's been years and you know it."

"And yet, here you are."

"I had to stop by the bar to pay my respects. Jesus Christ, a man is dead."

"You know what your problem is, Joe? You just can't say no. You're like a bomb waiting to go off. I can feel it, the tension from you. I want to do something with my life. Don't I make you happy anymore?"

"Of course you do! But you don't make a decision like that without discussing it with me first. We have obligations. How long is the program?"

"Two weeks."

"You really want to leave Anna for two weeks? You're her mother. It's not right."

"Fuck you about what's right. Look at you. And don't bring Anna into this. I'm a great mother."

"Great mothers don't leave for two weeks."

"You're a son of a bitch, Joe." She turned and walked away before I could say anything else. I heard the front door slam, and the car pull away.

I put my head in my hands, regretting my words. I had a gift for driving people to blinding rage, finding the one thing that hurt the most. But with Sarah and me there were no innocents. It was all nails and bile and viscera. Kill shots. The heart of things revealed that had no business being revealed. The gift of adulthood is that you know when not to speak, but add enough emotion or alcohol and we become children without the benefit of cuteness or innocence.

She was a good mother. She was ten times better than my own mother, and she was the best mother I knew. Everything was for Anna, had always been ever since the day she was born. So why did I say it? Because ever since the day Anna was born, Sarah had been an inadequate wife. Motherhood, for her, was a death sentence. She'd had dreams, ambitions, then found herself tied to a young man that she may or may not love, and a baby on the way. She'd talked of going to school but that was only talk. I never thought she meant it, not really. And so she was pregnant and stuck, and she was too good a person to hate the child so she hated me and loved the child. She loved Anna with everything she had, and there was none left for me. But I didn't resent her for this. I admired her for it. Because my mistake was that I loved Sarah too much, would do anything for her. And this, in time, had bred resentment. A woman says she wants a man to dote on her, but in fact the opposite is true. A love you don't have to work for is as flighty as a warm April day.

And now she was gone, and I knew in my heart that this was it, that something had changed and I wouldn't get her back without a fight. But I had to go to work, and what did she know about real responsibility? What kind of a person was she to dump that on me first thing in the morning in the state that I was in? There was a coldness to her that broke my heart because I would never be so cold. And as I sat there on the bathroom floor, the white porcelain pressing against my spine, I asked myself how far I was willing to go for her. For the first time since I'd been with her, I felt apathy. Where once there was fear and anger there was an edge of indifference as I realized that her resentment wasn't because of the booze or Anna or even me. It was because of the world, and everything she didn't know about it.

But she'd left me coffee. God bless her.

10

It was after nine when I arrived at the landing, and Paul was already there. Two-day old rain lingered in puddles along the rough-shod strip road. Without the forest canopy, the water found no exit lines. Everything cut had turned to swamp. The road headed through a small valley, and that made the problem worse.

The buzz and clank of machinery carried through the cut. Terry Pike was clearing trees with the feller-buncher while Paul talked to the skidder operator, an old-timer named Walsh. Terry cleared the edges of the road, leaving cut trees for the skidder to drag to the landing. I radioed to tell him I was coming in and he put the machine into neutral so that I could pass. His eyes were like two pissholes in the snow. I crossed his path, and he flipped the engine into gear. The saw whined high and loud.

Paul gave me a look. "Jesus, you look like shit," he said.

"The boys had a thing for Dan."

The skidder's cowling was up, and Walsh was standing in front of the engine looking bewildered. He might as well have been looking at a rocket ship.

"Pooched," Paul said. "Mechanic is on his way out."

"Where's the Timberjack? That Deere's been nothing but unreliable all year."

"Had to bring it back to the shop. The cop came asking about it yesterday."

"What does he want with it?"

"No idea."

"You brought it in this morning?"

"It's after nine, Joe, what the hell do you think we do all morning? He said he wanted to talk to you."

"He wants to talk to me?"

"That's what he said."

The skidder was across the end of the strip road, and the cut bundles were already piling up. Terry would keep working but without the skidder to haul the trees out, the delimber and slasher would be sitting idle at the landing, not to mention the haul trucks. It was a problem. We had a schedule and orders to fill; the down time would kill us.

There was a dark pool of oil under the belly-pan, most of it leached into the ground. Bled out like a gut-shot animal. It didn't look good. If it was a blown gasket, it would need to be transported back to the shop. The company had four skidders and two were being overhauled in preparation for the new cut. Now we were down a third, with the fourth commandeered by the cop. Paul looked at me and I knew he was thinking about all this too. The stress was there on his face: the constant frown, the deep lines on his brow.

"I shouldn't have had two skidders overhauled at once."

"Not your fault. You made the right call getting them prepped. But get me a machine out here today. I don't care what it takes." He pulled me aside. "Joe, I tried your radio all morning. No answer at your house either. I had to come out here myself when I should be on my way to Quebec. You understand that? Terry called me because he couldn't get a hold of you. Don't leave me hanging again. You want my advice? The next time they ask you out, tell them you can't make it. Keep that separation. If it's a one-off, I understand. We all got to blow off some steam once in a while. But I don't want to have to start worrying about you just when I need you the most."

I headed into town, the sunlight through the driver's side window beating down on my arm and the left side of my face. I felt like half of me was baking in the sun, the other half cold and parched, sun-starved, thirsty like an old dog.

I walked into the police station and Officer Taylor was sitting behind the reception desk drinking coffee from a takeout cup and reading the local paper. His face was clean shaven and soft. He was wearing a vest that said POLICE across the chest.

The police station was small and cramped. It was a one-storey building with a peaked roof and backyard that reached the shores of the Black River. It looked more like a house. There was a small waiting area with a single, ratty chair, and a hallway that led to two tiny cells that I remembered well.

I knocked on the counter and he didn't even look at me. I stood while he finished his paragraph, his lips moving with the words. He folded the paper and placed it on the desk.

"Paul said you wanted to see me."

"I've got some questions."

"Well I've got a concern of my own. I need that skidder back."

"You can have it back when the investigation is complete."

"I've got a broken machine and a contract. I need it today."

He smiled. He was happy to screw us over. "That's not possible. It needs to be processed. An investigator is coming from Thunder Bay later this week."

"Later this week? You must be joking. What am I supposed to do?"

"I don't know. I'm very sorry, but there was a death. I need to follow procedure."

"I told you what happened."

"You told me what you think happened."

I shook my head. "This is ridiculous. Do you know what this contract means to the company?"

"I don't care. My concern is how Dan Lacroix died out there all by himself."

"It was an accident."

"So you say."

"I say, Paul says, anyone will say the same thing."

"It doesn't matter. Do you see the problem, Joe, if I just take everyone's word for anything?"

"Yeah, we wouldn't need you at all. Because we don't. All you're doing is messing things up, slowing us down because you don't understand."

He stood up. I could see the contempt he had for me. "No, you don't understand. This is an investigation. How experienced was Dan Lacroix?"

"He was new, but he was trained."

"He was out there alone."

"He was ready to be alone."

"And that's documented?"

"Yes."

"And the skidder, what state was the skidder in when Dan was using it that day?"

"We have a strict maintenance schedule we adhere to. That's also documented."

"Were you aware that Dan often operated his skidder without wearing a seatbelt?"

"No I wasn't. We have a strict policy on that."

"Also documented?"

"Yes. Why aren't you asking Paul these questions?"

"I already have. But you're the supervisor, the foreman. It falls on you to make sure policy is followed."

"Anything else?"

"Not at the moment."

"Then call me when you're through with our machine."

I was nearly out the door when he said, "I looked up your record."

I knew it was only a matter of time. "So?"

"Assault, DUI, drunk and disorderly. Seems like you have a problem."

"I made mistakes. I was a kid."

"If you were a kid, then you wouldn't have an adult record."

"So I was nineteen, twenty. That's not me now, and I don't see what it has do with anything."

"You left your truck at the hotel last night. You ever go into work drunk? Or too hungover to do your job? People think they can just go home and sleep it off, but a lot of times they're still drunk in the morning."

"I don't drink anymore."

"I heard you were drinking last night. That's why you walked home, isn't it?"

"First time in a very long time. Anything else?"

He shook his head.

The other cop was pulling in as I was leaving. He had a paper bag on the passenger seat, donuts from the coffee shop. They were so far out of their element. Officer Taylor wanted me to know he called the shots. There was nothing I could do and that's what burned the most. My father always said that a man in uniform is to be feared, because his only loyalty is to his own. He has nothing to lose while you have everything to lose. And you can say that a cop has taken an oath to protect the innocent, but a cop is just a person. They might be strong or weak, have prejudices and discriminations. The oath is worth nothing because they're human like the rest of us.

Paul's mechanic was sitting on a chair outside the shop eating his lunch. It wasn't even eleven, and he was sitting in the sun in his blue overalls with a ham sandwich hanging out of his mouth. His face was tanned. He looked like he'd been lapping it up all summer.

"Nice day," I said. "You hear from Paul?"

"Ya, heading out after my lunch."

"It's leaking oil like nobody's business. I don't know for sure but I think it's a blown gasket."

"If it's an oil pan gasket I can't repair it in frame. Need to pull the engine. But I won't know until I have a look at it."

I stared at the sandwich, looked at my watch.

"You want me to head out now?" he asked.

"How about those two rebuilds? Where are we at with those?"

"One is in parts. The other I was planning to have done by the end of tomorrow."

"You have all the parts?"

"Ya, just elbow grease now."

"Can you have it done by the end of the day?"

He shrugged. "Be a long day. After midnight for sure."

"Time and a half after five."

He considered. "Alright. What about the John Deere in the cut? I'll need all day on the skidder here if you want it done."

"Just get the machine here ready to go and worry about the one in the cut later. I'll have a float outside the shop for five tomorrow morning. Any problems, let me know so I don't have a truck coming out here for nothing. And finish that goddamn sandwich; it's not even eleven."

I radioed Paul and told him my plan. It was a wasted day but at least it was a plan. He was heading to Quebec that afternoon. He said I had the keys.

Across the yard was the old beehive burner, a sixty-foot incinerator used to burn slash piles of bark, debris and sawdust. It was shaped like a flask from a high school chemistry class, with a conveyor belt that ran from the ground to about a third of the way from the top.

I remembered passing it with my father when I was a kid. It was always smoking then. Two, three men burning the slash of logs destined for pulp and paper mills on the north shore. Men in the yard, machines in the bush, and the taste of dust in your mouth. Back then, it seemed impossible that there could come a time when there wouldn't be enough work. There was more work than the company could handle, and if you pulled your weight there was always a job. But the success of these northern towns is cyclical. Stay here long enough, and you'll see it for yourself.

There are two types of people in these towns: those who stay and those who go. The stayers are connected to the land and will do whatever it takes to ensure their survival here, in place. I have always found these people to be of warmer nature than the other type, because they are secure in their place and their land, and in that security they find comfort. They surround themselves with family and like-minded people, and in this tight-knit group they overcome. They help each other out. They give work when they can afford it, and ask for it when they need it. And the sense of humility that comes from the situation, the willingness to put in work, makes the person. There is a freedom to poverty that the rich can never know, to holding onto something no matter the cost. It is based on ideals, and not money. To be beholden to no boss but the one you chose is a courageous choice, even if it makes you poor. They are not rebels, but idealists, and as their numbers dwindle their core becomes stronger, more persevering. The town becomes their own little dustbowl.

I have seen people lose their jobs, and run five small businesses from their garage to make ends meet. I don't judge a person for leaving. I have a family and I understand the need. But I wonder if they realize what they're giving up.

One thing I know is that when people leave they rarely come back. When they're gone, they stay gone, and on the rare occasions I see them in town they either look at me with contempt or they look at me with envy, but they never look at me with indifference.

In October of 1950, my grandfather Lucas Adler walked for three days and nights through the bush to get to his first job in Canada. He had arranged the job from Germany, confirmation through letters, and a reservation on an upriver boat. He took a steamer across the Atlantic, a train two thousand kilometres north-west, and arrived at the jump-off point to be told that the river had frozen a month early, that there would be no more boats that season. Sorry, sir, for all your troubles, but the next boat won't leave until May.

But he had no money and couldn't wait until spring. He had a wife and child to bring over. He had travelled across an ocean. The boat captain told him that a power line went to the logging camp. It was new, put in only two years ago, and that he could, conceivably, walk the power line to the camp. But nobody knew how long it would take or what to expect because it had never been done.

So he headed off into the unknown wilderness, the edge of civilization, with the clothes on his back, and the shoes of a clerk. He was a foreigner; I can only imagine the guts this took. He slept on the ground, huddled against a tree with his hands under his armpits. No gun, no shelter, just the biting cold and the gray October sky. He told me once this was the most terrifying thing he had ever done. Six years in the war, but his first three days in Northern Ontario were the worst.

It seems unbelievable now, but back then I think it's what most people would have done. The Europeans who lost everything in the war were a hard-nosed bunch. This hardness molded a generation. And the generations since then? Well, I can't imagine anyone I know making that walk. It would be out of the question.

But sometimes I wonder what it was all for, his walk and the walks of countless others. The country is different now. People are different. They don't wait for things anymore. They spend and they borrow and they spend some more so they can have things they believe they deserve. They've got payments coming out their ears. Sometimes, they borrow just to stay above water. The image of wealth is a lie. Dig deep enough and you'll find the truth.

They say the kids don't want to work, but I don't buy it. A person is no longer the sum of their output. Somewhere along the line that got lost. You want a union job? Good luck getting in. You want to go to University? Better have a lot of money and time and brains to go all the way because otherwise it's a gamble. Want to work in the mine? You're hired! One hundred and fifty thousand a year but your lungs are shot by age fifty and your hands too. Me? I'm just a lucky son of a bitch. Right place, right time. But I often wonder if I'd have made that walk, if I could make it now.

I want to tell all this to my grandfather as he slogs his way through the muskeg and swamp and sleeps on the ground not knowing how much further he has to go. I want to show him what the future holds, how my generation measures happiness. I want to tell him that the Canadian dream is a pipe dream, unattainable for the average person. I want to show him what all his hard work was for. I wonder what he'd say.

11

I drove to an old tree stand that I'd helped my father build when I was a kid. I hadn't been there in years, and the trail was grown in. I felt old for the first time in my life.

I climbed the ladder and sat in the weathered seat that was covered in lichens. The wooden platform was gray and warped, and the orange rug was still there, faded and chewed at the edges by some kind of rodent.

There were wear-marks on the rug from my father's boots. He loved that stand, and went there every day after work during hunting season. My mother was happy when he was out in the bush because it meant he wasn't drinking. The days he came home late from hunting were the best days to be around him. All his anger drowned in the lake. I saw the man that I think he wanted to be, that he might have been.

In the beginning he was good. That's what my mother used to say. The beginning meant before I was born, when they first met, when they were young. Then something happened. That's all she ever said about it.

The sun descended and the sky turned orange-red. Leafless birch trees looked painted on the horizon in black ink. For half an hour after the sun sets, there is enough light to hunt. This is the witching hour when the bush is silent and the patchwork of fall colours turn to shades of gray, the edges of things blurred by encroaching darkness. You listen for an animal crashing through the bush, walking along the shore. You listen more than you look because movement is easy to see but hard to hear. You familiarize yourself with the small animals, the birds and chipmunks that live around you, that chirp and prattle, annoyed by your presence.

I'd helped build that stand, my sweat ground into the grain of the wood. But that was long ago. The trail had since grown in, and I was a stranger. Better to be a stranger when your intent is to kill. Many years had passed, yet the place still resonated with me. It was different, but the same. My father killed two moose out of this stand, and each time he was a different person. This is the measure of the place, this crown land, which allows you to be all things at once and whatever you want to be. This is why the stayers stay. It's in their blood. It's the land that makes the person, never the other way around.

12

A week after the funeral, I came home to an empty house. Sarah's car was gone, and so was her suitcase and her clothes, only the good ones. There was no note, no nothing, and I thought how typical.

I drove to Anna's school to pick her up. Sarah's mother was standing by the fence, and the way she looked at me I knew my surprise and hurt were obvious. I was never good at hiding my emotions.

"You're off early," she said.

"I had an early day, thought I'd surprise the girls. Linda, what are you doing here?"

"She didn't tell you?"

"Tell me about what?"

"Her class."

The bell rang and the students came out. I leaned on the fence, watching as the double-doors opened and closed, the children running and laughing. "All I knew was that she was thinking of going. She mentioned it, that's all. When did you know?"

Tears pooled in the corner of her eyes and I knew it had been an eternity, and that if Sarah could keep this from me, she could keep anything from me. "Weeks," Linda said. "I've known for weeks."

At that moment I hated Sarah more than I ever have since. And even though I'd half expected her to leave, now that it had happened, it was not how I had imagined it. It was foggy and unclear. I had questions. I couldn't understand how she could leave Anna.

"I was done work early, and when I got home and she wasn't there. I guess she just assumed that I'd know you had Anna."

Linda put her hand on my shoulder. She was never afraid of work and had the hands of a gardener. "Oh Joe, I thought you knew. I wouldn't have gotten involved otherwise. What the hell is she thinking?"

"She said I don't support her."

"Nonsense. You've supported her for years. Some men would've left. But not you. When Sarah got pregnant you were a man about it. You got a job, got a house, got your act together. You were always there for her. So don't go blaming yourself for this. I know my daughter. I know how selfish she can be. And what's all this for? Something that's got nothing to do with family, or putting food on the table. If she were here I'd tell her myself."

For Linda, a mother's loyalty was to her family and everything else was a distant second. Sarah had betrayed that loyalty, and dragged her mother into the middle of it, made her witness to all our shit. Of course mothers make assumptions. They know when things aren't right with their children. But the way Sarah had involved her, having us here staring at each other, wondering if the other had the full story, was unforgivable.

I liked Linda and she liked me. She said I reminded her of her late husband, and I took that to heart. He was a miner, a real salt of the earth kind of guy. She understood exactly who I was even if Sarah didn't. My indiscretions never fazed her either. The first time I got arrested it was Linda who bailed me out, shaking her head with a little smile, asking if I gave as good as I got.

She understood me, but she never understood her own daughter. She came to me with questions about Sarah, hoping that I might have some insight, and when I didn't she revealed that Sarah had always had her head in the clouds and thank God she had me now to put some sense into her. And as much as Linda wanted to know Sarah, Sarah never wanted to know Linda. Linda was everything Sarah never wanted to be—alone, ordinary, and still in town.

When Sarah got pregnant, Linda said it was a blessing in disguise because she'd have to think responsibly for the first time in her life. Of course this only succeeded in driving her further away.

"Did she say how long?"

"She told me two weeks."

"Do you know if she said anything to Anna?"

"I don't know, hon."

And then Anna appeared. She was standing beside me, and I hadn't seen her leave the building. She looked up at me, her eyes full of concern. "Where's Mommy?"

Seven years old and already she sensed the failure, the collapse of our marriage. We were here and her mother wasn't and that meant something awful had happened. I forced myself to smile so she wouldn't think it was worse than it was.

"Your mom's gone on a little trip," I said. "Just a couple of weeks. Grandma will be picking you up from school."

Her eyes lit up. "Oh yeah! Did she go to her writing class?"

"Yes. Did Mommy tell you about it?"

"Oh yes. She told me she had to leave for a few days, and that I shouldn't be sad because she won't be gone long, and that Grandma will pick me up from school. But you're here too, Daddy."

"I got off work early today, sweetheart. What do you want for dinner? Feel like French fries?"

"Ya! Bye, Grandma." She ran to my pickup.

"Thank God," Linda said. "What time you off for work in the morning?"

"Six," I said.

"I'll be there."

Anna was standing beside my truck. She was beautiful, and I held her. "We're going to have a great time together," I said.

We drove to the restaurant downtown. She had questions, but she was holding back. She was so much like her mother. She thought about serious questions before she asked them. She was emotionally perceptive beyond her years. When she was two, if I was thinking about something, she would tell me not to cry. Don't be sad, Daddy. I never knew I looked sad when I was being serious. But like I said I was never good at hiding my emotions.

Anna poked at her fries, and I couldn't find my appetite either. I didn't know what to say to her. I asked her about school. I couldn't talk about her mother so we talked about soccer. I said I was the proudest dad in the world.

I gave Anna a bath and read her some stories. I put her to bed. She said the house was quieter without Mommy and I agreed. I said that Grandma would be there in the morning to take her to school, and I would be gone early.

"You're always gone early," she said.

"It's my job, sweetheart. The guys expect me there at sun-up."

"Is it dangerous? Mommy said your job is dangerous."

"It's not dangerous if you're careful."

She thought for a moment, then looked at me. "Was Gracie's Daddy not careful?"

"Sure he was. But sometimes things happen, and my job is to make sure nothing happens to me. Remember when I told you that we are all responsible for our actions? That you always need to think about what you're doing, and how it might affect other people? Well that's what I do. Everything I do out there, I'm thinking about you, about how much I love you and want to come home and see you. And when I'm thinking like that, all the decisions I make are clear and careful. Everything I do, Anna, I do with you in mind. Now how could anything happen to me when I've got your beautiful face on my mind?"

She put her arms around me. "Please don't ever leave, Daddy."

"I promise you I never will." I turned out the light.

I grabbed a beer from the fridge. One thing I know is that a parent should never appear weak to their child; it changes them forever. Sarah had told Anna that my job was dangerous. She'd said it on purpose to sway her, maybe to win her over. She'd been waiting for an out and when Dan was killed she witnessed her own mortality, or maybe mine, and it was like a kick in the ass. Now a clock was ticking inside her brain, and I was in her way.

She said two weeks, but I knew she had a bigger plan. She didn't want to be here anymore, and the only question was what she thought she could do about Anna. She had no money to care for her now, but eventually she would. She'd wait until it suited her and then she'd drop a bomb in my lap. But if she thought I'd just let Anna go, then she had another thing coming. And for those who say you can't separate the mother from the child, I say bullshit. It's the one who breaks up the family who should suffer. If she wanted out, I couldn't stop her, but I wouldn't let her drag Anna around while she found herself in the big city. I just couldn't allow it.

I finished my beer and opened another. I watched the end of the Leafs game and they'd blown another lead. I drank until there were no more beer, and then I watched Sportscentre. I stumbled to my room and crawled into bed and Sarah's side of the bed was flat and cool, and I stretched my arms into the space where she should have been. I smelled her pillow. The more I drank the more I loved her. I hated her but loved her more. And I knew that if she were there, I'd forgive her. I'd talk tough, but inside I'd be relieved. I'd make love to her.

13

The strip road was punched through and we began cutting. The bunchers and skidders worked out from the beginning of the strip road, clearing the trees inside the boundary of the cut, which was marked by pink flagging tape. I brought in an excavator and bulldozer to build the road. We needed a good solid road to support the haul trucks and machinery that would pound and batter it for the next few months. We needed to cut, limb, and slash the trees before spring when everything thawed. We were on the clock.

Paul called me from a hotel room in Quebec and was happy about the progress. Everything was on schedule despite being down a machine. He'd secured another contract, and that was good to hear. It had been two weeks since the accident, and I said I would enquire about our skidder. He said don't bother.

"There are rumours," Paul said.

"What rumours?"

"The cop is fishing for a negligence charge. He called in an investigator from Thunder Bay. He's been talking to our guys. He's bent on hanging the company out to dry. You didn't hear any of this?"

"I've been busy. I thought the MOL cleared us."

"They did. It sounds like he's going solo."

"What the hell. Who's he talking to?"

"Terry Pike, some others. Mostly Terry because he worked close with Dan. Terry seemed eager to talk to him is what I heard. I don't like it. The guy's a loudmouth."

"It doesn't matter. He can't pin anything on us because we didn't do anything wrong. Everything's by the book, Paul. The machine was maintained, and Dan was trained up. I had Terry do the certification himself. If he wants to implicate the company, he'll be shooting himself in the foot."

"Maybe not the company. Maybe just you. You guys have a history. I heard what happened at the hotel. It's all bullshit. Don't believe a word of it. That kid was more than qualified."

"There was the seatbelt."

"It worked fine. Dan wasn't wearing it, and that's out of our control. Once a person is certified, it's on them." He paused. He was getting all worked up. "This is such bullshit. We're finally making some headway, and now we have to worry about the cops. Negligence? Is he trying to sink us?"

"Nothing will come of it. He's new and he's out of his element. Did you see his face out there in the cut? The land terrifies him. We've never been negligent. I'll carry on without the machine, and we get it back when we get it back. I won't let it slow us down. We're making good progress here."

Paul was more of a hothead than I ever was, except that his rage was mostly bluster. Fake charges and smoke rings. He would blow his stack and then come around immediately. This was one of the reasons he was such a good operator. He showed emotion but it didn't cloud his judgment. But he needed that balance on the other side of the table, and that's where I came in. The job was the only place in my life where I was able to make rational decisions every single time. Paul was too close. The company was his baby, and whenever there was a big problem he would get worked up. He had the weight of a company and a town on his shoulders. Families depended on him to make the right calls. He'd given his life to the business because he believed in it and because he didn't want to see it evaporate like everything else around here. He was one of the old-timers now. He'd grown up in town, worked with the men of my father's generation, and when the company went tits up in the nineties, Paul bought it with the money his father had left him. He was in his late thirties then but he knew the business, knew the bush, and people were happy to see someone step up to the plate. He'd bought the business with its debt and old machinery and shrinking market, and turned it around. He took risks, but they were smart, calculated risks. He invested in the future, saw opportunity where others never did. He paid well, didn't take shit from anybody, and was well-respected. He was insulted by the cop's intentions, and pissed that Terry wouldn't keep his mouth shut. It would burn his ass for days.

Paul said, "How about you? Everything okay at home? Amy said that Sarah left town for a while, that Linda is picking Anna up from school."

"Sarah went to Toronto. She'll be back in a couple of weeks."

"Toronto? Shit, man. She drive or fly from Thunder Bay?"

I didn't know. Her car was gone, and I assumed that she'd driven the whole way, but I didn't know. I got the feeling that Paul knew more than I did. It had been three days, and I still hadn't heard from her. But she was just arriving, I thought, she'd call once she was settled. She would want to ask about Anna.

"Drove. She said she could use the time alone. I don't blame her, really. It's about time she did something for herself."

"Well if you need anything, help with Anna or whatever, I know Amy would love to." The receiver crackled, he hesitated. He was choosing his words. "You know I worked with your dad for a lot of years. He was a good bushman, and a good man."

"He was an asshole, Paul."

"Maybe, but I figure I knew your dad pretty well. He was one of the reasons I made you foreman. He knew everything about the bush, just like your grandfather. The Adler name holds a lot of water in this town. I saw the same potential in you that I saw in your dad, and I knew if you didn't piss it away on the drink, like he did, you'd be a damn fine bushman. And that's what you are now. But you're like him, kid, and you got to be careful. He kept to himself, too. Bottled things up, and I know that's what got the best of him. Holed up in that damn cabin too long thinking too much when he should have realized he had people to talk to. That's what I'm saying to you. I've known you for a lot of years, since you were a kid. You got people to talk to, talk to them. Talk to me. Hell, I'll come over with a case a beer and we'll figure it out. But don't do it alone. We both know what's down that road, and it ain't anything good. You got a problem with the missus, shit, who doesn't? But being alone ain't no way to be. You hear me?"

"It's fine, really. Sarah left for a couple of weeks and that's it. The other night at the bar was a mistake. I'm not drinking again. I just got my hands full trying to take care of Anna and everything. I can't remember the last time I made dinner."

"Neither can I. I'll have Amy bring something over tonight."

"That would be mighty kind."

Paul didn't know my father like he thought he did. He didn't know how dysfunctional it really was. My parents would fight, vicious fights, and after a few beers my father was capable of saying anything. My mother, stubborn and proud, wouldn't let him get away with it, so she gave it back as hard as she could. He never hit her, but he wanted to. He said so all the time. Instead he channelled his rage into the alcohol consumption that eventually consumed him. They would fight, my mother would cry, and he would drive off into the pitch black forest leaving us to fend for ourselves. We never knew when he was coming home. Me, my mother, and my younger brother Thomas. If he did that because he didn't have anyone to talk to, well then to hell with him. The truth was that my father was an alcoholic and a loner. I couldn't imagine that he ever felt close to us. If he did I never saw it.

My father once said to me: I have a lot of acquaintances, but few friends. It was his legacy to me. He made me careful about who I got close to and who I confided in. But when I met Sarah, I fell for her hard. She was my best friend, my only true friend, and I told her everything. With everyone else there was a veneer. To the world I was the hard bushman, the drinker, the fighter. But to Sarah, I was a man with fears and insecurities and weaknesses. She loved me once, I was sure of it. And now that she was gone and my world was breaking apart, I didn't know where to turn. Paul was right about that. I'd never been able to talk to anyone but her, not even my brother Thomas. Thomas who moved out west the day after he graduated high school and never looked back. The last time I saw him was at our father's funeral. We didn't talk much, didn't seem to have anything in common but the memory of our father's anger. I didn't know much about him. I didn't even have an address. All I knew was that I had stayed while he had left, and so there was a line drawn in the sand. His pity or bewilderment about me, and my resentment of him. I stayed to shoulder the burden of our family, of our mother, while he got away scot-free. Free to piss away his tar sands money on beer and cocaine. My younger brother, whom I had protected from the worst of our father's wrath, didn't give a shit about any of it. He didn't recognize the sacrifices I had made. He didn't have a family. He said to me at the funeral: I don't know how you do it, being a father, I'm terrified of turning into Dad. At least when I get wasted, nobody gets hurt unless they have it coming. He smiled, took a long swig of beer. He could put it down, just like the old man. But it looks good on you, he said. You're a good father, I can tell. But that woman, she'll be the death of you. Cut her loose before you're in too deep. I see the way she looks at you in a crowded room, when you're looking away. I see how she looks at other men. She's got eyes for anything but you. Cut her loose, man.

Of course I didn't believe it, didn't want to hear it. I told him he was jealous, resentful that I had a happy marriage. He just shook his head and said he shouldn't have brought it up. That was two years ago and it was the last time we talked, not even an email between us. I blamed him, but inside I knew it was my fault. I hated him for what he'd said and for being smart enough to leave when he did. I am the older brother, I should have been more responsible.

And my mother. She lived alone in a house on the other side of town and I went to see her every couple of weeks. I would bring Anna. There was love, but there was a wall. There were mountains of pain. I wanted to move on from my father's darkness, and all I could see in my mother's eyes was sorrow and guilt, endless guilt. She wanted to talk about the past, her eyes big and glassy, the smoke from her Du Maurier swirling around her wrinkled head and stinking up the house the way I remembered it. She looked like a skeleton. I would arrive and thrust Anna upon her lap and escape to the backyard where I wouldn't have to feel her pain, and even out there everything screamed of my father—the grass, the peeling deck, the rotting fence, the tiny hole in the siding. I couldn't escape it. I began to realize why Sarah hated the town so much—it was a fucking black hole.

I called Sarah's cell phone from the office and she didn't answer. I left an angry, desperate message. I yelled and pleaded for her to call the house, leave a number, an address, something. It's been three days, I screamed, don't you care about your daughter!

I got into my truck and drove to the cut. I had it in mind to give Terry an earful, but the more I pushed him the harder he'd push back. It was an endless loop where I knew I'd eventually have to bury him, and I wasn't there yet, so I took the turn off to the cabin instead. I needed something to cool my head. I parked beside the black ruins, leaving the engine running. I took a pry-bar and flashlight from the tool box in my truck, and walked to the rusted pickup. I knelt beside the driver's side door, and brushed the grass and weeds that had grown over the trap door on the ground. I found the lock and wedged the pry bar underneath and lifted until it popped.

Back in the eighties CP Rail tore up a section of an old line that was rarely used, and left the ties in scattered piles where the line crossed the highway. People pilfered them for all kinds of uses. The oil-drenched wood would never rot. My grandfather built the cellar out of these ties and parked the old pickup over it, and that's where he let it die.

I shone the light inside and the glimmer of two dozen bottles of Irish whiskey shone back. I took out three and placed them on the ground beside me. Underneath the whiskey was a metal ammunition box, and inside that was my grandfather's forty-five wrapped in an oiled rag and a few boxes of rounds. He'd bought it on the black market from a Finnish war memorabilia dealer in Thunder Bay. He never had a proper permit for it, kept it hidden in the ground. I took it out, felt its weight. I remembered shooting it with my father and brother, emptying the clip into the side of an oil drum. I wrapped it in the rag and put it back in the box. I closed the trap door, and pushed the tall grass over it. I put the bottles behind the seat and sped down the single-lane road with the grass in the middle and the wind in my hair. My family legacy, I thought: the only things worth burying were whiskey and guns.

Linda was doing the dishes when I arrived home. "You don't have to do that," I said.

She just smiled at me. "It's no bother. Nothing but a few breakfast dishes here." Her arms were submerged in the soapy water. She wasn't wearing gloves. Sarah always did and I found it weak. It made me wonder what my grandfather would say.

"You hear from Sarah yet?"

"No."

Anna was in the living room watching television and eating cheese and crackers. She was wearing her soccer uniform and a thick hoodie and toque and I remembered that she had practice. In Black River, the soccer season ran until the end of September, but the last few years Coach McCarthy had run a fall program through the month of October, and all of the kids played through, despite the cold.

"Hi Daddy!"

"Hi sweetheart. What time is your practice?"

"Six."

"Did you eat dinner?"

She pointed at her snack.

"That's not dinner, Anna."

Linda called from the kitchen, "Do you need me to make something?"

"No, it's fine. Amy is bringing something over."

Linda dried her hands and came over. "You look tired."

"I'm fine, just a long day."

"And now you have to take your daughter to practice, feed her, clean up, and put her to bed."

I shrugged. "I'll be fine."

"Well, you were never one to complain."

She gave Anna a hug and said she'd be back in the morning.

I grabbed a beer and sat beside Anna. She was oblivious to everything but the television. A commercial came on, and she turned to me. "I have to go to practice, Daddy."

"I know sweetheart, we'll leave soon."

She looked at me skeptically. "But you're in your work clothes."

"It's okay, they won't mind."

"Were you careful at work today?"

"Of course I was, just like every day. Just like I told you."

"That's good. I hope Gracie is at practice today. She was at school and I asked her if she was coming to soccer and she said she might, if her mom lets her. I miss her."

"I know you do, honey."

I finished my beer and we drove to the soccer field. Anna drew stick figures in the dust caked on the glove box.

"When are you going to clean your truck?"

"In the spring. Once a year is plenty. The dust gets every-where. I clean it today and five days from now it'll look just like this."

"So why bother?"

"That's right," I smiled. "So why bother."

We arrived and the other kids were already on the pitch, running laps around the half-field. I looked at my watch and it was 6:03. She ran onto the field and took her place in the circle of cleats- and sock-wearing children. Coach McCarthy looked at his watch as she ran onto the pitch. He saw me looking at him look at his watch. He gave me a nod.

I sat on the benches with the other parents whose conver-sations were about the positions their kids played and what the coach wasn't doing right. I wanted a beer right then and there. I looked for Jenny Lacroix but didn't see her. It was windy, and the trees behind the field bent and swayed. The coach blew the whistle and the kids gathered to hear his instructions. He was shouting over the wind. I heard only broken phrases and syllables.

Then I saw Jenny Lacroix. She was crossing the field with her baby in her arms and Gracie beside her. The wind blew her hair back and made her eyes squint and pressed her dress tight against her belly. Her chin was low and her hair was dark and wild. She looked like she was walking from a plane crash or a hurricane. She looked like a survivor.

Gracie ran to the kids gathered around Coach McCarthy, and knelt beside Anna. The other parents looked at Jenny, they gossiped; this was the first anyone had seen of her in a while. She stood off to the side and stared with those faraway eyes that I remembered from the funeral, looking at nothing in particular. The trees swayed, a front was moving in. The coach blew the whistle and the kids scattered to their positions for the start of the drill. Jenny turned and looked at me, and this time she was looking right at me, like she had the day I told her about her husband. There was sadness there and pity too, not for her but for me, as though she felt sorry for me, was reaching out to me, and I wondered why she was looking at me like that.

We arrived home after practice to find Amy's foil-wrapped lasagna on the counter. There was a note taped to it that said: Call if you need anything. We're always here for you, Amy.

We ate, and Anna watched television and played with her Barbies while I cleaned up. I drank a beer and read her some stories, and once she was asleep I retrieved the bottles of whiskey from my truck. I hid two under the workbench in the garage, and opened the third. I drank it sitting on a lawn chair in my garage thinking about Dan Lacroix and the way his body looked on the roof of the skidder, his face under the pool of reddish water, the life pushed out of him. I wondered if his death was instant or if he'd suffered. Maybe he'd fractured his skull and was dazed when he breathed the water into his lungs. I wondered what that would feel like.

I thought about Jenny crossing the field, the wind in her hair, pressing against her body. I poured drink after drink of Irish whiskey, and passed out in the chair wondering if whiskey ages something like wine.

14

I stood on Jenny Lacroix's porch tasting whiskey in the back of my throat. I knocked and she answered quietly, inviting me in. We sat at her kitchen table as the aroma of strong coffee filled the room.

She wasn't surprised to see me; she'd been seeing people for days, each asking her the same exhausting questions. She wore faded jeans, wool socks, and a Roots sweatshirt. The socks were gray with an orange stripe across the top. They were pulled up over the cuffs of her jeans, and were well-worn and pilled. I figured them to be Dan's.

She held the cup of coffee like she was sitting at a campfire, cradling it under her nose. She had dark hair and dark eyes, and when she put the coffee on the table and brought her knees to her chin I realized how small she was. A petite French girl with subtle French features and a sorrow that ran deep but wasn't desperate. It was practical, measured. She had a family that she needed to take care of and that came first.

"Maggie's still asleep," she said.

"I'm sorry, I shouldn't have come so early. I was driving by and saw the light on, and didn't know when I'd have another chance, figured it was as good a time as any."

"It's fine. I was up, just kind of puttering around. I'm used to getting up early. It's nice to have some time away from the girls."

"Maggie," I said. "I never heard her name before. I like it. Gracie and Maggie."

"It's short for Margaret. A nice, simple name. We never went for those new names the kids have these days, names that make no sense. Parents try to put all this meaning in the name and the opposite happens. Who knows where they get these names from. It's like they forgot who they are, where they come from, giving their children names like that. Nobody's happy with what they have anymore; everybody wants to be a celebrity. At first, Dan thought that Gracie was a bit much. I had to convince him that it's still pretty normal. Grace. Grace Kelly. It has a classical feel, don't you think?"

"Margaret too."

She smiled and looked out the window to her driveway. The sink and counter were clear of dishes, and I thought how she could keep everything so tidy when things were so bad. "Our girls are good friends. Gracie talks about Anna all the time. Dan thought it was great." Her smile faded. "He looked up to you. He said of all the guys in the bush, you were the one he trusted most."

I sipped my coffee. It was black and strong. "How are you holding up?"

"I might say good days and bad, but it's a lie. Every day is bad. The worst part of it is not knowing. Not knowing where the money will come from, not knowing how I'll take care of my kids, that's the worst part. I loved Dan, and I miss him, but I've realized I'm on my own now."

She glanced down the hallway at the bedroom door that was open a crack. I knew what she meant. She had a newborn and couldn't work. She wasn't on maternity leave because she wasn't working before she got pregnant. The town was old-fashioned that way. That's just how it was. Wives raised the kids, ran the household. Some worked, but there wasn't much beyond nursing, a faltering service industry—a handful of stores and restaurants and a couple of gas stations. Northern Timber had a life insurance policy, but it was small, and paying it out took time. She was relying on family, and it couldn't go on much longer.

"Everything will work out," I said. "It always does."

She looked at me long and hard, and I realized that was the wrong thing to say. I looked away from her, feeling my hangover creeping in, the taste of old whiskey and a splitting headache. I looked at the clock on the stove, one of those old stoves with the coil elements and foil plates. I needed to be in the field.

"Terry Pike came by," she said abruptly. "I understand he doesn't like you very much. I'm telling you this because I want to be clear about things. I say what's on my mind now. I figure it has something to do with Dan's death. I don't hold anything in anymore. If it upsets you, I apologize. But there is something unsaid between us. If that's what you came here for, I want you to know I don't put much stock in what Terry Pike says. He was Dan's friend, not mine, and I always thought he was a loudmouth, one of those people who like the sound of their own voice. And Dan trusted you. You believed in him, he said so. And that means something to me."

"Dan knew what he was doing. He was a good worker and a good man. What happened out there was an accident."

She looked at me hard. "If he knew what he was doing then he'd still be here with me and his daughters. If he knew what he was doing then he'd have put his goddamn seatbelt on. I get so mad when I think of it. The simplest thing. The easiest thing. But that was Dan now, wasn't it? Walking on a tightrope his whole life, pushing everything to the edge, like all you guys. These jobs and what you do. If it's not the bush then it's the mine and what extra you make in salary you lose in quality of life. Isn't that the way of it? I don't know why we put up with it, but I guess we have to since this is where we were born, where we came from. What's the alternative but leave and start over, and that would mean that we assume that other places don't have their own problems, that pain and hardship and death don't happen in other places. But it does. It has to. There's no way the good lord would leave us to our little pile of shit if it was the only one in existence. Can't be. No, I'm convinced that things are bad all over, and you either deal with it or it deals with you. How does your wife deal with it?"

"You'll have to ask her that."

"I heard she left."

"She went to Toronto."

"For how long?"

"That's up to her."

"Sorry to hear it. Must be tough to manage with your daughter. But isn't that just like Sarah Adler? Taking off for the big city when she's needed here. She always had her head in the clouds. Sorry to say it, but I guess it's my unapologetic truths coming out again. You can blame Dan again for that."

"I didn't know you knew her."

"I know enough, figure out the rest. Our little girls are friends, we've crossed paths enough times. It isn't hard to figure when someone walks with an air like they're something special, like they don't belong here even though they were born here just like you were, and your husbands work the same stretch of bush. But you don't have that air about you. No, you know exactly who you are, don't you, Joe Adler?"

The baby cried. Jenny said she'd be right back, but I told her I had to get going. She thanked me for stopping by, and walked silently down the hallway. She opened the door, and the smile on her face when she saw her daughter was like nothing I have seen. Maybe death makes us appreciate what life we have left. For that brief moment all Jenny Lacroix knew was the love she had for her daughter. For a moment her life was perfect.

15

I was laying line—flagging the furthest, most remote boundary of the cut—and misjudged the terrain. It can happen, when your head's not in the game like it ought to be. It creeps up on you like a bad feeling, and the next thing you know darkness is on the horizon and you've still got miles to go.

The valley was thick with alders and scrub brush, and the going was slow. I thought of the Amazon jungle, guides hacking with machetes through impenetrable vine. The sun went down and with it came the cold. I abandoned my flagged trail for the logging road two kilometres away.

Dusk in the bush gets you by the short and curlies, I don't care who you are. Panic tells you to get the hell out of there as quickly as possible, but this is a trap. Bad things happen when you hurry in the bush—a stick in the eye, a twisted ankle, a fall through the ice. I used the old-time orienteering technique of taking a compass bearing on a fixed point, proceeding to that point then taking another bearing. It takes a bit longer, but I'm of the mind that a man should be able to function without any kind of gadgetry, especially when the chips are down. Skills rarely used are quickly forgotten, was one thing the old man taught me. When I stopped, the silence was overwhelming, and so I didn't stop, just pushed through until I needed a flashlight to read the compass and my points were as far as a beam of light would allow.

I checked my position on the GPS. My truck was a little dot on the little screen, the first waypoint of the day, and my tracks looked something like a flattened circle, not quite complete. Other waypoints marked other places of significance: a crossroads, a creek, a big flat rock. The road was between two hills, where two sets of elevation lines met like colliding sound-waves. I made for this spot in the pitch black, the bush and everything in it nipping at my arse.

But my fear was dulled by the task at hand. It's why they tell you to keep busy if you're lost in the bush. Still, there was something about it that I thrived on, a subconscious desire to push myself, to exist inside the fear to see what I was made of. Life's routines can be terribly boring, and sometimes you need a shot of adrenaline to get your head right. One winter I broke my ankle playing hockey, and Paul had me riding a desk. There was never a position more unsuitable to me. I found myself staring at the clock waiting for lunch, waiting for the day to end. When I got back in the bush the freedom was overwhelming. The truck, the space, the logging roads covered in spring melt-water, and the machines buzzing in the cut. I smelled spring in the air and knew I had to live my life outside. But even that becomes predictable. You start to take it for granted; it happens to everyone who's ever loved their job, and every now and then the mind needs a jolt back to basics. Raw fear forces you to block out everything but what you need for survival. It forces you to live in the moment, everything else a muted pinprick of light. This is when you know yourself best.

It was after eleven when I pulled into the driveway. Linda met me at the door with the cordless phone in her hand and a panicked look in her eyes. It was exactly how Sarah would have greeted at me.

"Where were you?" she demanded.

"Bit of a tough day out there. Sorry to worry you, Linda."

She stood in the doorway with her arms crossed. "You're goddamn lucky. I called Paul Henri and got his answering machine. I was about to call the police. I thought you were in trouble."

I wanted to get by her but she was blocking my way. I don't think she even realized it. "Paul's not home, you probably woke up his wife."

"Doesn't bother me much when you could have been lost out there, or dead."

"I overextended myself. I should've known better."

"I had a fine time calming Anna down. She was frantic, thought you were hurt. She kept saying we needed to go find you. She wanted to go herself! I called the hotel bar looking for you."

"You called the hotel?"

"What was I supposed to do?"

"Thanks for the vote of confidence, Linda."

"Is this what you put Sarah through? She has to worry about you coming home late, worried that you're not coming home at all."

"I'm sorry Linda, I don't know what else to say. I'm here and I'm okay, and I'm sorry I left you hanging."

I squeezed by her into the kitchen and grabbed a beer from the fridge. I stood at the sink while she calmed down. She looked at me the same way she did outside the school when I went to pick up Anna: sad, pitiful, now resentful. I hated that she saw me like that.

After a few quiet minutes she sat at the table. "I shouldn't have called the hotel. I just… I got to thinking and wondering what could've happened and everything played through my mind. I wasn't thinking straight."

"It's okay, Linda."

"You must be hungry."

"Starved."

"There are leftovers in the fridge."

"Mighty kind of you."

There wasn't much else to say. We stared at the floor avoiding each other's eyes. After a while Linda said, "I have a doctor's appointment in Thunder Bay this Thursday, a specialist. I'll be there for two days. The appointment's been booked for six months otherwise I'd change it. You know how hard it is to get in to see these specialists."

"Anything serious?"

"Just old age creeping up on me, happens to all of us. I can try to find somebody to watch Anna. I have a few friends I could call."

"Anna's not your responsibility. You're helping out here, and I'm grateful for that. But I can handle it."

"Who do you have in mind?"

I took a sip of beer before I answered. "Jenny Lacroix."

"The widow?"

"Anna is friends with her daughter, and I figured Jenny could use the help, financially."

"I don't know what Sarah will think of that."

I looked at her. "What does it matter? We haven't even heard from her."

"Yes, you're right," she said, but she wouldn't look me in the eye. She was hiding something.

"Have you heard from her?" I walked across the room and sat in the chair next to her. "Linda, I need to know."

She hesitated. "She calls to talk to Anna after school, before you get home. She didn't want you to know."

I couldn't believe it. Actually I could believe it, but that didn't lessen the shock. This woman, my wife, whom I once knew very well was now a complete stranger to me, doing things to hurt me, on purpose it seemed. It didn't make sense. It was absolute betrayal. "I never saw any numbers on the caller ID."

"She told me to erase them. I'm sorry, I knew it was wrong to keep this from you, but I didn't know what else to do."

"She must have told Anna to keep it secret because I know she would have told me."

"This is good, don't you see? It's progress. I was only doing what I thought best to get her back."

"And how is that working? The program ended a couple of days ago, right? So where is she?"

"She said she's staying with a friend."

"A friend."

"She'll come back, I know it."

"She's not coming back, Linda, not ever. That's what this is all about. She's wanted out for years, and now she's out. A real fine mother, isn't she?"

"Joe, don't talk like that."

"You shouldn't have kept this from me."

"I'm sorry."

"I can't trust you, Linda."

"Don't say that."

"I don't want you back here anymore."

"You don't mean that!" she cried, sitting in the chair with her face in her hands.

I felt no empathy for her. I wanted to hurt her. I finished my beer and leaned back in the chair, my arm on the table. "I don't know what's worse, the fact that you've been lying to me in my own home, or that Sarah told Anna to lie to me. Sure does run in the family, doesn't it?"

She had a pained look on her face and I knew we'd never be the same. I didn't care. I wasn't giving her a pass. "How could you say that to me? I've always respected you. Sarah's my daughter, and if I'm not on her side then who is?"

"You know, at one point I would have said the same thing, but now I just don't give a fuck."

I took the leftovers out of the fridge—spaghetti and meat sauce. I had an appetite despite everything. I figured why waste a decent meal considering it would probably be my last one for a while. It was good, too. I had to hand it to Linda, she could cook. Whenever Sarah made sauce she never put meat in it, which always left me hungrier than a bear. When I told her this she just rolled her eyes. Big strong man, she'd say, needs meat to survive. So I'd pound down two helpings of her vegetarian creation just so I wouldn't be starving when I went to bed, and she took this as a sign that I couldn't get enough of it. You see, she'd say, you like it just fine without meat. The sauce became a sore point in our marriage. Her unwillingness to put some meat in it for whatever reason (it's not like she was a vegetarian), and my end of the day relentless blue collar appetite. If she'd have put a dozen steamed hot dogs in front of me, I'd have eaten them all too, and at least they'd have had some weight to them.

I thought about Linda, her anger and desperation as I came through the door. It was exactly how my mother reacted when my father returned home from his long stretches in the bush. But over time she became less afraid, until all she cared about was how drunk he was when he returned. If he was in good spirits, the house could carry on as normal. If he was angry, we got the hell out of his way. My mother didn't even try to change him anymore. She avoided him and did everything she could to keep him contained: dinner on the table, a cold beer in his hand, she played her part to keep the family from imploding completely.

My father died in the run-down geriatric ward of the Black River Hospital. They called it a hospice but it was no more than a few rooms with a few old geezers breathing their last breaths. He was fifty-eight, which made him the youngest patient in the ward by a country mile, but he looked like the oldest. He was thin, gray, weak, and mean as a viper to the bitter end. There were wires and drips attached to him. His gray stubble shone like polished silver. His front teeth were broken and chipped from bar fights and beer bottles. His hair was long and gray the way my grandfather used to wear it. He looked like a dying George Carlin.

He was born Friedrich Adler, but in Canada he was Freddie. Freddie Adler, the drunken son of Lucas Adler died like a trapped dog, skinny and gravelly, sneaking shots of whiskey behind the nurse's back. I'd visit and he'd stare out the window like a convict. I knew he'd sooner put a bullet in his own head than die like that, and more than once I'd thought about doing it. I didn't hate him anymore, just pitied him, the way you pity a sick animal before you put it down. Even after everything he'd put us through, I couldn't bear to watch him die in a hospital bed like that. He deserved to at least take his final breaths in the bush, a log to the back of the head or a fall through the ice. He deserved to die in the bush like his own father did. That was two years ago and I vowed I'd never die like that. After Sarah went to see him she poured all our booze down the sink and I didn't blame her. I was completely dry for six months after he died. When I pushed myself in the bush, I always had my father in mind. Maybe I was looking for death out there because the alternative was unthinkable. Maybe that's what he was looking for too.

16

I called Jenny Lacroix before I left for work in the morning. It was still dark outside but I knew she'd be awake. Streaks of rain reflected off the streetlight. She answered after the first ring.

"I'm in a tight spot here. I have nowhere for Anna to go. I don't mean to assume anything, but I figured that maybe we could help each other out."

"It's no problem. Bring her over on your way to work. Gracie will be thrilled."

"I'll pay you whatever is fair."

"We can talk about that later."

"Thank you, Jenny."

I arrived at the yard and found Paul in the meeting room. Cut maps, and shelves of occupational health and safety books and binders of industry documents lined the walls. The stained coffee maker sizzled beside a half-dozen used teaspoons and an ancient container of whitener. It was the boardroom of a small lumber company and it smelled like a kitchen in the morning.

I poured myself a cup of coffee and stood at the map wall. There were detailed boundaries of the cuts, everything from the last two years. New roads, winter roads, planned cuts, it was all there. There were enough trees to keep the company going for years, but that was never the problem. The problem has always been the market.

"One contract. Not huge but not small either. I figure we've bought ourselves another year." Paul was happy. You get used to small victories in a dying town. His one-week trip had turned into two and a half as he stayed in a motel in a Quebec town, visiting the owner of a medium-sized paper mill every morning to pitch his offer, tweaking it until he got him to sign.

"He was worried about us being able to deliver, said he was hesitant to sign with such a small company because I was just as apt to close up and declare bankruptcy as I was to deliver what I said I'd deliver. I sign with you, he said, that means I don't sign with someone else and what happens when you don't come through? I told him he was small potatoes too and why should I trust him to buy my wood once I cut it down! He had a good laugh at that. I mean, we're the same, after all. Small-timers looking to carve out our own path when the big fish are eating what's left. We need to stick together, I told him. Solidarity. Solidarité! In the end, though, it was the price that got him, because isn't it always? We signed and then his wife made us dinner. We drank rye and Coke and talked about Les Canadiens."

"The great equalizer. Therrien has pulled that team together."

"He's a tyrant, Joe. Back in the minors he used to smoke on the bus and tell the players he's the coach and can do what he wants."

"Where did you hear that?"

"Read it in the news."

"That was in the nineties."

"Says a lot about his character."

"Maybe he was trying to toughen them up."

I studied the map of the Laurie Lake cut, all the cliffs and creeks and gullies and everything that made it unique. Every location has its problems, and you have to understand the land to work it efficiently and smartly. You have to do this from the ground because a map only tells you so much. Paul rarely walked these areas so I needed to be the one who pointed out things that weren't obvious or didn't make sense.

"I heard you got turned around in there. Forget which way's north, Joe?"

"Who told you that?"

"A little birdy."

"Terry?"

He nodded.

"Son of a bitch. Can't do anything in this town without it being everybody's business. The terrain is difficult, at best. You could go through there with a friggin' bulldozer and still be there till next Sunday. Alders, scrub brush, like walking through the jungle. Plus the distance from where we're working now. Winter's the best time to cut in that mess."

"Exactly what I was thinking. We'll get that winter road punched through and haul ass until spring."

"There a year's worth in there?"

"No, but I have some other areas in mind. I heard something else too, about your friend the cop."

"Go on."

"I have a buddy in the Thunder Bay OPP. He grew up right here, in Black River. We go way back. You know his name so I'm not going to tell it to you. I know you keep your mouth shut, but when I give someone my word, I mean it. I guess Officer Taylor isn't too well liked out that way, by his own. The higher-ups caught wind of his investigation and blew a gasket, collectively. Said he was wasting money requesting a forensic unit to drive four hours to come look at a dinged skidder and some photos of something everybody knows was an accident and that the MOL and coroner cleared. So this unit was half-way to Black River when they were told to turn around. Officer Taylor got his hand slapped pretty good for that one. I guess he went above his supervisor."

"No shit. When was this?"

"Last week."

"So he's been sitting on the machine ever since."

"He's pissed off. He got written up, and if he didn't feel like an outsider then, well he does now."

"Acting like he's still got cause to hold it."

"He has none."

"I'll go down today, get it back."

"No Joe, I'll go down. How was the meal Amy brought over?"

"Fantastic. Please thank her for me."

"Of course I will. I'm your friend, you know."

"You're my boss, but you're right, maybe the best friend I've got."

"Why are you so hard on yourself?"

"Because she was my friend. Who do I talk to if I don't have her?"

"You can talk to me."

"You sign my checks, best to keep it that way."

"Alright then, play it hard if that's what you want. Just don't roll into work all lit up."

"Not my style. I get ripped at home, after the job is done."

"So did your dad, until getting ripped became the job, and everything else was the distraction."

"I gotta get to the cut, we're finishing off the east block and the boys will need some direction."

"You're doing great work, Joe."

"I do my job, Paul, the best way I know how."

I sped down the bush road thinking about Sarah. I felt pressure inside my chest, like steam with no place to go. It climbed higher and higher and I knew I had to expel it or else lay waste to something. It was a familiar feeling from my childhood, all my anger repressed and bubbling to the surface. A kid would look at me the wrong way and I'd be all over him. I couldn't fight my dad so I fought anyone who crossed me. After a while guys knew to stay clear of me, and the ones who didn't, the ones who came looking for a fight were the same as me, pissed off about something or other and looking to draw blood. I recognized them a mile away; it was like looking in the mirror.

Terry Pike was on the buncher. He looked at me and I knew he had something to say, but didn't have the guts to say it. He was the type to call you out when his pals were around so things wouldn't escalate too much. But no people around was exactly what I wanted. If something went down it would be his word against mine, and I was alright with that.

He swung the boom around like he was busy working. I ran up behind him and jumped on the track. I banged on the door beside his head, and he jumped in the seat when he saw me there. "Jesus Christ, Joe! Have you lost your mind?"

"You saw me coming, Terry, don't act like I would've ended up under the track unless you wanted it that way."

He flipped the machine into neutral. "What the hell are you talking about?"

"I'm talking about your big mouth. Telling people that I had some hand in Dan's accident, that it was my fault. You were talking to that cop."

"He came to the shop, talked to everyone."

"You were the only one trying to sell me down the river. Are you trying to get me in trouble, Terry? Want me to go to jail? You talked to Jenny Lacroix about me too, and that I can't abide. She has enough to deal with."

"I heard you been to her house a few times. What sort of business you conducting, Joe? Have a thing for the widow now that your wife has split?"

I reached into the cab, pulled the hard hat off his head and threw it as far as I could into the bush. I grabbed the front of his denim jacket, twisting the material in my fist. I turned until my fist ground into his sternum and the torque brought his face close to mine. "The next time I hear some rumblings behind my back and it's you who's behind it, there'll be no place you can hide."

"Go on and hit me, see where it gets you. You ain't a kid no more, and assault is a serious offence, especially when I've got the ear of a cop who has it out for you."

"You don't have shit."

"Pop me and see what happens. See how fast you'll be in a cell downtown and your kid shipped off to your wife in Toronto."

"Keep on that track Terry and I might just bury you out here, make it look like an accident."

"You don't have the balls."

I reached across his waist and unbuckled his seatbelt. I grabbed him by the jacket, pulled him out of his seat, and threw him over the track to the ground below. He landed hard. It was a good four feet down, and if the buncher weren't idling I'm sure I would have heard the thud of his body hitting the ground.

"You son of a bitch!" he yelled.

"I told you to wear your seatbelt, this is rough terrain here."

"You did it now."

"Did what? You fell out. And you know what else, you smell like booze. I don't know if you had a few for breakfast or if you're just hungover, but I'll be sure to tell the cops about my suspicion when they come talk to me."

"You son of a bitch."

"And another thing: I don't get lost; I never get lost. I'm just a hard fucking worker." I hopped off the track. "Make sure you don't operate that machine without a hard hat. That's a critical offence, and I'll have to write you up. See you at the shop."

I arrived at Jenny's after six. Anna and Gracie played in the living room while Jenny prepared dinner. She offered me a beer so the girls could hang out a bit longer and I said sure, what the hell. She dug in the fridge and said there were still some left from Dan. She handed me a Canadian and I thought: so this is what Dan drank. It was strange to be drinking another man's beer when he wasn't there, stranger that he was dead.

Jenny was cooking stew or soup in a big pot. I missed coming home to the smell of dinner on the stove. "So, how's she been?" I asked.

"Anna is a good girl, Joe. You should be proud of her. She's a leader, too. I watch them together and hope that some of Anna rubs off on Gracie. She's all you, you know."

"She's way smarter than me, and I hope it stays that way. I want her to go to school for something decent, something that she can be proud of so she can get the hell out of Black River. There's nothing here but hard work and pregnancy. If she's lucky she'll get a man who isn't mean or drink too much and has enough energy at the end of the day to pamper her a little. What kind of life is that?"

She looked at me. "Sounds okay to me."

"Sorry, I didn't mean to—"

"Sorry nothing. I understand you clear and you have nothing to be sorry for. Of course I want more for my girls, but it's not as bad as you make it out to be. It's a choice, living here, just like everything else. You have to know what you're in for."

I watched the girls in the living room. They were playing with Barbie dolls, dressing them up and making them walk and talk. They had made a little shopping mall out of milk cartons. "They really do get along, don't they?"

"They're the best of friends."

"Well that's great."

"You're welcome to stay for dinner."

"We can't. Gotta get home, you know."

"What have you got planned for dinner?"

"Not sure yet."

She laughed. It was nice to see a smile on her face. I knew the money I'd be paying her would go a long way, cover her groceries and gas and maybe a little more. If she was lucky Dan's insurance would take care of the mortgage. One thing about living up here is that houses are dirt cheap.

"Take some stew with you. Plenty in the pot and I was just going to freeze it."

"You're very kind."

"It's nothing."

"Have you thought about a rate?"

"How's twelve an hour?"

"Make it fifteen. I don't want the person watching my child making less than that."

"I won't argue with you."

"You shouldn't."

"Hey, Joe, thanks for everything."

"Don't thank me. This is what they call a symbiotic relationship. You, me, the girls, well, everybody wins."

17

A month to the day after Sarah left, she called the house, like she had the date circled on her calendar, like it was just another appointment. "Joe?" she said. Her voice was faint, almost a whisper.

I looked at the clock and it was past eleven. "Nice of you to pick a reasonable time."

"I didn't realize."

I sat up in bed. "I'm just glad you called."

"I can't talk long. Why isn't Anna with my mom?"

I heard voices in the background. It was loud; it sounded like a dormitory. "Because she lied to me. A lie that you put her up to. Are you coming home?"

"I called to talk about Anna. I want my mother to watch her before and after school, not some woman I don't know who's probably a mental wreck."

"That's not your decision to make. You gave that up when you left without telling me. Why didn't you just tell me?"

"Because I knew you'd talk me out of it, and I had my mind made up."

"I would've let you go."

"It would have been another fight, and I can't do it anymore."

"When are you coming home?"

There were so many voices, shouting and laughing. I pictured her in some college dorm with teenagers and young adults. She was in her late twenties, not too old, but not young either. But Sarah was a talker. She was cunning. She would win them over and was probably a mother figure to somebody. "It's complicated. See, the profs here really like my work; they say I've got potential. Isn't that great? There's this retreat, a writer's retreat that starts in a few weeks out in B.C. The air out there, it really gets you going. It's a great place to work on your craft."

"What are you talking about?"

"I want to enrol in the winter semester. My teacher says I'll get in no problem, and that my work's strong, really strong. They all want me to stay at the workshop here until it starts. I want to stay. I was thinking that you and Anna could come down for Christmas. We'll have Christmas in Toronto, just the three of us. It'll be great! I've heard the ice rink at Nathan Phillips Square is the most beautiful thing in the winter. Bring all our skates. Anna will love it."

Something in her voice reminded me of when we were teenagers, the way she would talk, full of hope and possibilities. Sarah had wanted things. I had always known this, but never truly considered it. All those years a fire had been building in her. I never understood because I'd never wanted more than what I always had. "Christmas in Toronto? Have you lost your mind?"

She didn't answer.

After a while I said, "You're not coming back." I stared into the darkness of our room. It was pitch black but for the red numbers on the clock-radio. It was empty without her, and I didn't know if I missed her or the idea of her, if she could have been anyone, if all those years she was simply a warm body that I needed, a woman to share my life with. Sex and conversation. Dinner and drinks. Fight, make up, argue, fuck. But isn't that what marriage is? Once the honeymoon is over and the child comes things change forever. You spend years trying to get back that spark. But isn't that what people have done for centuries? Isn't it part of the deal? You stick it out, work through the bad times because you made a commitment.

"Sarah."

She breathed into the phone. I knew she was going to say something final. "I'm sorry, Joe, in my mind I was already gone. That town, those people, the way we lived, it was never me."

"What about Anna? What am I going to say to her?"

"I need to talk to her. I'll explain things in a way she can understand. I need time to build myself a life I can live. She will understand that."

"This is her home. Black River is her home."

"You need to be reasonable. We need to be reasonable about this."

I heard a deep voice, a man talking to her. "Listen, I have to go," she said.

"You don't have any money, no job. How are you getting by?"

"Joe, we have a joint account and you can't just cut me off."

"I haven't done that, but you can't keep using our money to fund whatever it is you're doing. I have Anna. I have a mortgage and responsibilities."

"I know that. I'm staying with friends until I know about B.C., then I'll probably rent a room in a house near school. I'm applying for a student loan once I get accepted."

"This is crazy."

"Crazy is doing something for somebody else for most of your life, that's crazy. Listen, I need to be able to talk to Anna, you have to give me that. I was doing it when my mom was watching her because I didn't want to hurt you. But you have to give me that, Joe. I need to talk to my daughter."

"Fine. Call tomorrow at six."

"Thank you."

"Sarah, is there somebody else?"

"No."

"Whose voice is that?"

"Nobody, just a friend."

"Please don't lie to me."

"I have to go," she said, and then she hung up.

I lay there looking at the ceiling. My bed was empty, the spot where Sarah's body used to lie, cold. I put my head on her pillow and could smell her in the fibres, the goose down embedded with her scent, its permanence. I would have given anything to have her back. I thought: so this is what it's come to.

WINTER

18

My mother's house was always cold and damp. Oil for the furnace was expensive, so she turned it up only when it became unbearable. She had a little electric heater that she carried from room to room, along with her pack of Du Mauriers, Bic lighter, and black coffee.

"Christmas, Mom, in Toronto. We're having Christmas in Toronto this year."

She stared out the window at the concrete walkway covered in melting snow and ice. The ice was thick, so I had put down salt when I arrived and would shovel it on the way out. It was warm for December, hovering around zero degrees and it felt like spring, even smelled like it.

"Mom."

She turned and looked at me, and I put my hand on hers. Her skin was thin and freezing. Her face was wrinkled and drawn out and her eyes had that cloudy look of cataracts, though she'd never been diagnosed or if she did, she never mentioned it. She was old beyond her years. "Mom, you have to turn the furnace up, this place is freezing. It's not good to live like this. You'll catch pneumonia."

"Last time they filled the tank you know what the bill was? Five hundred dollars. Can you imagine?"

"What about the woodstove? I brought in wood the last time I was here. You haven't forgotten how to make a fire, have you?"

She shrugged. "It takes twenty minutes to get it going, and you have to feed it all day, and then it only really heats the basement and I hate sitting in the basement. It's too dark."

"It will help with the oil cost, Mom. I can bring in all the wood you need, but I can't come here every day and start a fire."

"I don't need a fire."

"Well I'm going to make one because this is ridiculous in here."

"Suit yourself." She took a cigarette from the pack and turned back to the window. She waited until I was halfway down the stairs before she lit it, the strike of the lighter and crackle of burning tobacco strings the only sounds in the empty house.

The basement was exactly how my father had left it. This was why my mother never went down there. Remnants of him were strewn about: rifles and fishing rods piled into corners, hunting gear and packs on the workbench beside an open tackle box and a case of empties. The old television and beaten-up easy chair were an arm's reach from the beer fridge. Nothing had changed. My mother never cleaned up my father's things to punish herself for allowing him to infiltrate our lives for so long, keeping his ghost alive by never moving on. She had dealt with his death by not dealing with it. All the things she failed to say to him while he was alive she failed even to say to him now, in his death. Beer, whiskey, hockey, and a workbench. He was home long enough to prepare for his next outing and to get blind drunk. He slept on the couch for as long as I could remember, wrapped in my grandmother's afghan, an old bear right to the end.

I opened the woodstove and piled kindling over some cardboard and balled-up newspaper. My mother still got the paper even though I'm sure she never read it. The papers were stacked up at the landing near the entrance. I brought them downstairs every time I visited. I lit the newsprint and the pile quickly went up. I loaded in some small pieces of birch, then closed the door to a crack to keep the oxygen flowing.

I walked upstairs to a haze of blue cigarette smoke and sunlight through old white lace curtains. I sat across the table waiting for her to speak first, to offer me a coffee, to say anything, and when she didn't I knew her mind was bogged down in the past. Every time I came I made it harder on her. She was too old for sixty, far too old. She was gray and wrinkled and exhausted because she didn't take care of herself. She smoked like it was still the seventies. She barely cooked and lived off canned soup.

I took a cigarette from her pack on the table, and she gave me a funny look.

"I thought you quit."

"Years ago."

"Then what are you doing?"

"I don't know, Mom."

"Well you shouldn't smoke, it's bad for you."

"I remember when I was a kid, I used to steal them. I'd go outside and smoke them with my friends, or with Thomas. You never noticed."

"You don't think I noticed? I noticed. I noticed everything. That was my biggest problem. I noticed everything. What do you think, Joe, we lived off your father's skimpy paychecks, whenever he decided to work. And when he wasn't, when he was off in the bush, we had to make do. You don't think I knew everything we had in the house? How long my pack needed to last?"

"You never said anything."

"What was I supposed to say? You were going to smoke anyway, and I figured it was better you take them from me than from your father."

"I took them from him too. He never noticed."

"No, I suppose he wouldn't have. Where is Anna, why didn't you bring her?"

"Because we need to talk about things."

"About Toronto?"

"About Sarah."

She was quiet for a moment, and then looked at me. "She's left you."

"Yes."

"She wants you to bring Anna to Toronto for Christmas."

"Yes."

"That's hard Joe, when did she leave?"

"A couple months ago."

"You should have told me earlier."

"I didn't know what to say."

"One never does, but I'll tell you this: it's better now, like this, than any other way. I knew she wasn't cut out for this life, and if she's not happy then it's best she move on."

"What about Anna?"

"What about her? This is her home, Joe, nothing changes that. Sarah made her choice to leave."

"So then Anna gets no mother?"

"Anna gets what Sarah will give. Take her to Toronto, don't deny her her mother because she will never forgive you for it. Let her see her, but when it's over, she comes back here. Always her home is here, with you."

"I love her."

"She's all you've known. I remember when you were teenagers, you would have done anything to make her happy. But she was young, Joe, you were kids."

"We were kids but we were in love."

"*You* were in love. You were blindly in love. But she didn't love you. I think you knew it, too, all those years, but you couldn't admit it. That's understandable. We all take the time we need. And look at that beautiful girl of yours. She's something special. Better that she doesn't see the fighting anymore, the negativity. You need to be strong for her. You need to be attentive and pay attention to her when you get home. This is the best thing a parent can do for their child."

"You were good at that, Mom."

"Are you drinking?"

I didn't answer.

"I said are you drinking, Joseph?"

"Sometimes, but I don't know how else to forget. I can't fall asleep at night. I think."

"Thinking's good. You'll need your wits about you. But the drink will destroy you, just like it did your father. It runs in your family, the Adler side. But I don't buy that. A person is either weak or they are strong. Your father was weak, your grandfather was strong. So then there's you. You're strong, but now you face your first big test. This is what will determine you."

"What about when Dad died?"

"You were relieved, we all were. He was never meant for this world. He was an aberration."

"Is that how you feel about your life, your family?"

"You and Thomas are the only things I ever did right. If your father existed simply to bring you and your brother into the world, then his life was not wasted. He spent years searching for something out there in the bush and at the bottom of a bottle, when all he had to do was come home and look into his sons' eyes, really look, and he would have known that all his searching was in vain."

"I feel his anger."

"I know you do. That's why the whiskey has to go, for Anna's sake. Who is watching her before and after school? Why not bring her here?"

"Because you smoke like a chimney, Mom. Jenny Lacroix."

"Ah, the widow."

"It's not like that."

"I suppose it wouldn't be, not yet. But remember this: the second time around you really know what you're looking for. Trust your heart, whatever it tells you."

I lit the cigarette and we smoked together in silence. It tasted horrible, like chemicals, not like the one I had outside the bar. Probably because I was sober. She closed her eyes, exhaling out her nostrils like an ancient dragon and ground the butt in the overflowing ashtray.

"Please bring her by soon," she said, staring out the window. "I miss my little pancake."

19

We drove south on the only highway out of town, a rundown road scarred with potholes and cracks that grew deeper and more abundant each winter. Up here, the highways are all like this; I've never seen a cent of my tax dollars at work. At the Trans-Canada we turned left and continued east, and the highway was black and sleek and damp. The black spruce were snow covered, and the leafless poplar and birch looked dead or dying because you can only see their buds up close, the new life in the dead of winter.

By White River it started to get light. I pulled into Robin's Donuts to get a coffee and so we both could pee. The exhaust of idling trucks hovered low, its stink permeating the morning air. Overnight, the temperature had dropped to minus twenty and the bush workers were drinking their coffees before heading into the field.

We passed the Winnie the Pooh statue and the giant retro thermostat marking White River as the place where the bear cub of the children's stories was sold to Lieutenant Harry Colebourn, and the town that holds the record for the coldest spot in Canada with a temperature of minus fifty-eight degrees Celsius. It was an hour to Wawa and the giant goose, and I settled in with my coffee.

The sun climbed higher, glistening off the snow and shining into my eyes and I flipped down the visor and watched for moose. In cold like this they'd be on the move, walking through the deep snow with hot breath like clouds of smoke and frost on their noses, herded up for protection against wolves. A few years ago I came across a dozen moose in a plot of planted jack pine bordering an old cut. It was near the end of hunting season and the bull I was tracking led me right to them. I'd never seen so many moose in one place. I took my bull and when the dust settled, I saw the tracks and beds everywhere. Four feet of snow packed down flat like in a schoolyard. I'd never seen anything like it.

I drove while Anna slept. There's nothing between White River and Wawa except endless conifers and a single gas station that is closed in the winter. The stretch is notorious for snow storms and moose collisions. The haul trucks blasted by with loads of black spruce destined for the mill in White River.

I played hockey in all these towns when I was a kid: Hornepayne, Chapleau, Marathon, Dubreuilville. There was a tournament nearly every weekend and the rivalries were fierce, the hatred mutual. We didn't see all the things we had in common, only the things that made us different: they spoke French, their arena was colder, they wore Doc Martens. In a small town everything you do is harshly judged and you learn to conform early on.

We went to Toronto once when I was a boy. I remembered being awed by its size, but mostly I was amazed at how progressive it was and how it made my own town look like a hopeless backwater in comparison. There was a freedom to the big city that I admired. My father never liked Toronto, but then he never liked any city, or any place south of Sault Ste. Marie. We arrived at night and the eight-lane highway and towering lights stretched off into forever. I had never seen so many people in one place, and the size of it, the magnitude of it was something else. My first impression was not to hate it but to embrace it. It wasn't until I was a young man that the indoctrination had taken hold, and I disliked the city for everything it stood for just like my father and grandfather before him. It was this childlike sense of wonder that Sarah held onto that scared me most—the impulsive way she was doing things, like she didn't have a care in a world, like she was on some sort of drug.

Anna slept with the sun on her face. Her coat was rolled up for a pillow beside the frost-covered window, and her blond hair was bright and shiny. She looked peaceful and content. There's nothing like a nap in the early morning sunlight.

I watched her in the light and promised that I wouldn't burden her with my judgements. I wouldn't criticize the city or what her mother was trying to do. We would have a nice dinner. We'd go to the Ontario Science Centre and the Royal Ontario Museum. I would be supportive, but firm that this was a visit and not her home. I wanted her to be in awe the way I was when I first hit that eight-lane highway. I wanted her to have a great trip that she would always remember.

Sudbury has the Big Nickel and smokestacks that are tall and ominous with gray streamers turning westward in the afternoon sun. They say the trees don't grow large because the bedrock is pervasive and they can't get hold, but one look at the giant smokestacks and you think something different. The place looks windswept and deserted. Anna looked out the window and was unimpressed. I asked if she wanted to see the Big Nickel and she gave me a look like I was from another planet. She was too young to give me that look. Kids grow up too fast, girls especially. She wanted to put distance between us and those smokestacks. She wanted to see the big city and Sudbury was like a bigger version of Black River. I told her about the nickel mine and how many people from Black River had moved here when the gold mines were downsized. She rolled her eyes. All she said was: I think it would be nicer to work outside. She kept asking about Toronto, about where her mom was staying. She had all these ideas in her head. She was building it up to something triumphant and I hoped she wouldn't be disappointed.

"Mommy says Toronto is a great place to live. Are we going to stay there too?"

"This is a visit, sweetheart. After, we're going home."

"But what if we love it? Mommy says that I will just love it."

"Well I hope you do, but remember that this is a visit."

"But Daddy."

Past Sudbury the trees were taller and the landscape hillier as we entered Muskoka. I pointed out the window. "Look at those huge trees! Silver maple. We don't get anything that big where we're from. Just look at the trunk of that one, has to be four feet across. Enormous!"

Anna sighed. "They're trees, Daddy. *Trees*. It's nothing to get so excited about."

She was growing up before my eyes. Not yet even in the city and her past was already something to be ashamed of. Moving on to bigger and better things. She gazed out the window with pretension in her eyes, and I wondered where it came from. I realized I was hopeless to the ways of a young girl. The thought of her as a teenager scared the shit out of me. Sarah always handled Anna, and here I was stepping into the role and I was lost. I hoped that once Sarah saw her she would change her mind and come home with us. I mean, how could she not?

At Georgian Bay the snow thinned and the trees were huge and varied. There were species that didn't grow up north where we were from: oak, maple, white pine, weeping willow. We crossed the French River and I remembered the beauty of the place, so we parked and walked through the visitor centre and crossed the suspension bridge, and Anna got a kick out of that. It was cold, but sunny and wind-still. We looked at the river far below, the ice that covered everything but a small and fast-moving current. It was the white pines that made the place, I decided. The way they perched and towered over the steep cliff of the river gorge, the way they guided the path to the suspension bridge.

"Now this is somewhere I could live," I said.

"Me too," Anna said.

"You know the white pines, those big pine trees there, about two hundred years ago they used them for masts on sailing ships. Because they are so tall and straight, they make perfect ship masts, you know, where they attach the sail."

"I know, Daddy."

"Thousands of them, from here to Ottawa and farther still. They felled them and sailed them down the St. Lawrence, across the ocean to Europe and Britain."

"Do they still use them for that?"

"No, because ships don't sail anymore. Not the big ones anyway. They use engines."

"Like in a car?"

"Like in a car."

"I'm glad they don't cut these trees down anymore, because I like them."

"I like them too."

We hit the eight-lane highway north of Toronto and the night was clear. We could see all the way to the downtown core, the lights running along Yonge and Bay Streets, and the headlights of a million cars like a snake winding its way to the heart of the city and to Sarah. It was late, but Anna was awake, the lights reflecting off her eyes. She was quiet, watching. She was tired but in wonder, content with the moment, the way she could be sometimes. I didn't say anything, just drove the way I knew to get downtown. It was December twenty-third and there wasn't any snow on the ground. I rolled down the window and the air was damp and hovering around zero. It wasn't Christmas like I knew it, or like Anna knew it. It was warm and muggy. There was too much concrete. The highway was wet and sounded wet and even the light and the darkness were wet. Two hours south of Georgian Bay and the world I knew had disappeared. Two hours between knowing and not knowing. The city was a rainy day and the black highway heading south, widening and growing wetter. It glistened in the night; it was the loudest thing I'd ever heard. I drove and my heart pounded in my chest and there was nothing comforting about this place, not a single grain of something redeemable, something I could say I liked. I hated it all. I hated its business-like December warmth. I hated how the lights blocked out the stars. I hated the way it made Anna stare in awe. But most of all I hated what it had done to Sarah, the mother of my child. It had sweet-talked her, fooled her, and anything that could convince a mother to abandon her child was heartless and callous, and that's just what this place was.

I had visited Toronto once with Sarah. We watched Phantom of the Opera and stayed in a fancy hotel with a view of other hotels, the CN Tower, and the long bright Yonge Street strip. The next day we went up the tower and had lunch in the revolving restaurant; Sarah had the duck. The weekend trip cost me two weeks' pay, but it was worth it. Everything first class. She really loved me after that trip, had the biggest smile you could imagine. She'd make elaborate dinners and dance around the house with Anna in her arms, listening to the Phantom of the Opera soundtrack she'd bought after the show. And at night, she made sweet love to me. She wanted to go to New York to see a real show, she said, and dine in Little Italy, and I had promised I'd take her. Spring, I said, we'll go in spring. But spring rolled around and work was busy and it never happened. And then summer in the north is beautiful and I didn't want to leave and then came fall and the long winter. By about February, Sarah had settled into a mood she never recovered from, a quiet sort of sadness. She didn't complain, she never complained, but I could see the gears turning in her head. She clung to Anna like she was the only thing keeping her alive. Dinners became routine. She had a menu that she rarely deviated from, that you could set your watch to. Anyone in a marriage knows that food prepared without love tastes hollow. She didn't talk about New York anymore and I was relieved, but I could see her banking it, remembering. In bed, she didn't want to touch me. I told her we could go in the spring and she snorted into her wine, nearly dying of laughter. Have a beer, she said, and watch the game.

Anna and I stayed in a hotel off Evans Avenue, about fifteen minutes from downtown because it was half the price. Anna had a bath and went to sleep, exhausted from the drive and the excitement. I filled the little bar fridge with the twelve-pack I'd brought and drank beer, ordered chicken wings from the restaurant downstairs, and watched the end of the Leafs game. If there ever was time for a rebuild for that godforsaken team, it was then.

The next morning, we drove to Bloor and Spadina where I paid fifteen dollars for parking and waited for Sarah in a dodgy-looking restaurant populated by undergraduate students. The variety of people, hairstyles, clothing, colour, sexual orientation, everything, was overwhelming, and I felt like the small-town hick that I was. This was the New York of Canada; this was where you came if you didn't fit in back home, if you were young and ambitious and wanted to freely express yourself, if you wanted to *make* it. I gathered in all this even though I didn't want to. I wondered how Sarah saw herself in this place, how she believed she fit in. I watched the people on the street from our table by the window. It was Christmas Eve and it was warm. The stores were open and the street was packed. There was a great Christmas mood, and as I watched these people,

I felt a touch of admiration for the place. In a small town you get used to the same old thing and learn to distrust anything a bit different. But I was never a hater, not really. I played the part, but the truth was that I admired the will to be different. I understood, just a little bit, what Sarah was after.

It was morning but Anna wanted fries so I ordered her home fries and ordered myself The Big Breakfast with three kinds of meat and a Caesar because I was hungover and needed the salt. Anna dipped her home fries, one by one, into a great pool of ketchup and watched the sidewalk parade. She sipped her apple juice, wide-eyed, occasionally asking me questions about what she'd seen. Sometimes she just blurted it out. Purple hair! Those girls are kissing! That's a man right there, a *man*!

"Is it like this here all the time?" she asked.

"Yes."

"Why?"

"Because this is the big city, sweetheart. It's a little different than our town."

"You bet it is!"

Sarah walked into the restaurant twenty minutes late. She was wearing trendy new clothes, and her hair was cut short and dyed dark. She looked ten years younger. The crush of this city had actually breathed new life into her.

Anna let out a shriek and ran to her. Sarah lifted her up and buried her face in her neck, kissing her over and over. I looked at my watch.

"Nice to see you, Joe."

"You're late."

"I'm sorry. I was working this morning and lost track of time, but that's when you know it's good, when you forget yourself in the moment."

"I didn't know you had a job."

"Writing, I mean."

"Not really work, is it?"

She looked at the empty glass on the table. "Drinking already?"

"Anna, please go wash your hands after your fries."

"But Dad."

"It's right there, down the hall. I can see the entrance."

I waited until she was in the bathroom before I looked at Sarah. "What would you have me do? Actually I'm proud of myself for not being blind fucking drunk right now."

"And Anna, who's watching her? Jenny Lacroix? Why not my mother?"

"Because she lied to me. But you don't have a say in any of it anymore."

"Do you have a thing for her?"

"She just lost her husband."

"And you lost a wife."

"Fuck you, Sarah."

"It's okay, I know you. I understand what kind of man you are, how you require a woman to keep your head straight. Some men are like that. My father was like that, but aren't they all up there? I would actually prefer that you had a woman so that I know you're keeping your head about you. You do have a history with the whiskey, Joe."

"I've got responsibilities. I've got to work and take care of a little girl when I get home. Real work, you know, something you'll never understand. You couldn't even do one of those things for very long before you bailed. Now here you are, not working, not raising a child. You're here finding yourself. Well I hope you like what you find. I won't tell you to come home, because I don't want you if you don't want to be there. And I won't tell you you can't see Anna, because she deserves a mother. But I'll tell you this: Black River is her home. That will never change, and if you go putting ideas in her head that maybe she should go live with Mommy for a little while in B.C. or Toronto, or fucking Kathmandu, I'll make sure to bury you in legal battles that I know you can't afford. See, I don't make much money, Sarah. But I make more than you, which is nothing. And anyone who knows anything about the law knows that it has nothing to do with right or wrong, but who has more money, and in this case, I'd be right and I have more money so you wouldn't have a chance in hell now, would you."

"I expected this from you."

"I bet you did."

"I won't fight you on it. But you have to let me see her. I don't want her to forget me."

"You'll have nobody to blame but yourself."

"Damn you, Joe."

"Anna is coming."

And just like that Sarah put on a big smile and Anna crawled up on her lap and they were smiling and laughing, and I was sitting across the table scowling like an asshole because I could never hide my emotions the way Sarah could, the way many women could.

"The winter," Sarah said, "isn't it nice and warm here?"

"It's beautiful," Anna said.

"I prefer the cold," I said, and they both looked at me. "I'm going to the washroom."

I walked to the washroom, and once inside the stall I put my head in my hands and it took all my power not to punch a hole in the door. She was never coming back. This was how it would be now. Visits to Mommy. She had plans: travelling, writing, seeing everything she had missed while she'd been stuck in our town. But I knew that she meant it when she said she wouldn't fight me on Anna. She didn't want the responsibility anymore. She was twenty minutes late to see her daughter after months apart. If she still loved her, it was a kind of love I didn't understand, a selfish kind of love that says something like you must love yourself before you can love others, or you must help yourself before you can help others, things that should never be said when there are children involved. Sarah was acting like a child, finding herself, and I was left to gather the pieces. She was in the other room playing mommy for the day because she wanted to have her cake and eat it too. I was so close to burying her in it, forcing her to make a real choice, to saying: don't call us again, and the only reason I didn't was because I couldn't break Anna's heart. So I splashed some cold water on my face, gathered myself and walked into the restaurant to spend the day with a woman I could no longer look at without hating because I had to make it good for Anna. And from that moment, I knew that everything I did now would be for her.

We went to the Ontario Science Centre. It was Christmas Eve and the place was mostly empty, but Anna didn't know the difference. There was an IMAX about lemurs and one other family inside the theatre. We went to the electricity demo and Anna's hair went all staticky. A college-age employee commented that this was really the best time to visit for lack of crowds, and I knew we looked like the broken family that we were. We walked on either side of Anna, trying hard not to look at each other. From behind I could barely recognize Sarah. Her short dark hair in some kind of pixie cut, part of her head shaved. She looked either ridiculous or right on the money. I didn't know which.

Anna ran ahead to the cave exhibit and Sarah turned to me. She was still so goddamn beautiful. "Not that I expect you to care or anything, but one of my teachers thinks I have a lot of talent. He's really pushing me to go to this writing program on Vancouver Island. He says with my portfolio I'd definitely get in."

"And then what?"

"What do you mean?"

"What will you do after that?"

"Well, I'm hoping for some publishing credits by the end of that, so, I don't know, maybe I'll write a novel, or try to anyway. I feel like I've got this great story in me, that I just need to get out, you know what I mean?"

"No. Is he fucking you?"

"Excuse me?"

"I said is he fucking you. Seems like a fucked-up thing to encourage a mother to leave her child, and I can't understand why else he would do it."

"It's none of your business, Joe."

"I heard a man's voice the night you called. Isn't that what these teachers do? These failed artists? Don't they all try to bang their students, put crazy ideas in their heads?"

"You're unbelievable."

"I'm here, that's more than most would do."

"You were never one to compare yourself to others, why start now?"

"If you expect me to keep it together this whole time, you're farther gone than I thought."

She took a deep breath, and looked at me. "Well he's not. He's a friend."

"Yes, at your place late at night."

"So what if he was? And how do you even know it was him?"

"Because I can tell by the way you're speaking about him. Stars in your eyes like some pathetic teenage girl. You're twenty-nine, young but not that young, too old to start over. But a man with tail on his mind will say anything to get it. So tell me the truth, is he fucking you, or does he want to? Because if he is you can't trust anything he says."

She glared at me. If I'd said something like that before she left I would have chased her down, apologizing, blaming it on the booze. But not anymore. I'd had two Caesars with breakfast and felt good. I wanted to be the brute she married, the uncultured bushman because that's what I was and that's what I would always be, and I never tried to be anything else.

"You know, I would never call Anna a mistake because I love her to bits, and one day she will understand why I had to do this, that it was the only way for me to survive. The truth is that you were the mistake. I was young and foolish and I should have followed my heart when it told me that a life with you would be full of pain and sorrow. It's not your fault. You are you and I am me, and we should never have been more than a fling."

"But you have a child who needs you, don't you understand this? Anna needs you."

"She will have me, Joe. Of course she will have me. What I'm asking for is some time to get my life together, my life without you. Then I can be her mother again, really be her mother. I know she can't live with me during the year, but there are holidays, there is March break. Summers could be spent with me, too. I want to be her mother. I'm asking you to please have mercy on me, please help me to get better, so I can be better for her."

"So you want it all."

"I just want to get my life together. You're a good father, you always were. A good man, honest. So find another woman. It won't be hard for you, believe me. Find a good woman and raise our daughter, and when I have her I will raise her the way I can. Now when you look at it like that, the prospect is not so terrible for Anna. She will get to travel, she will have her town and her father, and also her mother, a happy mother. She will get to see things. March break she can come to Vancouver Island, if you will allow it."

"I hate you."

"No, you love me more than you ever have. If you didn't, you wouldn't be here."

"I can't do this."

She looked at me with something like pity in her eyes. "We're fine here if you need to get away for a bit. We can meet you at the CN Tower this afternoon."

"But you don't have a car."

"This is Toronto, nobody has a car."

So I gave Anna a hug and told her I wanted her to spend some time alone with her mother, and headed back downtown along the Don Valley Parkway. I wanted to hate Sarah but the truth was that I hadn't seen Anna this happy in months. Maybe it was for the best.

The Don Valley Parkway twisted and turned like a racetrack, and I pushed the pedal to the floor on a big turn with the valley down below. The engine growled and the truck's weight shifted as the tires grabbed the asphalt. I'd heard there were deer in the valley and rainbow trout in the river during spring. I felt for the animals that lived here.

The tall buildings of the downtown core rose out of the ground like concrete trees, and I imagined them to be the remains of a great forest, the surrounding smaller buildings the cut. Everything cut away but the corridor along Yonge and Bay all the way to the lake, a place for the wildlife to thrive, for the bankers to hide. I needed a drink, something stiff, so I took the Gardiner back to the hotel in Etobicoke, parked my truck, and took the Evans Avenue bus to the subway and the subway downtown. I got off at Union Station and walked around until I found a cool-looking bar in a pie-shaped building jutting out into the street like something from a Dickens novel (I'd read Great Expectations in high school and the setting of Industrial-age London had made an impression on me, its bleakness comparable with this city's).

It was one o'clock, and I sat at the bar and ordered a pint and a shot of rye. The World Junior hockey tournament was starting in a couple of days, and the talking heads on TSN were discussing the imminent pummelling of some unfortunate Eastern European team. The bar was busy, and I didn't feel too bad about being there on Christmas Eve. Dozens of men escaping family obligations, like we were all keeping the same secret. I drank and watched hockey highlights. I enjoyed the mood. No matter what else went on in my life, there were always hockey highlights. I felt this applied to most men in this country, certainly most of the men in my town and in this bar. It was the one point of kinship I felt with these Torontonians, for it is true that Toronto is a hockey-first town, and when hockey is on or being discussed, where you're from is not as important as what you can contribute to the conversation.

After many drinks I headed to the CN Tower. This was to be our special Christmas dinner. I was from a German family. We always had Christmas dinner on the eve. Sarah hated this tradition, but by conceding now I knew that she was reaching out to me.

The concrete beneath my feet was hard and unforgiving. My head was swimming. It was warm but cold at the same time. The temperature hovered around zero but the chill went right to your bones. It was a different kind of cold that came off the lake and flooded the city and made it miserable. No wonder everyone wore black. I could see the tower to the west and headed toward it like it was a lighthouse and I was a sinking ship. I was determined not to ruin Christmas. I wanted to show them I could have a good time despite everything.

I took the elevator and watched the city melt into dusk as the daylight became a foggy grayness flecked with weak colourful lights. I felt like I was atop the mast of an ancient ship, the choppy sea all around me, and the city lights were candles floating in the water, survivors of a shipwreck. Water droplets formed on the glass windows of the elevator shaft. The rain got harder the higher I went, and at the top the city and its lights were no longer visible. At the top the world had disappeared. I took the stairs to the higher observation deck for one last look at the frothing wet gray before I gathered myself and headed into the dining room to find my wife and daughter.

The moment Sarah laid her eyes on me she knew I was hammered. I knew how I looked: my jackass half-grin, my head on a tilt, glassy-eyed. But I smiled at her like everything would be okay and she relaxed a bit. She knew me well enough to know the bad drunk from the good one, and the distance it took to cross the two.

I ordered a bottle of wine and Sarah drank her share, and soon we were talking like it was old times. Anna was happy to watch the city pass far beneath us through a swirl of fog. Sarah drank her wine and talked and I listened, but mostly I watched the movement of her lips. I told her I liked her new hairstyle and that she looked good, that the city seemed good for her. She told me she missed me, missed Anna. She told me that there was nobody else, that the voice I heard that night was a just a classmate. A gay classmate, she said, so you don't have to worry. I didn't come here to have an affair, I came to find myself.

We finished dinner, drank a second bottle and by then Anna was tired and wanted to go back to the hotel room. Sarah suggested we stay with her for the night so she could see Anna first thing in the morning. Christmas morning, she said, I can't miss it. I conceded and we went back to her tiny one-room bachelor apartment with a red curtain strung across the middle to separate the futon from the rest of the room.

It was dark, and she put Anna to bed. She came through the curtain with her pajamas on and sat beside me on the couch.

"So this is how you live."

"It's not terrible. I have everything I need."

"Except your family."

She sighed. "I miss Anna so much, Joe. But this is how it has to be for now. You understand that, don't you? You see that I need this for my own sanity?"

"Do you miss me?"

"Sometimes. Mostly I miss our talks. Having you beside me in bed. But I don't miss the town, that's for sure."

I walked to the window. There wasn't much of a view, an alley down below and the corner of a neon sign. "I understand. But I still hate you. And I still love you."

"You're the father of my daughter. I will always love you."

"I hope you make something of this. I hope it's all not for nothing."

She shook her head. "But even this is something, isn't it?"

"I don't know."

"Thank you for coming."

"Anna deserves her mother."

"I will make it up to her."

"You better."

"And you?"

"The same. Except everything is a hundred times harder by myself."

"Don't hate my mother. It was my fault. Let her see Anna."

"Do you have anything to drink?"

She retrieved a bottle of wine from the counter and poured us each a glass.

"You don't miss me at all?" I asked.

She looked at me and I could see that she was tipsy. She put her hand on mine, and then she put it down my pants and we were kissing on her couch like a couple of teenagers. She reached behind her back and took off her bra but kept her shirt on. She slid off her pants and I took off mine, and I'd never felt her that wet before, not even when she was eighteen and I was a horny kid. She rode me quietly, both of us careful not to make a sound. I felt her body around me, the warm comfort of her. It was the closest I'd felt to her in years, and it was the last time I would ever feel her. I came inside her and then we drank her wine, talking about the old days and the town. She showed me her writing and I told her I liked it, and I really did. I couldn't hate her because she was the mother of my daughter, and I loved her for bringing Anna into this world. And I knew that without them, both of them, I wouldn't have amounted to much. Sometimes a man needs a good woman to keep him straight. This is the type of man I am.

In the morning Anna opened her presents. Most of them were from Santa, but were really from Sarah, and I don't know where she hid them in that tiny apartment. There was a small plastic Christmas tree beside her bed, decorated with ornaments that I recognized from home. It meant that the day Sarah left, she had thought to pack them. She had known then that she would be gone for good.

We had Christmas dinner at an Indian restaurant. Anna was watching us closely, she knew something was different between us. The mood was relaxed, we bantered like the old days. I think Anna thought it meant that we would get back together, when all it meant was that we could stop hating each other. And despite it all, it was the nicest Christmas I could remember.

20

In the dead of winter, the bush slows to a standstill. Black trees and white snow and a deathly quiet except the howl of the wind, the grains of snow blowing across the hardened snowpack. In places it was a metre deep with a four-inch crust, and with a pair of snowshoes I could fly across the top like a rabbit. When I was a kid, I'd hunt them with a twenty-two. I'd head out on a cold Saturday and follow their tracks through the black spruce and leafless alder, watching for their outline, the white on white. There's something about the winter hunt. Maybe it's the stillness, the quiet. In the winter bush you can feel like the only living thing, and to come across another living thing is invigorating. But I never really liked the taste of rabbit, so I gave up hunting them. Because, if you don't respect the land, it will eventually turn on you.

The Laurie Lake cut was rolling. Haul trucks were pushing deep on a winter road that would be impossible to cross once the spring melt began. It was a race against the changing of the seasons. Paul had trucks coming in from Marathon and Dubreuilville and another skidder and feller-buncher. We were operating two shifts, and I needed to be in the field for part of both to make sure the boys were keeping pace. We had contracts to fill and Paul was on the road again, selling. The shop was mine to run and the men looked to me for direction. I didn't want to let them down.

I drove to the end of the winter road to scout the remaining trees. The forest of black spruce gave way to a stand of huge poplar, and on the far side was a sheer rock face that the machines couldn't negotiate. A natural boundary, like everything in the north.

In the fall those poplar, ripe with leaves, would sway like blades of tall grass on a windy day. It would be a great spot for a tree stand—where two stands of forest and a cliff came together. This was the way my grandfather taught my father to hunt, the way my father taught me. You look for places of intersection: where a creek meets a lake, where a stand of trees opens into a bowl, where a road ends. Places of transition, because you will catch them in transit. A smart moose won't show itself unless it has to. It will walk along the periphery, dart across an opening, make itself scarce.

My grandfather, Lucas Adler only hunted in places that other people couldn't find, or didn't know existed. He would sit for hours in a spot, emerging after dark with his faded orange hunting hat cocked to the side and his rifle cradled in his arms. He knew the bush better than anyone. He said that Northern Ontario was built for solitary animals. The true hunter, he said, isn't afraid either. He pushed himself to go to the remotest places, staying out longer and longer until eventually he would spend the entire night in the bush, sleeping under a tree with his rifle in his lap.

And then one day he never came home. That's how my father always explained it: he just never came home. I can see him now all misty-eyed (as far as the old man got misty-eyed) holding his beer bottle by the neck, resting it on his chest with his feet kicked up on the pine coffee table. He just never came home, and that was that. What happened, Dad, what happened to Grandpa, my brother Thomas would ask. Then my father would take a swig of beer, inhale quickly like something had irritated him, and say: nobody knows because they never found his body.

For me, there was never any mystery. The bush was immense, endless, a vast swath of green and blue as far as Hudson's Bay, as far north as my mind could imagine. It wasn't improbable that he had been lost out there; it made perfect sense. The land had swallowed him up just like it was meant to. He always talked about being one with the bush, well maybe he got his wish.

But for others, it was a mystery indeed. Because everybody knew that my grandfather was the bushman of bushmen, and how could such a man get lost or killed in the world he so resembled. When someone got lost the COs called Lucas Adler. He had disappeared because he wanted to disappear, struck off for the hills to live off the land the way he always wanted. His kids were grown and his wife was dead, and he wasn't much of a family man to begin with; so why the hell wouldn't he? That was how the town saw it, at least.

I remember that time well. There were search parties sent out from the cabin to scour the surrounding lakes and cutovers. My father sneered at them all, saying it was a waste of time, saying the big bear had finally got the old man. He loved that cabin, built it with his own two hands, and would never leave. No, he went out too far one night, and he never came back. The only thing that could've taken old Lucas Adler was a monster bruin, that one percent of predatory males that will kill you just because. That's the thing to fear up here in the north. Not a pack of wolves, or a bull moose in the rut, or even a sow with cubs, but the solitary male black bear that has never seen a human being before. Cross the wrong one of those, and you're as good as dead. And what about his clothes, the evidence, they asked. Well, that's the easy part, my dad said. Old Lucas Adler went to places that nobody had ever set foot before, so that's why we would never find him. And that was the story my father stuck to for as long as he lived. There were questions, because there always are. The cops didn't buy it and they let him know. They hauled him out of the bar one night and he was meaner than a wolverine, cussing and spitting and kicking. His relationship with my grandfather was never a good one and the cops told him they knew about that too. So they took him in when he was piss fucking drunk and tried to question him and when that didn't work they made him sleep it off on the cold jail cell floor, then hammered him again the next morning. That must've been what really settled it for him and the cops.

Bunch of goddamn bullies, he said when he got back the next day, heading straight for the fridge for a cold one. They're looking for a body and they'll be lucky if they don't find two out there wearing Gestapo uniforms. I knew my father, and I knew that he couldn't have done it. But there was a fight, the cops had said, everybody in the bar that night saw you two nearly going at it. Didn't one of your colleagues have to break it up? Some fight, my dad answered. My father coming to the bar to get *me* out, to send *me* home! After everything he did to us, after never being there, he had the nerve to come get me because my wife was worried and I hadn't seen my kids in a while. Now that's the biggest joke I ever heard! So you didn't go? You're damn right I didn't go. Think I'm gonna take life pointers from my father? I mean, it's obvious what kind of job he did now isn't it?

And this is when the cop really crossed the line. He leaned in and said, in my experience, Freddie, a man is responsible for his own self, and everything else is an excuse. So my father said: either let me call a lawyer or let me go, but I'm done talking to you pricks.

Even then, years ago, the cops were shipped in from the south. They hailed from places where political correctness ruled the day. They were fresh and clean and young and they weren't prepared for the likes of my father, who had so much hatred for them they just couldn't make sense of it.

Never trust a man in uniform, he'd always say, because his ideas are not his own. And young cops, well they're the worst, because they haven't lived long enough to see things for what they are. They take the company line of bullshit and swallow it whole. Hook, line, and fucking sinker.

I heard the groan of heavy machinery. Terry Pike was down the final leg of the cut on the feller-buncher. He never told anyone about our encounter, but there was something in his eyes I didn't trust. I didn't want to see him, but I didn't want to avoid him either. I walked down the skidway led by the sound of his machine. This was my yard he'd pissed in, and I had to keep reminding him it was mine.

21

I watched Anna and Gracie playing in the living room. They were laughing and giggling. It was nice to see my girl so happy. It had been five months since Sarah left, five months since the death of Dan Lacroix. In my mind I had linked the two events, as though one could not have occurred without the other. If it was his death that had driven her away, the truth was that she was already gone and had been for years. Dan was just that final push she had needed to get out the door. When I watched Anna now, I was beginning to think less about how she had lost a mother and more about how she was gaining a family.

We often ate dinner at Jenny's house. Work was tiring and I was hopeless in the kitchen, and she said it was nice to have a man around to eat her cooking. She was good, too. Either you cook with love and passion or you don't, and it always shows.

We talked a lot. We talked about everything. I learned that she had married Dan after Gracie was born, and that she did it to appease her mother who was old school and couldn't stand the thought of her having a child without being married. She loved Dan, but not in the usual way, not the way she dreamed of as a girl, the way girls dream of falling in love. Dan was a good father and a good man, but they were married too young. What do you know when you're a teenager, she asked me. I was just a kid making a life decision with so little life experience. I smiled at that. I told her I understood completely.

Sometimes the neighbours gave me looks, my truck parked there first thing in the morning to drop Anna off and after work to pick her up, longer if we stayed for dinner, which was just about every night because when I made dinner it was hot dogs or spaghetti or pizza. But their looks didn't bother me. I'd grown up in this town, and I'd never hidden anything from anyone. We were doing what we had to do to make our lives a little easier, and if we happened to get along while we were at it, well then that was fine with me. And the more we talked, the more I realized how much we had in common, more than I ever did with Sarah. She was happy with what she had and didn't try to be anything else. When you marry the first person you fall in love with, either you're meant to be or you're not, and how the hell can you tell the difference if you've got nothing to compare it to? You can go blindly through life thinking that your differences are part of a normal marriage because you don't know any better, and because you watched your parents do it. But eventually the cracks turn into canyons and the distance across is too great, and nothing in this world can ever bring you back together.

"People are saying things," Jenny said.

"About what?"

"About you, me, the girls."

"Gossip's what makes this town go around."

She sat down. She was so small in that chair. Slight shoulders and dark hair, her lips and cheeks, French Canadian. She was beautiful and confident, and comfortable in her own skin. She made me feel welcome, and that was the best part of her, the way she made people feel.

"The last time I saw Sarah was at Christmas. She said something to me about how it would be okay if I found another woman because a man like me needs a woman to keep him straight."

"She said that?"

"Yes, but that's Sarah. That's exactly what she would say to try to make herself feel a little bit better. I can tell you she never had an arrangement like this in mind. I almost think it would make her angrier, that we could just be friends, just eat together and talk and let our girls play. It would drive her crazy that we were friends. But you've been good for us, for me and Anna, and whatever this is I'm grateful for it, because I don't know how we'd manage without you."

"Thanks Joe."

She smiled, and I wondered what it would have been like to grow up with her. She was a few years younger than me, but if we were the same age we would have been friends. That is the thing with a small town, from the moment you're born your options are limited. It makes you wonder about all the marriages, if they really found the right people or if they just settled or were confused. If Jenny settled, and I was confused.

"Do you miss her?"

"I miss her company. I miss her presence, her heat. But I don't miss the fighting, the second-guessing. Sometimes I would come home and she'd be so worked up about something. It could be anything, and she'd be so worked up that I could see she'd been thinking about it all day, playing everything out in her mind. I'd come home and she'd have made a decision, and that was that and there was no changing her mind, and I'm talking about a life-changing decision, a big decision that needed to be discussed and thought over. It was crazy, and it happened all the time. I know she resented me. It's like all she ever wanted was an excuse to leave. And the day she left she didn't even leave a note. Her mom was there to pick up Anna and that was it. But I felt it, you know, the storm coming. For years I felt it, I just didn't want to admit it."

She picked up Maggie and held her in her arms. She closed her eyes and rocked her back and forth, and after a while she said, "Did you ever think about how different your life would be if you were born someplace else?"

"This town is all I've ever known. When I was a kid I knew that this was going to be it. My grandfather, my father, me, and hopefully if there is a God, not Anna. When I was in Toronto there were so many people; it was overwhelming. And I've got nothing against them, I think that people are people wherever you go, but I just couldn't live there. I like my space, I like the bush. It's the only place I feel at peace. What about you?"

"I don't know. I've got two girls and I'm doing the best I can, but I feel like the rug is being pulled out from under me. I have a mortgage, Joe. There was a small life insurance policy but it will run out quick. What kind of prospects do I have here? I loved Dan, I did, but being alone wasn't part of the deal, it wasn't supposed to happen. And maybe we weren't the best fit, but I would have stayed with him because he was good and I am loyal. Now, nothing makes sense. The town seems foreign. I walk downtown and people give me funny looks, like I'm doing something wrong. They don't have any idea what I've been through, what it's like at home without your husband there, the emptiness, the fear. I'm twenty-five years old and I have two kids and a high school education. What options do I have?"

I looked in the living room. Anna was so happy, the happiest she'd been since Sarah left. "I don't know. The only thing that makes sense to me is that little girl in there. And I'll do whatever I have to do to make her life a little bit better, because she didn't deserve any of it. Not the flighty mother, not Christmas in a dorm room. This is her home, the one stable thing in her life, and I have to make sure it stays that way. Listen, I will pay you more. And once school is over Anna will need a sitter for the summer. That's full-time work."

"I'm not asking for a handout. You've been amazing already."

"It's not a handout. Look at her—she's happy. And you deserve to get paid for the work you do."

She looked at me. "Do you feel sorry for me? Do you feel responsible for what happened to Dan?"

"It was an accident. I don't feel sorry for you because I see strength in you. I saw it the day I showed up at your door to tell you he was gone. If that was Sarah, she would have folded over and given up, and in a way she did. But not you. You don't need pity, and all those people that look at you like that have no idea who you are. I like you, Jenny. I like being here. That's why I'm here."

22

That Friday was cold. I remember because I was scouting a new cut and the sun rose in the clear sky as I took the bush road out of town. The coldest days are the clearest, the sky, a thin blue membrane separating us from the endless vacuum of space.

I hadn't had a drink in weeks, and I don't mean just the whiskey. Maybe Sarah was right in leaving, or maybe my mother was onto something— that I had loved the wrong woman all along. Not that I blamed Sarah for my drinking, or thought that I was falling for Jenny, but the right woman can make all the difference. And if we were looking for something beyond friendship, we never said so. I think we both knew we had a good thing going, and didn't want to screw it up. And of course there was Dan. He wasn't even gone six months and it would look cold. But like Jenny said, who were they to judge her. They didn't know a goddamn thing.

I parked on the side of a snow-covered road that wound its way up a clear-cut hill dotted with stumps and slash piles. It was minus thirty-two and wind-still. I strapped on my snowshoes and headed east into the sun, my breath rising above my head like exhaust from a tailpipe. The cold air pierced my nostrils and burned my lungs, and in minutes my nose hairs were covered in frost. I wrapped a scarf around my face to warm the air a bit and soon it was covered in frost too and stiff like cardboard. In cold like this you don't want to break a sweat. A deliberate, steady pace, keeping your heartbeat under control is the best way to work. One night when I was a kid I ran from the cops.

It was minus thirty and I ran flat out down a pedestrian way, the cruiser on my tail. I never got caught but I froze my lungs. For days the pain was excruciating, but I never told a soul.

I cut into the green bush and took a reading on my GPS. I headed for a creek about seven hundred and fifty metres from the main road that marked the eastern boundary of the cut. One hundred and fifty metres from the edge of the creek was the limit of the riparian zone, where the land remained untouched to prevent erosion and waterway contamination.

The creek was frozen, but the water still flowed under the ice and snow. It was thin, dangerous ice, and more than once I'd fallen through on the coldest days and had to make my way back to the truck as my feet and legs cramped up.

At the edge of the boundary, I tied my first ribbon and continued north. It was eight-thirty and the sun was low, peaking intermittently through the trees. I came to a clearing where the creek bed descended and snow-covered grass stretched out from the frozen water. I stood in the clearing letting the sun wash over me and poured a cup of tea from my thermos, the warm liquid trickling down my throat and into my gut. I felt its heat inside me like the sun itself. I tried to picture the place in the spring, when we'd be operational. The clearing and the grass meant it was a swampy area, and the spring meltwater would flow off the high ground I had come through and pool in here. We'd have to leave this section until at least June, which was fine, there was plenty of workable land in here until then. I made a note on the map, and then marked a waypoint on my GPS. The more detail the better. The reason so many of these logging companies go under is because they don't walk the ground. They study the map and figure they know what's what, but that is a mistake. You need to walk it, know it intimately. You have to have a back-up plan for when things go south, because more often than not, they will go south.

A dark spot at the far end of the clearing caught my eye. It looked like it didn't belong. I watched and waited and when it finally moved, I saw it was a cow moose and calf walking along the shoreline. They were browsing on the tag alders that grew close to the water. They would walk a step, eat, walk a bit more. The cow raised her head and looked in my direction, ears perked up, and I knew I stood out to them just as they stood out to me. I didn't move for a few minutes, just watched them go about their business. They ate, plodding along, while the cow kept watching me. The calf was big and healthy, and had survived most of the winter, which was something. She turned and walked into the treeline and the calf followed. I put my thermos into my packsack and continued with my work.

Each time I come across an animal in the bush, I wait for the moment to run its course. I become part of the landscape because I know I'm only a visitor. Even after all these years, a lifetime in the bush, I'm still just a tourist. Because the moment you take the land for granted it will turn on you. Maybe that's what happened to my grandfather, Lucas Adler. Maybe he forgot his place and figured the bush owed him something. A few years out here can do that to a person. You walk a few trails, paddle a few rivers, shoot a couple big bulls and think you've got it all figured out. And it's true the natives have more cause to call the land their own, but I'll be honest when I say that my grandfather could hold his own with anyone in the bush, even the Ojibwa who still lived the old lifestyle. I'd put my grandfather up against anyone. The land sees no cultural differences. It doesn't see experience, or recognize confidence. All it sees is a human being out of their element, and it waits for the slightest mistake to pound their expectations into dust.

It was Linda's night with Anna, so I was home early to pick her up from school. I had kept my promise to Sarah. I couldn't blame Linda for protecting her daughter, because I knew how far I would go to protect Anna. And it was good for Anna to have something of her mother in her life. There were telephone calls and holidays, but it wasn't enough. It would never be enough. Sometimes I saw the sadness in her, recognized its impact. A little girl needs her mom more than she needs her dad, and I was a piss-poor consolation prize.

She got into the truck and slumped in her seat with her feet up on the glove box.

"You okay, sweetheart?"

"I don't want to go to Grandma's."

"I thought you liked going there."

"I want to go to Gracie's instead. Why can't we go there?"

"Monday you can. Maybe tomorrow if Jenny says it's okay. But you have to see your Grandma because I promised your mom. Don't you usually talk to your mom at Grandma's?"

"Yes. But sometimes I don't like talking to her."

"Why not?"

"Because it makes me miss her more."

"What does she say?"

"I don't know. She says things."

"Nice things?"

She rolled her eyes. "Of course nice things, Daddy."

"Well that's good."

"Daddy?"

"Yes?"

"I miss Mommy."

"I know you do."

"Why isn't she here with us?"

"Because she needs to be somewhere else right now."

"But I'll see her on March break, right?"

"Of course you will."

"Daddy?"

"Yes?"

"Does Mommy love us? I mean does she love me?"

I looked at her and saw the tears in her eyes. It was so innocent, the question and how she asked it, like she'd done something wrong. She was a tough little girl, but she buried things deep the way her mother did. And now I saw how she'd hidden everything inside, all the emotion, putting on a brave face while her insides were being torn apart. I pulled over and hugged her close. As a parent, you feel as if it's your fault, as if maybe there was a moment you made her think she was the cause of all the bad things. I held her and told her I loved her. I said that nothing in the world could take me away from her.

"But why did she leave?"

"Your mom loves you very much. She wants to be here with you, and someday soon she will, but right now she needs to do something for herself. That's why she left. And we need to support her in that, even though it hurts. Do you understand what I mean?"

"Yes, I do."

"You need to be strong. And you need to talk to me when you're upset, like now. That's the most important thing."

"But you're always gone to work."

"I know, and I'm sorry. But we have the weekends. And I'll try to be home earlier so we can have dinner together, just the two of us, what do you say?"

She smiled. I wiped the tear from her cheek. "Okay, Daddy."

Linda was waiting inside the screen door. She'd been standing there awhile because there was frost on the window of the door, where the cold air met the warmth of the house. Anna hugged her and ran inside and Linda gave me a grateful look and I knew that she wasn't mad at me and understood what I was going through, but that her loyalty would always lie with Sarah. Because that's the way it goes.

"Anna's feeling pretty upset about her mom today. Can you make sure she's okay? Just make sure she's having lots of fun and that kind of thing."

"Of course. I always do, dear. You'll get her tomorrow before dinner?"

"Yes, the same as last week."

"Thanks, Joe."

"You're all she has of her mother right now. She needs to know that Sarah loves her. That's what she asked me on the drive over, if her mom loved her."

Linda shook her head. "I don't know what to say."

"Just tell Sarah that when she calls tonight, tell her what Anna said. She needs to hear it."

"There will be March break."

"Yeah, I really hope so."

I paid Jenny on Friday, and I paid her in cash. I had no intention of claiming any of it, and Jenny didn't either. Not paying tax on something is one of my small victories in life. I took the money from the only cash machine in town then headed to her house. It had snowed a few days ago and her driveway was still covered. There were tracks from her tires and a foot path from her minivan to the house. I took a shovel from the back of my truck and cleaned out her driveway. I looked up and saw her in the kitchen window. She was holding Maggie. She mouthed the words "thank you," and waved Maggie's little hand at me. She was wearing a white tank top and her hair was down. I came to the door with the envelope in my hand. She looked concerned about something and asked me to come inside. It was strange being there without Anna, so told her I couldn't stay long and took off my boots and sat in the same chair I always sat in, the one with the view out the window over the kitchen sink. I wondered if it had been Dan's chair, the way it faced the room, the fact that she never sat in it. But I had taken my cue from Jenny, and if she didn't want me sitting there, she would have said something. I put the envelope on the table.

"Do you want something to drink?"

"No, thank you." Without Anna, it didn't feel right, like I was taking advantage of Jenny. I felt Dan's presence in the house. There was a family portrait in the living room; I'd looked at it many times. Jenny and Dan were smiling, but there was something under it, something hidden. I could tell there were things between them: arguments, frustrations, fights, differences that ran deep. I'd lived it for ten years and knew the signs. You can't hide that kind of animosity. You bury it because of the kids but it never goes away, you're never able to fully sort it out. Concessions are made and life goes on, but the resentment stays. I felt Dan watching me through the living room wall. I saw his body lying on the roof of the skidder, his face submerged in the reddish water. I wanted to tell him I was sorry for what had happened. I wanted to tell him that I cared about his wife and knew something of the pain she felt.

The way she looked at me I knew something was wrong. "It's nothing," she said.

"I've known you long enough to know when it's something."

"You're not going to like it."

"I don't like it already."

"I feel like I've done something wrong."

"What happened?"

"I ran into Terry Pike at the grocery store. He said he was sorry that he hadn't come over since Dan died, but he just doesn't want to run into you here."

"He said that, did he?"

"So I told him that's fine, that if he didn't want to come by it was alright with me. Then he said something else. He said that I was dishonouring Dan's memory by being with another man already, worse that it was with you, because it's your fault that he's dead. I told him we weren't together and he laughed at me, said the whole town knew."

"The whole town knew what?"

"That Dan's not even gone six months and I'm sleeping with you. He said he was embarrassed for me. He said it was disgraceful."

"Jenny," I said. But she had her face in her hands, trying to hide the tears from me.

"What have I done wrong, Joe? Tell me please. Tell me why I'm such a bad person, why a friend of my husband would say this to me."

I didn't answer; I couldn't. I was numb. I pressed my fingers into my temples, but I couldn't feel anything. I wanted to touch her, to hold her but it didn't feel right. Nothing felt right. I felt like an imposter, more than I ever had before, that maybe in some fucked-up way this was Dan's doing, that he was ending it before it started, because he foresaw the inevitable. She was saying something but I couldn't make it out. I felt like I was underwater. All I heard was the blood flowing in my ears, the rush of white noise, and I knew what I had to do. There was no choice, really. Either you're a man and you stand up for yourself or you don't, and if you let it happen once it will happen again and again. It will never stop. They will keep at it until you're less than them, until their thumb is pressed down on you so hard, you're less than a man, less than a human being. The old man taught me that too. Maybe he was good for something. I got up to leave and she was pleading, holding my arm, telling me not to go. She knew now that it was a mistake to tell me, but it was too late. He couldn't take back what he'd said, and I had to make it right. I took her hands in mine and told her everything would be okay, and then I left.

It was Friday night and I knew where he'd be. I walked into the hotel bar and he was sitting right where he was always sitting surrounded by his friends, a couple of guys who worked for Northern Timber and a couple who didn't. He looked at me, and his eyes grew wide and he knew exactly why I was there. I must have had some crazy look on my face because as soon as I made for him, he jumped out of his chair and went for the door. I grabbed the back of his collar and pulled him back in. His shirt tightened around his neck as he fell to the floor. He stood up with a beer bottle in his hand and swung hard for my face. I dodged it and grabbed his wrist, smashing his arm on a chair. The bottle clanged on the ground. He took a swing and caught me on the jaw, but I didn't feel a thing. I punched him as hard as I could, and he stumbled back. I moved in and swung two, three, four more times. I swung until he hit the floor and then I straddled him and kept swinging until he stopped fighting back, until his face was red and bleeding. I felt something crack under my fist. Finally, they pulled me off and I was relieved because if they hadn't I'd have killed him for sure.

I stood up, and leaned against a pillar. Terry was motionless on the floor. His friends looked at me and the bartender said, "Jesus, Joe. I think you killed him."

"No, he's breathing alright. Do you have a cigarette, Karly?"

She handed me one with a shaky hand and I got into my truck and it felt like I didn't take a breath until I was speeding down the industrial road, streaking through the pitch black, the black trees and the white snow, the filth of the industrial road in winter. I floored it and the engine roared, and I wondered how fast I could go before I put it into the ditch. The trees and the snow banks flew by; I could barely see a thing. I lit the smoke and felt the tires spinning on the packed ice and snow, the thin sheen of gravel laid on top. The landscape blurred, became one endless streak of gray, the white and the black, the darkness and the light, and I knew where I was heading, aimed my truck there like a goddamn compass needle. It felt right. It felt like I was going home.

I hopped out of the still-running truck and opened the cellar door. I grabbed the closest bottle and let it pour down my throat. It was the desperation, the urgency that was the worst part. This is when you know you have a problem. All I could think of was getting that liquid into my body to dull the hurt that had started at Jenny's house, because I was responsible for her pain, and after tonight there was a good chance she wouldn't want to see me again. I remembered thinking the exact same thing as Terry Pike's face was splitting under my knuckles, when his skin tore open and the inside of him spilled onto the barroom floor. And in the moment I told myself I didn't care, but now it was different, now there was Jenny.

I walked through the remains of the cabin with the liquor bottle in my hand. The snow was to my knees, and I knew it would take some time for the cops to get out here. Still, it wasn't much snow for Black River.

The moon was bright and the stars were out. It was a beautiful February night. I shut off the truck and stared into the sky as I drank my grandfather's Irish whiskey. Not sure why Irish. He was a Kraut, after all. He drank beer, but after a few cold ones it was always onto the Irish. It was the same with my father. As a boy it made me think of crooked New York City cops, paddy wagons, and billy clubs. Gangs of New York. Maybe because it was cheaper than scotch.

It was minus thirty but the more I drank the warmer I felt. I had half a mind to start a fire in the middle of the cabin, but realized it would be too much work and abandoned the idea. I felt whiskey heat my core like a furnace. Maybe that's why he had liked it so much—it went with the environment, like a St. Bernard in the Alps.

I opened the cellar door and took out the forty-five and a box of rounds. The smell of railroad ties was overwhelming and reminded me of hot summer days walking the railway line with my friend Pat Dermody, before they tore it up. I loaded the gun and pointed it at the cast-iron stove in the middle of the cabin's ruins. I held it there for a minute before I took aim at the bright, full moon that had peaked above the treeline, the edges of black spruce and jack pine, and emptied the clip into the night sky, the sound echoing through the clearing, ripping through the stillness of the night.

I drank until my fingers were numb, and I could no longer feel my face. I laughed because I knew I was really fucked up and I should have felt the cold more, and for some reason I found this funny. I put the gun back inside the cellar. I pushed some snow across the cellar door. I stumbled to the truck and started it and the clock said twelve-thirty. Fucking Terry Pike. I could have killed him. A guy like that won't stop until you bury him, and I hoped that's what I'd done, because the next time I knew I'd kill him for sure. There was just no other way for it. And it didn't matter anymore because Sarah was gone and she wasn't coming back. She'd left me to raise Anna by myself and a hell of a job I was doing. Drunk in the bush like my old man. I tipped the bottle, the final drops fell into my mouth. I realized I didn't have any water, and I knew that would hurt in a few hours. I started to nod off, but before I passed out I cracked the window a couple of inches, because everybody up here knows you don't sit in an idling vehicle without the windows rolled down a bit.

I dreamed of my father. He was walking through the bush with his old Italian army pack. I was behind him, trying to catch up. I was just a boy, and the snow was deep. He looked back a couple of times, telling me to hurry up, and no matter how hard I tried I couldn't keep up. He got farther and farther away, and then he disappeared and I was following his tracks in the snow. I walked through the forest following his tracks, and the sky turned gray and it started to snow. I marvelled at the beauty of the big white flakes even as I knew they were covering the tracks, sealing my fate. The snow got heavier, and soon the flakes were everywhere, covering everything. I walked until the tracks were completely covered, then I walked the way I thought I needed to go. The sun was going down and it was getting colder. Suddenly I had the realization that my father was gone and I was going to die out there, but I wasn't afraid. I was a kid, had the mind of a kid, and still I wasn't afraid. The bush wasn't terrifying anymore, it was just the bush, and all I thought was how beautiful the snowfall was. The bright white snow on the ground and the branches, flakes the size of toonies, falling perfectly without wind, barely falling, floating to the ground in a bright white light.

There's nothing like the sound of a billy club on a window. It wasn't the first time I'd heard it, not by a long shot. There was the time we hot-boxed my dad's truck, or the time Sarah and I got caught doing it in the gravel pit. A couple of horny teenagers. I can still remember how wet she was that night. Goddamn it I missed her.

I opened my eyes and it was a bright gray morning. The pain in my head started immediately, and I knew it was going to be a bad day.

"Come on out, Joe. I've already driven all the way out here, so don't make me come in there and get you."

"Have the paddy wagon, do you? Because I know you didn't make it with a cruiser, not in this snow."

"Open the door."

I opened it and Officer Taylor took me by the arm and pushed me against the hood of my truck. "Got any weapons?" he asked.

"No, but Terry Pike did. Came at me with a beer bottle. I was just defending myself."

I heard the handcuffs come out, felt them on my wrists. "What about my truck?"

"Not my problem."

He read me my rights and put me in the back seat, and for once I was glad that Sarah had left. I asked Officer Taylor if Terry was okay and he never answered. He just drove, staring straight ahead, trying to keep the tires in the ruts.

A voice came over the radio and Officer Taylor said, "Ya I've got him, we're on our way." He put the radio down and turned the rear-view mirror on me. He watched me for a while before he said, "A guy can pretend to be lots of things. He can pretend to be reformed, all better, but it never works, it's always a lie. Because guys like you never change. You fuck it up sooner or later. And in the end, the authority that you hate so much is the only thing protecting you from yourself. So you got a tough go right now, well, don't we all? You nearly killed a man over something he said, over words. Now where would that have left your daughter if you'd killed him? Seems to me this is just about the last chance you've got left. You're a father, Joe, act like it."

I leaned against the cold window and thought about Anna. For the first time in a long time I felt like my father.

"Assault, evading arrest, drunk driving. Quite the tally, Joe." It was late afternoon when they finally let me make my call. Sarah was gone and Paul was out of town, so that left one person.

"Just like the old days, eh Mom?"

"What is wrong with you, Joseph?"

"It's bullshit, Mom. Everything but the assault charge."

"And that?"

"I cracked Terry Pike a few times. But if ever a person had it coming it was him. What did Dad always say? You let one person talk to you like that and that's what you'll get for the rest of your life. I couldn't let him get away with it Mom, not now, not ever."

"Taking advice from your father? That would be a first."

"He wasn't always wrong."

"I beg to differ."

"Did you talk to Linda?"

"I filled her in."

"What did she say?"

"She said she wasn't surprised. She said she'd keep Anna until you were out, which looks like it won't be until tomorrow morning."

"Jesus, that's what he said?"

She nodded.

"Great. More fuel for Sarah."

"I don't think the officer likes you very much."

"How's Terry?"

"In the hospital. He's got a broken jaw and some cuts on his face. Maybe a concussion. From what I hear it's a good thing they pulled you off him. Christ, Joe, what did he say to you?"

"He said some things about Jenny."

"Do you love her?"

"What? Mom, God no. We're friends, that's it. But you know how people talk."

"So let them talk."

"I can't let anyone say that."

"They say it because it looks like you're trying to keep it a secret. If it was in the open, there would be nothing to talk about anymore."

"I told you we're just friends."

"Men and women can't be friends, Joe. It's impossible. There is either a mutual connection, or one is in love with the other and it's not reciprocated. Obviously, from your position here in this jail, you love her or like her, because only a man with feelings does what you did. What you have to ask yourself, is does she feel the same way? I love you Joseph, and I don't want to see you get hurt again. You can't handle it. Anna can't handle it. Make sure it's the real deal or move on with your life. And let Linda watch Anna. She's a good person, she was only doing what any mother would."

"It's not like that."

"Okay Joe, then it's not. What do I know? You know you can leave Anna with me, too."

"You smoke too much, Mom. That's the only reason."

"So you keep saying. I'll see you tomorrow. Take care of yourself."

She left and I was alone and I was a like kid again, a dumb teenager doing dumb shit who thinks he knows everything. How many nights had I spent in this cell? Too many to remember. The other cop brought me food and was kind enough to bring a book. I told him I didn't read much, so he brought me the sports section. There was pity in his eyes. Maybe he'd heard enough from Officer Taylor to last a lifetime, and maybe he sympathized with me a bit.

I spent a lonely, quiet night in jail and Sunday morning Officer Taylor opened the door and marched me out with a look about him like this was all for my own good. It was the same look my father used to give me. He told me I'd get something in the mail about a court date in Thunder Bay.

"Great," I said. "I love a reason to drive four hours."

"Terry Pike's going to be okay. Consider yourself lucky."

I turned and looked at him, and I must have had some kind of look in my eyes because his eyes got wide and he took a step toward me, his hand beside the nine millimetre in its holster.

"Go home," he said.

I walked through the front door of the Black River OPP detachment, and my mother was waiting in her car. "That's the cop that doesn't like you very much." She handed me a salami sandwich wrapped in plastic. It was late morning and I hadn't eaten anything. I unwrapped it in a hurry and ate it in about four bites.

"Let's go get my daughter," I said.

23

"I'm not going to fire you, if that's what you're asking. And not because I don't think you deserve it. I mean, what the hell Joe, he's twenty years older than you. What were you thinking?"

Paul's office was tiny, an extension of the map-filled, coffee-smelling boardroom we usually met in. There were maps everywhere: on the walls, across his desk, rolled up in tubes in the corners of the room. There were GPS's charging on a shelf in the corner, and a dust-covered computer. Paul and I never communicated via email. He preferred conversations one on one. He liked having you in front of him.

"Don't forget that Terry took the first swing, with a beer bottle."

He folded his hands on the desk and there was plenty of power in his arms for a man his age. "It was you who went looking for him, not the other way around. But as far as I can see it, you did what any man would have done. And if Terry can't see it that way, and take his lumps and keep his mouth shut, then I'll deal with him. I want you to take a few days off. Call it a paid vacation. Terry's back to work the day after tomorrow, and I need things to settle down before I send you out in the field."

"How long?"

"A week, come back next Monday."

"What the hell am I going to do for a week?"

"I don't know, Joe, figure something out. I'm paying you. Take your little girl to Disneyland. Enjoy yourself."

"If that's the way you want it."

"That's the way I want it." He looked down at his hands, wondering what to say next. They were rough, gnarled. They were the hands of a farmer or a blacksmith. Knuckles thick from a lifetime of gripping heavy things, from tying ropes, lifting logs, raw from cold steel in the dead of winter. They were the hands of every man who'd ever lived in Black River, from my grandfather to my father, from miner to bush worker. They were the hands that had built this town and the hands that would die with it.

Finally, he said, "When Sarah was around, she inflicted some kind of *control* over you. What I mean, Joe, is that when she was here you managed to keep yourself together. The worst part about this whole damn thing is that you drove all the way out to the middle of nowhere for a bottle of whiskey. That's a problem. Because I can't have a bloody drunk running my show. Understand that. If you fuck up with the booze again, that's it. Have a couple beer if you can; if you can't then maybe it's time you got some help. I'll help you get help. I'll stand by you. But Joe, this is your last chance. That's all I'm going to say about it."

He handed me an envelope. "That's your week's pay in advance. For God's sake get the hell out of here."

"What about the cut?"

"I'll handle it."

"I need someone to take me to get my truck."

He looked at me. He wasn't impressed. "Let's go."

So I took my check and we walked out of his office, and the boys I saw in the yard either nodded like they were with me or didn't look at me at all, and I was fine with that, because with me there was no in-between. Either you loved me or hated me, but you were never indifferent. I took that to mean I had a strong character. It wasn't the first time two guys who worked at Northern Timber had a dust-up, and it wouldn't be the last. In a small town things like that are bound to happen.

A reasonable person needs to see the forest for the trees, and Paul was a reasonable person. I knew he meant it too, about the booze. He meant every damn word. I needed to keep my head straight. I needed to keep my cool, and I knew if I saw Terry Pike or Officer Taylor or heard another word about Jenny, I'd do anything but that. I needed to lay low for a while.

One more thing about my grandfather's disappearance I never told you. The night my grandfather and father had that fight in the bar, the night the cops questioned him about, well my father came home alright, but he never stayed home. I remember it because TBS was running a Sergio Leone marathon and I was halfway through Once Upon a Time in the West, my favourite western of all time. I always thought of my father as the Henry Fonda character, the quiet angry man, the man in black. As soon as I heard his truck in the driveway, I turned off the television and ran upstairs so I wouldn't have to face him. He came inside, grabbed a beer from the fridge, and settled in front of the television. He turned it on, and wouldn't you know it he kept watching the movie. It was he, after all, who'd turned me onto those old westerns.

He watched it for a bit, while I listened from my bedroom at the top of the stairs. I wanted to watch it so bad that I sat on the floor by my bedroom door, opened a crack, and listened. There is little dialogue in that movie. It's all long, dramatic shots and dramatic music and hard stares. But I knew it off by heart. I knew when Harmonica was on screen, Cheyenne, and Frank. There is so much said in the music that I didn't need to see the screen.

I could hear my father too. Mostly I heard the sound of beer bubbling in the neck of the bottle with each long swig. Him, too, I could see without seeing. I knew exactly how he'd be sitting, how his feet would be up on the coffee table, at which parts of the movie his lips would curl up ever so slightly in a reluctant smile, and a grunt.

I heard him grab another beer, heard the cap snap and hit the floor like a coin, skidding off into the corner. He sat down again, and after a while I heard him say something. He was talking to himself, repeating the same words. He just kept saying, "That son of a bitch," over and over until finally I heard the bottle slam on the table (It was empty; this sound, too, I knew without seeing). Then he stood, and I heard him take the keys from the kitchen counter, the door close and the truck start, its tires crunching on the gravel driveway, its engine revving as it accelerated down the street.

At the time, I thought nothing of it. It was completely normal that my father would leave the house in the middle of the night after a few drinks to go God knows where. And I have to say, I was relieved, because I could sneak back downstairs to finish my movie.

I don't know when he came home. It could have been the next day, or it could have been days later. Thomas and I tried to ignore the old man as best we could, and my mother was much different then, more distant. Now I realize that her coldness wasn't from lack of love, but an incomprehensible frustration and sadness regarding my father. She spent a large part of her life trying to keep her family together. She had to manage him as best she could, keep the house functioning on some sort of level. So it was ironic that we only became close after my father died, after the years she spent protecting us. Once he was gone, it felt like we could all finally exhale, and let our guard down.

It was a few days later when they questioned my father about Lucas. Lucas hadn't come home in a few days, but the police were only alerted after that time because he had a history of not coming home—they had to make sure this was the real deal. It was one of his friends that had told the police that he was missing, and you can bet that got them thinking too.

I listened from my bedroom as they questioned my father, asking him about Lucas, about their relationship, and finally about that night in the bar. My father told them that he came home. They asked him specifically if he stayed home, and he said of course he did. So there it was, the big lie, the one that I remember clearest from my childhood, that everyone in our house buried so deep we never spoke of it. And I wouldn't have dared say otherwise, not then, not ever. The old man would have knocked my head clean off my shoulders if I ever contradicted him. And to be honest, I never thought he didn't come home because he was out killing my grandfather. That thought never once crossed my mind. I just thought he went out drinking in the bush somewhere. It wasn't until years later, after my father had died that I told my mother about that night, and she looked at me and told me that she knew too, and that Thomas did as well. She felt the same way I did, at least she did then. Thomas on the other hand, well he had his own opinion of the old man.

Thomas left home the day after he from graduated high school. I mean exactly the day after. He got his diploma, got shitfaced, and first thing in the morning drove his beat-up F150 all the way to a Northern Alberta oil rig. A friend had set him up with the job, said all he needed was his high school diploma. Even a hard case like Thomas knew his options would be non-existent without that piece of paper, otherwise he would have been long gone before then.

I was at his graduation, so was Mom. Sarah was at home with Anna, who was only a few months old. And my father, well, after all his humming and hawing and about Thomas taking off, about him betraying the Adler name by leaving town to actually make some bank, never showed. I wasn't surprised, and neither was Thomas. It was actually a relief to not have to see him there. So Thomas graduated, got hammered, and early in the morning, after not sleeping a wink, loaded his pickup with the few essentials he figured he needed to start a new life. He was in the driveway when my father pulled in behind him, and instead of a firm handshake and a good luck, son, my father started about Thomas being a failure and a quitter and a disgrace to the family name. Thomas had no intention of returning and my father knew it, could see it plain as day, as clear as a highway billboard. And Thomas being Thomas, being eighteen and with that Adler bone-headedness, told my father where to go, and what kind of father he was.

I wasn't there for that little exchange, and in a way I'm glad I wasn't. There's only so much hatred you can spew at a man before you start to feel a bit sorry for him. I didn't feel sorry for my father, but I think it would've hurt to see Thomas lay it all out. I was older, and had been living with Sarah for a few years, carving out my own life in the bush, and maybe I felt the same way my father did, just a bit, and I would've said as much. But I have to hand it to Thomas, he had some balls.

Thomas and I were never very close. We never talked about personal things, especially our father, which is strange when I think about it now because the effect he had on our lives was so total, so constant. We grinned and bore it, like the old man would have wanted, instead of standing together, at least colluding somewhat, organizing our defences, and providing some kind of support to each other. No, he was good at creating division, and each person suffered quietly and alone. We each had our own private little hell that we never talked about. We lived in silos, each one disconnected from the other, each one unaware of the pain the other was experiencing. And after all these years, I truly believe he had no idea the effect his drinking had on the family, which makes it even sadder. My mother and I only started to talk after he died. Thomas and I had no relationship at all. And there I was, scrounging buried Irish whiskey like a hopeless drunk, which I might very well be. But I don't blame him for that. A man makes his own decisions in life, is responsible for his own failures. But some days I wish he would have showed us an ounce of love, showed us that we mattered more than the booze and the bush. I have my own problems with the old man, but I know they are nothing compared to Thomas's.

So Thomas and my father were going at it in the driveway at six in the morning, and in a last-ditch attempt to save face, and that's all it was: to save face, my father told him that he wasn't allowed to leave, that he could leave over his dead body. So Thomas said: just like Grandpa, you mean? My mother was listening from the window but wouldn't dare get between them, never had, which is why Thomas hated her too. My father, stunned, angry, sad maybe, said: you're a real piece of shit, Thomas, I always thought that about you. You want to go, then go. But don't ever come back. And Thomas spit and said that he never would. And that was that.

Once Thomas was gone we never heard from him again, not until the old man's funeral. I heard things through his friends. They knew what was what and would tell me things whenever I ran into them. Thomas hated us because we didn't protect him, and I couldn't blame him for that. If I could barely hold it together, and my mother was a chain-smoking wreck, then I can only imagine what Thomas went through. Remarkable, the pain a person can cause simply by not caring. For years I'd wished my father would've just left, because then we could've at least had some kind of a normal family. Instead, he destroyed us one by one, separately but together, like a bomb.

24

The next morning when I dropped Anna off at school, the teacher on yard duty gave me a look that said she knew what had happened. The whole town knew by then. But I have to admit that it felt good, to be the incarnation of the man you are, to have everyone know it. I had nothing to hide, never had. I had hurt a guy for talking bad about Jenny, and there was no shame in that. No shame in a little frontier justice.

I went by Jenny's to say my piece. I knocked on her door and she opened it and kind of shook her head and turned and walked into the kitchen leaving the door open for me. She poured me a cup of coffee and sat at the table. Her place was clean, tidy. Everything in its place. Maggie was on the living room rug, a colourful show on the television.

Jenny was wearing a faded red checkered shirt with the cuffs rolled to her elbows, and a thin silver bracelet around her tiny wrist. Her still-wet hair rubbed the collar of her shirt, darkening it in places. She looked at me without anger, and I knew right then that she expected nothing of me, that we could sit here in her kitchen and drink coffee and things would go back to the way they were. And I thought for a moment the best way forward was to pretend it never happened, just play it off like it wasn't really about her. But I wanted her to know that it was. I wanted her to know that she could count on me. She was a quiet, thoughtful woman who considered her words before she spoke. I'd never seen her fly off the handle and I didn't think she knew how, or if she did it would be a long time coming, and it would be like cannon fire.

"I'm sorry if this made it harder on you. It wasn't my intention. I just, I couldn't let it go, Jenny."

"You know the funny thing is that people are a whole lot nicer to me now. People think we're together."

"Do you tell them the truth?"

"Nobody asks. Everybody assumes. But the way they look at me now is different. That's all."

"So, where do we go from here?"

She shrugged.

"If they think—"

"I don't care about them. I don't care what they say. I don't like what you did. You could have killed him, Joe. But what you did means something. The only other person who would have done that for me was Dan."

I sipped my coffee. Milk, no sugar. So many things between us went unsaid. "What do you think about that?" I asked.

The stress of the situation was there on her face, furrowed in her brow, embedded in the lines around her eyes, which made me sad because the last thing I wanted to do was cause her stress. "I think that Dan's only been gone six months."

"Yes, there's that."

"And I loved him Joe, I really did. He was a good man. He would have done anything for me. I cry for him, every day. I miss him. I don't let you see it, but I do. I don't let anybody see it. I'm sad that my girls don't have a father. I'm sad that I didn't love him better while he was alive. But then I think about you, and that makes me happy. I'm confused. I don't know how I'm supposed to feel."

"I'm not asking for anything from you Jenny, nothing at all. But I see beauty in you, in your family, and I like being here with you. And if somebody talks bad about you I can't let it slide, because I care about you."

"Terry Pike is an asshole. I'm glad you did it. I mean, I'm not happy that you hurt him, that you spent the night in jail, but I'm glad you stuck up for me." She put her hand on mine. "But Joe, don't go to jail again on my account. That's not fair."

"I don't intend to."

"You're crazy, you know that."

I laughed.

"But he won't say another word to me."

"No."

"I remember you from when I was a kid. You had a reputation."

"All good?"

"No, not really."

"I guess some people forgot."

"I didn't. I need some time. I have to sort it all out. I have to consider things, like Gracie."

"Fair enough."

"Thank you for sticking up for me."

"Anytime, Jenny."

"What about you, what did Paul have to say?"

"Paul wants me to take a week off, take Anna somewhere nice."

"Where are you going to go?"

"I'm not sure."

"I think you should go somewhere, get away from this place for a bit."

"I have no idea where to take her."

"C'mon Joe, you're not that hopeless, are you?"

"I haven't seen my brother in a while. He lives in Alberta, the oil fields."

"Yeah, that sounds like a dream vacation. I'm sure Anna will love it."

"They must have rides there. A whole oil village."

"They just might."

"Actually I don't think we're going anywhere. What Anna needs right now is stability. And that is school, and her life here. The last time we took a trip she saw her mom and God knows what kind of shit that put in her head. I think I'll take her ice fishing, been a while since we've done that. We'll go on a warm day. I'll build a fire, roast hot dogs, make smores, that kind of thing."

"That sounds really nice."

"See? I'm not that hopeless."

"I never doubted you for a minute." She looked at me, considering her words. She was beautiful, there in the morning light streaking through her kitchen window. "Joe, I want you to know that I'm not saying no. But at some point we will cross a bridge that we can't come back from, and we need to be sure of what that is. Because we have a good thing going here, and whatever happens we can't screw it up."

"We do, don't we?"

"Yeah, we really do."

25

The last time I saw my brother Thomas was at my father's funeral. We barely spoke. There was a wall between us; there were things unsaid. One day I realized it was the same relationship that my father and grandfather had, and I thought: what a shame.

I was three years older than Thomas, which is a difficult age difference when you're kids. When I was in grade twelve he was in grade nine and we didn't have much in common. Thomas had his friends and interests and I had mine and that was that. And whenever the old man came home the tension was so unbearable that we separated and went into our own rooms to avoid him because it was safer to lie low. The living room was for when he was gone, and when he was we would sometimes watch the same show or the hockey game and tolerate each other's presence. When my father was gone we could sort of be friends, and we tried to be friends, but mostly I think we tolerated each other.

I pulled his phone number from the junk drawer in the kitchen and stared at it. The paper was torn from a lined three-ring sheet and the number was scrawled diagonally across the lines. Thomas had written it down at my father's funeral, and I had cleared it away and hadn't looked at it since. Now I studied it to get a feel for my brother, what kind of man he might be, if he was still partying like a maniac in those oil field dormitories.

I laid it on the kitchen table and took the phone from the receiver. I stood there with the phone in my hand, hesitating, and then I said screw it, and dialed. He answered after two rings.

"Hello?"

"Thomas, it's Joe."

"Holy Christ, Joe?"

"Did I catch you in bed?"

He cleared his throat. "No, I'm on graveyards, haven't gone to bed yet."

I looked at the clock on the wall by the window; it was nine-thirty.

"What's going on?" he asked. "Mom die? Is Mom dead?"

"Mom is fine. I just wanted to see how you are doing."

"You want to see how I am doing?"

"Yeah Thomas, that's why I called."

"You're sure Mom is alright?"

"She's fine, man."

"Just give me a second." I heard him moving around, heaving or sighing. I heard the clink of beer bottles and hoped he was just cleaning up. I could see his place now. A tiny bachelor apartment with empty beer bottles, half-eaten bowls of chips, and hockey on the TV.

"I can call back later if it's a bad time."

"No, it's fine. I mean, shit, there probably won't be a later, right?"

I heard cupboards open and close and figured he was getting the coffee on.

"Sarah left," I said.

"When?"

"About five months ago."

"And you're calling me now?"

"I don't know who else to talk to."

"I'm sorry to hear that. How are you?"

"Fine. I got booked for assault on the weekend."

"Who'd you pop?"

"Terry Pike. He had it coming, believe me."

"I don't doubt that for a second. What did Paul have to say about it?"

"Gave me a week to cool off."

"And now the phone call to your estranged brother."

"Something like that. I just … I just wanted to see how you're doing is all."

"It's okay man, I understand. No good reason we never talk, right? So many times I had the phone in my hand and didn't call. More than you can imagine."

"It was hard with Dad and everything. It was hard with Sarah."

"Yes it was."

"How are you doing?"

"I'm alright Joe."

"Really?"

"I mean it."

"I heard from some of your buddies you're hitting it pretty hard out there."

"Well, for what they pay me. All I need to worry about is getting my ass to work, and after that it's all gravy. But I don't go too hard. Not like some of the guys out here."

"Just be careful, man. You are our father's son."

"Listen to you. I don't need advice if that's why you called."

"That's not why I called. Sorry I brought it up. It's just, things happen in your life that cause you to take stock of what you got."

"I heard about Sarah. I thought about calling too. Had your damn number in my hand for about three hours one night before I gave up. I'm sorry about that, I really am. But some women aren't cut out for that life. Be happy that it's now instead of ten years from now."

"Yeah, I know."

"And Mom?"

"She bailed me out."

"Just like the good old days."

"Except now the stakes are higher."

"How's Anna handling it?"

"She's got friends and she's got school, so that helps. But it's hurting her. I see it. A little girl needs her mother. Would be nice to see her uncle too."

"Is that an invitation?"

"Like I said, there are points where a man takes stock of what he's got. The longer Sarah's gone the more I realize how important family is. Mom would like to see you too. See that you're still alive."

"You sure about that? Last time I saw her she called me some choice words."

"She's softened up, Tom."

"Still smokes a pack a day?"

"She hasn't softened up that much."

"Let me think about it."

"God knows you don't owe me anything."

"We don't have to talk about any of that."

"Then we won't."

"You sound different."

"Must be the circumstances changed my mindset."

"You've had your bridges to cross."

"Yeah, Tom."

"So like I said, let me think about it."

"Fair enough."

So Thomas thought about it and showed up two days later after a four-hour flight from Edmonton and four-hour drive from Thunder Bay because there hasn't been a direct flight to Black

River since Bearskin Airlines pulled out in the early nineties. I told him I would pick him up in Thunder Bay, but he rented a car instead. I think the idea of relying on me to get around was too much for him to handle. Independent since birth, my brother.

He came through the door with an army duffle bag on his shoulder, wide-eyed, hair dark and wild, and thick stubble on his face. He looked exactly like a man who'd come from the oil rigs. I could smell the bitumen, absorbed into his clothes and shoes and skin, and remembered that from the last time I had seen him. He had a crazy look in his eyes, but he was smiling, and when Anna wouldn't come out from behind me, afraid to get too close, he let out a big guffaw and said: I'm your Uncle Tom! And then he reached around me and gave her a hug. It was clear we weren't going to let the past ruin our visit, that we would put it behind us, and for the sake of Anna, try to have a relationship. I was glad that he'd come.

We shook hands and he laughed again. He reminded me of how we used to try to crush each other's hands as kids. How we'd squeeze and squeeze until Tom cried out and I let him go.

"But then you got stronger," I said. "And you gave me a run for my money."

"So who do you think would win now?"

"Maybe after a few," I said. I took his bag and coat, and put my hand on his shoulder. "It's good to see you. Come in, I made supper."

"Mac and cheese?"

"An actual meal."

"That a first?"

"Pretty much."

He sat at the table and I handed him a beer and Anna sat in her seat and couldn't take her eyes off him. "You look like Daddy," she said.

"Yeah, I suppose I do. Guess that's why I let this beard go. Don't want people in town thinking I'm your dad."

I laughed. "Maybe not these days, eh?"

He looked at Anna. "So, how's your father's cooking?"

She stuck out her tongue. "Blech! I'm glad we don't have to eat it much."

Tom came over and looked in the pot simmering on the stove. "I dunno, Anna, it smells pretty good. Looks okay too. What have you got going on there, Joe?"

"Irish stew."

"One of Mom's staples. Thought I recognized the smell. Moose in there?"

"I never got one last year. It's beef."

"Great," said Tom. "Because I hate moose."

"You could've fooled me," I said.

"You knew?"

"Of course. Mom knew too. She knew you hid it in your napkin and tossed it in the garbage, but she never said anything to Dad."

"Because he would have killed me."

"Yep."

"The good old days," Thomas said, and he leaned back and patted Anna on the head, ran his fingers through her hair. "Beautiful blonde, just like your mother."

Anna giggled and climbed up on his lap and gave him a hug.

"Well that's just about the nicest hug I've ever got, my dear."

"You're welcome," Anna said.

"So if your dad doesn't cook much, who does?"

"Jenny!"

"That so?"

"We eat there almost every night. Jenny picks me up from school too. I get to play with Gracie. I love it there."

"Jenny Lacroix?"

"Yeah," Anna smiled. "Gracie's mom."

Tom looked at me. "How long has her old man been gone?"

"Six months."

He laughed and shook his head. "Really, Joe?"

"Anna, go play in the living room until I call you for dinner."

"But Daddy, I want to visit with Uncle Tom."

"And you can, but right now we need to have some adult talk. Go on."

"Oh alright," she said. She walked into the living room with her head and shoulders slumped, feigning hurt, all bluster and hyperbole, like everything with a little girl.

I opened Tom another beer. "She takes care of Anna and I pay her. We also happen to be friends, which is great because Anna is friends with Gracie."

"And the dinners?"

"She likes having someone around to eat her food, and I'm a horrible cook."

"I take it that's what got Terry Pike popped and you a weekend in your old favourite hotel."

"Yep."

He took a swig of beer. "See, that's one of the reasons I left this place. Everybody in your damn business."

"Don't tell me it's not the same in those oil towns."

"Sure, but most of the guys live on site during the week. No families, no gossip, just hard work and a whole lotta partying."

"You keeping your head clean out there or what?"

"I get to work in the morning and I do a good job, a damn good job. Never had any complaints, no run-ins with the boss. I'm good at what I do, Joe. But it's the lifestyle, everybody hits it hard."

"Fair enough."

"You know I remember Jenny Lacroix from high school. A couple years younger than me. I knew Dan too. He was alright, a stand-up guy. But that Jenny, man. She's something else, isn't she? She still as gorgeous as I remember?"

"She is."

"And you're not sweet on her, you sure?"

I smiled and Tom laughed. "I knew it. Just like the whole town knows it. So why is it a secret then?"

"Because her husband died six months ago, and she's got a heart."

"So you give her time. Give her whatever she needs. A woman like that, a practical woman like that is what a man like you needs."

"You sound like Sarah."

"She's right. I never thought I'd say it but she's right."

"Why didn't I listen to you when you tried to warn me about Sarah?"

"Because you were young, and you were in love."

"But you were right."

"I don't take any pleasure in that. I never wanted to hurt you; I just wanted to protect you."

"Like I couldn't do for you?"

"Something like that."

"I guess, Tom, what it comes down to is that I don't want to go down as the failed son of a failed drunk. And the way things are heading, well it could be my fate."

"Do you love her?"

"Shit, I don't know. I like being with her. Anna loves her and that means a lot. But she's vulnerable, and I don't want to take advantage of that."

"Hell, that sounds like love. Nothing's predestined, Joe. You can change whatever you want. You just need the heart to do it. Drinking to solve things never much worked for me. I drink to take the edge off. Maybe too much but at least I know why I do it, and I'm not hurting anybody. But you, man, you got a little girl who needs you now more than she ever did. If you need any reason at all, that's it. You got more guts than I ever did because you stayed here and you had a family, the two things that scared me more than anything else. If you're scared of becoming Dad, well you ain't there yet, and you can't hang this all on a woman. If it doesn't work out with Jenny, you can't throw in the towel, hear what I'm saying? Because the worst thing you could do to that little girl is throw in the towel. She needs you, more than she needs Sarah, even if you don't see it. In twenty years, she's not gonna remember that you spent a night in jail. She'll remember that you stayed. That you were her father. Whatever happens between her and Sarah is out of your control, but she loves you and she will never forget that you were here and Sarah wasn't."

"I work a lot."

"Everybody works. I'm not a father, but it seems to me that all a kid wants is attention and love, and if she gets those two things, everything else will work itself out."

"I think you're right about that, Tom. Want to go ice fishing tomorrow?"

He smiled. "Hell yes."

I called Anna, and we sat down to dinner. The stew was piping hot and good and I was proud of the meal I'd made. I'd even found some decent bread in town to go with it. The fancy round bread, Anna called it. Tom and Anna talked and I was amazed at how good he was with her, a real natural. Some people don't know how to talk to kids. They get awkward or nervous or don't know what to say. But Tom was right: all they want is attention and love. It's not that hard to take an interest in a kid's interests, to ask questions. He asked Anna about school, soccer, her friends, and she loved every minute of it. By the end of the meal she was calling him Uncle Tom, and that made me smile.

I put Anna to bed while Tom cleaned up. I told him to leave it, but he insisted. What's gotten into you, I asked him, and he told me that maybe he had grown up a bit too. I couldn't remember the last time I'd sat with my brother and there wasn't unbearable tension, let alone that he would volunteer to do the dishes. I guess a crisis can bring that about in people, cause them to lay down their weapons, or at least try to bury a long-dead hatchet that nobody can remember the genesis of anyway. And I guess that's what it was, a crisis. Tom buried one drunken asshole and maybe he didn't want to make it two. I had never reached out to him before, but it seemed it was all we needed to reconnect and try to wash away the aura of our father and start new or just try to be brothers again.

I grabbed a couple beers and we sat in the living room. Anna's Barbies were lying all over the place in various stages of undress and I could see the smirk on Tom's face.

"Daughters," I said.

"Yeah."

"I couldn't imagine having a son. I think about Dad, the way it was, the fucking tension and I'm glad I have a little girl because I have to be gentle with her. Sure I yell and get mad, but I think there's softness because she's a little girl and I know there's aggression in me she ought not to see. If she were a boy I don't think I'd be as cautious."

Tom looked around the living room. It was mostly Anna's toys and some of her books, and a few pictures on the wall. "I'll tell you, it's pretty sobering, all this."

"What, my life?"

"The fact that you're able to keep it together. I'm sorry I was such an asshole."

"You know," he said after a while, "part of the reason I never came to visit was Sarah. I just got a bad vibe from her and figured if I came back I'd say something that I'd regret and that would be it for us. When I heard she'd left, I was hoping you'd call."

I patted him on the shoulder. "Really good to see you."

"So when are we going over there?"

"Where?"

"Jenny Lacroix's."

I laughed. "Like hell we are."

"C'mon, you want me to tell you if she's good for you or not, don't you."

"I think I'll pass."

"Alright Joe, have it your way."

We finished our beers and opened a couple more, and I felt the urge to get into the Jameson, celebrate a bit. But instead I stood up and told Tom that I had to get to bed. He looked at me and I thought he was going to goad me a bit but he just nodded, and said he might head to the hotel for a couple, see who's there.

I said goodnight and went in to give Anna a kiss. I sat on the edge of her bed and watched her sleep. She was so peaceful. She looked like Sarah, a spitting image just like Tom had said. I wondered which way she'd go when she became a teenager, that all-important time that decides the fate of so many kids. I hoped that she'd be smarter than her friends, because I knew most of them would probably party hard, make bad decisions, and end up in town for the rest of their lives, be a stay-at-home mom to a "stand-up guy." Not that I had anything against guys like that, guys like me, but isn't it just like a father to want more for his daughter? What kind of father would I be if I wanted her to marry a guy like me? No, I knew she was smart, probably got it from Sarah. Who am I kidding, I *know* she got it from Sarah. Sarah who read books and wrote and enjoyed the city and was out there finding herself. And for the first time I saw that Sarah's absence was Anna's way out. She had a role model that was more than this town, and that was a good thing, a damn good thing. And I decided right there not to hate Sarah for what she'd done, because she knew all along we weren't right for each other, and she had the guts to do something about it. And as long as she kept her promises, and saw Anna when she said she would, then I would support her. After all, she had given me Jenny.

26

I loaded the ice fishing gear onto the truck. It was February but sunny and not too cold and the day was going to be beautiful. I started the truck and let it warm up a bit, the defrosters blowing full bore before I took the ice scraper to the windshield. Tom helped me bring gear from the garage and Anna, bundled in her snow suit, played in the driveway with a shovel.

I could smell the booze on Tom and knew he'd had a late night. He must have run into an old friend. But he was up and bright-eyed and keen and had the look of a practiced drunk, because that's what he was. I knew how things were in those oil field bunkhouses. Guys spent entire paychecks on booze and coke and hookers in a single weekend, then lived off credit until they got paid again. All young men and testosterone, pent-up aggression. They worked hard and played harder and the evidence was there in the lines on Tom's face. Most of them made too much money too easily. I'm not downplaying how hard they work; it's goddamn hard work, but it's not particularly skilled and a young man can come across it pretty easily. They were like my miner friends who made one hundred and fifty thousand a year and owned a brand new truck, new ski-doo, and spent money at the bar like it was going out of style. But they didn't have a dime in the bank, and absolutely no thought as to what might happen if they lost their job. These were family men too, which makes it inexcusable. That's one thing I've always been able to do: save my money. I drove a ten-year-old truck and my snow machine was about the same. I made one-third of what others guys made but my house was nearly paid off, and I had a school fund for Anna. I drank beer but I didn't blow money in the bars. Could be the cheap Kraut in me, just like Sarah always said.

We headed out of town on the snow-packed gravel road and the sun was bright and the sky a brilliant blue. Tom hadn't been ice fishing in years and Anna was up for anything. I promised her a fire and hot dogs, and maybe if she was lucky, a pickerel. Anna sat between us and the space behind the front seats was filled with gear. Ice fishing rods and a short-handled net poked out of my army pack. The minnows sloshed around in the box of the truck. I'd thrown a few lawn chairs in too, because that's the thing about ice fishing: it's a whole lot of waiting around for things to happen, which usually they don't.

We passed a haul truck and I pulled to the shoulder to give him enough room. It was one of Northern Timber's, and I knew the driver would recognize my truck. It was guaranteed that everyone at work knew by now what had happened.

We turned down a road we weren't hauling out of and it wasn't plowed. But there were tire tracks, deep and well worn, and I knew the road wasn't too hairy. I stopped to put the truck in four wheel drive before continuing on. I glanced over at Tom and he was staring out the window, and I thought there was something like longing in his look, or maybe it was just a hangover.

"Recognize this?" I asked him.

"Should I?"

"Dad used to take us hunting here."

He grunted something of an acknowledgement. "Winter hunt?"

"Yeah."

"That was my favourite kind."

"Mine too."

"Why?" Anna asked.

"Tracks, darlin'," Tom said, and I had to agree. "But after being away, it all looks the same. The trees, I mean. It's that Northern Ontario bush, especially in winter. Trees as black as the ace of spades, roads of white. It really is endless, isn't it?"

"That's what I like about it."

"You sound like Lucas."

"I'll take that."

"Who's Lucas?" Anna said.

"That's your great-grandfather."

We drove and the tracks of small animals cut across the road. We cut a set of moose tracks, big and deep, and I thought about how I never shot one last year. That wasn't like me, not getting my moose. The sun was behind us and the tall winter poplars cut sharp shadows across the road. Anna was talking to Tom about her favourite subject in school, which was music (at least today it was). It was going to be a nice day.

We reached the lake and the vehicle tracks went right out onto the ice, fanning out and disappearing as they reached the windblown expanse of frozen water. Tom gave me a look and I knew he was wondering about us driving the truck right out on the ice.

"Middle of February," I said. "It's been a cold winter. Not a lot of snow."

"Gotcha."

I took a line that went straight out, then hooked right and hugged the shoreline, heading for a point of land that jutted out into the lake. The snow was deep in places, formed into drifts that rose and swelled like waves or dunes. We were driving in established tracks that were mostly blown-over but still visible and hard-packed so we wouldn't get stuck. The snow was deeper close to shore as the wind had blown it to the edges and corners of the lake.

About fifty yards out from the point of land I stopped and told them we were here. There were a few sticks poking out of mounds of ice, and I said we'd use the same holes as the last guy, because there was no sense in drilling fresh holes when we were going to fish the same spot.

There was only a thin layer of ice on the holes so I cranked up the auger to punch through while Tom and Anna walked the treeline gathering burnable wood and fire starter. It was unspoken, a quiet understanding of the tasks that needed to be done. I was setting the lines so Tom would gather the wood, that's how it always went when we were kids. My father would coax us into ice fishing with the promise of fire and smokies, not that we really had a choice when we were really young as the old man's final word was always the final word, but I suspect he wanted us to enjoy it a bit, and he was always a little giddy at the beginning of a day of ice fishing, before all the beer had been drunk and not a fish had been caught. So my father would drill the holes and set the lines while Tom and I scoured the shore for firewood. This was in the old days before he'd bought a power auger and he'd be turning and turning that thing for an eternity. In February, the ice could be a metre thick and usually he needed the twelve-inch extension on the auger, between the handle and the blades, just so it would reach the water. By the time he was done and began the business of setting the lines, Tom and I would have a massive pile of dry wood and the beginnings of a fire. On the coldest days the wood was a necessity, but by March we would gather it to keep out of the old man's way.

I punched six holes, two for each of us, and went to work setting the lines. I used a bell sinker and minnow, threading the fishing line through the skin at the spine of the minnow so it would stay alive and keep swimming, then tied on a treble hook and lowered the line into the water. I set the rod in a small pile of snow and ice beside the hole, then scooped water over the pile so it would freeze. I had three rods, so I set those first, and used sticks and fishing line for the rest. I looked at the shore and saw that Anna and Tom had a good bundle of wood collected. Tom was shovelling the snow from beside a big black spruce to make the fire pit, and Anna was scooping snow away with her hands, laughing at something that Tom must have said. It made me happy to see them like that, and I hoped this wouldn't be the last we'd see of Tom for a while.

I finished the lines and walked over to the fire pit. With a Bic lighter in his hand, Tom was huddled over a little teepee of sticks and old man's beard collected from the spruce tree.

"That's a good pile," I said, nodding at the firewood.

"It's the only way in hell I'll stay out here."

I laughed. "Nothing ever changes."

"You're goddamn right it doesn't."

I looked at Anna. She was hunkered beside Tom, their toques nearly touching above the small flame. "Don't listen to your uncle. Ice fishing is the most fun you can have on a Saturday in the winter."

"But it's Thursday," Anna said.

"Thursdays too, and Sundays, and definitely Fridays. Friday is an ice fishing day if I've ever known one."

"Don't listen to your dad. When we were kids, same age as you, our dad would drag us out to the lake and make us pretend like we were having fun."

"But it is fun," Anna said. "I like ice fishing."

"That's because we're making a fire. Ice fishing's all about the fire. We'll never catch anything out here. Where are those hot dogs?"

Tom got the fire roaring and I went to the truck to retrieve the lawn chairs and the hot dogs and a couple of beer. It was almost eleven and I was on holidays. I knew that Tom with his hangover would appreciate a beer too.

We sat around the fire roasting hot dogs and watching our lines out on the ice. Every now and then we walked to the holes and pulled up the lines and made sure the minnows were still alive and kicking. Anna was fascinated with the minnows, wondering how they didn't die. We ate hot dogs and we waited for the fish to bite. The beer was nice and cold from sitting in the snow, and beside the fire on a winter day it went down just fine. It was like all the bush parties I went to as a kid, the cold liquid in your gut and the heat of the fire on your face. I looked out to the ice and squinted at the sun's reflection on the pure white landscape. The only break in the scenery across to the opposite shore were the dark outlines of the fishing rods and my pickup parked on the ice. It was quiet, too, wind-still, the crackle of the fire and our sporadic conversation the only sounds probably for miles.

Tom was sipping his beer and poking the fire with a stick. He had no interest in fishing and that was fine. He was the same when we were kids, uninterested but happy enough to enjoy the things about it he enjoyed. Dad always called him the extra limit.

Sometimes I wondered about my own reasons for fishing and hunting. The thrill of the kill, maybe. The moment you hook a big pike or down a monster bull. Though the longer I lived the less of a thrill and more of a necessary evil those moments became. Not that the adrenaline rush is a bad thing; it's probably hard-wired from our caveman days, the excitement a reward for being able to survive another day. But it's more than the thrill that gets me going. It's the landscape itself, the snow and the ice, the cold. It's driving my truck on the ice and sitting by a fire with my daughter and my brother whom I haven't spoken to in years. It's the freedom of it that I value, being able to go where I please and do what I want. But it is the inborn respect for the landscape which I feel most, as though the land and I are each other's confidantes. I understand the environment better than I understand people because it is rational and predictable in its unpredictability. You prepare, and you know that when things go south you only have yourself to blame.

But the easiest explanation is that I was born into it. This culture is all I've ever known, what I've always done, and so it comes naturally. It's where we live and it's part of the deal. Growing up, we never ate beef because there was moose. The land provides, and as long as you respect the land it will take care of you.

In my grandfather's later years he kept a garden by the cabin. It was small and simple, but it provided everything he needed. It was a battle to keep rabbits and the like out, but he managed to grow his own food. He ate fresh in the summer and stored what he could for the winter. This, along with moose, fish, and other game, made him nearly self-sufficient. This was what he was most proud of in those later years: that he didn't have to rely on anybody but himself. Poverty, he once told me, is as close to God as you're ever going to get.

"So then I'll ask Jenny if she wants to come over for dinner."

Tom smiled. "You're going to cook?"

"I'm not that bad."

"You're getting better," Anna said.

"Hey look," I said. "We have a bite!"

One of the rod tips was bouncing up and down, the hard-packed ice and snow keeping it from falling into the hole. I ran to the hole with Tom and Anna close behind. I grabbed the rod and gave it a little tug, and sure enough there was a fish on.

I looked at Tom, grinning. "Want to reel it in, Anna?" I asked.

"Sure!"

She took the rod and I showed her how to hold it. She kind of pushed me away saying, "Geez, I know, Daddy!"

She reeled and I knew the fish wasn't that big because the rod stayed more or less where she held it and she was able to turn the crank. The fish dove and she nearly dropped the rod down the hole, but recovered just as I was about to help her. She gave me a look that said: let me do it on my own. I thought: good for you, sweetheart.

She kept reeling and the fish appeared in the ten-inch hole, a nice pickerel. She pulled and flicked the fish out of the water and onto the ice, where it flopped around for less than a minute before it stiffened up in the cold winter air.

Anna looked at the fish as I re-baited the hook and sent it back down the hole. She poked it with her bare finger. "He's getting stiff," she said.

"He's freezing."

"That's so weird."

"Maybe you can cook it when Jenny comes over," Tom said. There was ice clinging to the stubble on his face.

"Need more than one pickerel."

"Well the day is young." He walked back to the fire, jigging each of the lines for a few seconds along the way like he was in his own little world. He hadn't changed a bit.

I put a hot dog on a stick and put it into the fire. "Anna," I said, "see if you can find some more firewood."

She nodded and headed into the bush. Tom was on his fourth beer, his head cocked back on the aluminum frame of the lawn chair, the sun beating down on his face. I couldn't see his eyes beneath his aviator sunglasses but I knew they were closed.

"Listen, you need to make another visit while you're here."

"Forget it. Ain't gonna happen."

"Been thinking about it?"

"No, not much. You'd be surprised how little I think about any of it."

"Does it make it easier, being across the country?"

"Yeah. Too many memories here. The roads, this fucking lake. All of it."

"Was it that bad?"

He leaned forward in his chair, the old woven nylon creaking under his weight. "Is that supposed to be funny?"

"She's changed."

"Really? Tell me this: do you ever leave Anna with her?"

"She smokes like a chimney."

"Of course she does, and inside the house too. She won't even change for the sake of her granddaughter, so don't tell me she's changed."

"He was a tyrant."

"And she was absent."

"They were different times. What kind of rights did she have, Tom? What kind of rights did any women have then, here in this town where there's no work for them? The old man's word was the final word. If he scared the shit out of us just think how he made her feel."

He shrugged. "A mother bear, Joe, that's what a mother's supposed to be. Everything else is a bullshit excuse."

He stood up and walked out onto the ice, the beer bottle dangling in his hand. I knew he was right. He was right in leaving and he was right now. He didn't owe her anything, me either and yet here he was. But some memories are too painful, I suppose. At least we were in it together as kids, but she represented *him*, and *he* was the enemy. It took me years to see the effects it had had on her, and once I understood I was able to forgive. But not Thomas. He was still the stubborn kid standing in the driveway having it out with the old man at six in the morning. He'd lived his whole life with that in the rearview mirror and he was never able to escape it. My anger more or less died with the old man, but it wasn't enough for Tom. He wanted reparations. He wanted something that he knew he could never have. That's why he lived out there all alone with no wife, no girlfriend, no family, because it was easier to numb the pain and because he was terrified of becoming the old man.

He jigged a few lines, checked the minnows, and then walked farther out onto the ice. He walked to where the tracks petered out and sat down in the snow. He took a long swig of beer and set the bottle beside him. He stared out across the lake sitting cross-legged, his sunglasses-covered eyes turned to the sky and the heat of the afternoon sun. He looked like he was meditating and maybe he was. He was clearing his head out there in the middle of the frozen lake, trying to put the past behind him.

Anna came back with a few sticks and asked what Uncle Tom was doing out there by himself.

"He's thinking," I said. I stoked the fire up good and high and made us both another hot dog. We watched the lines but they weren't moving.

"I want to catch another fish," Anna said.

"You and me both."

"Is Uncle Tom okay?"

"He's fine, just needs some time to himself."

"Why do we never see him?"

"Because people take different paths in life. Not everyone you love will stay close to you."

"I know that," Anna said, and she took off running across the ice before I could stop her, because she knew I would. She ran to Tom and tapped him on the shoulder, and he turned and smiled. And then he was laughing at something she said and she tackled him, knocking him over in the snow. They laughed and wrestled, and I sipped my beer in front of the fire, watching them and the sun, which was piercing the treeline on the lake's western shore, orange and yellow peeking through the black spruce and leafless winter birch. They came back holding hands, and they were like brother and sister.

"Okay," Tom said. "You sent your minion to do your dirty work and I will go."

I looked at Anna. She was grinning in the sly way she did when she knew she was getting away with something.

"On one condition. You make that dinner with Jenny happen. It's clear to me that you need my wisdom more than ever, brother."

I laughed. "Done."

On the drive back, Tom leaned against the window and slept off his hangover. The sun and the beer had done him in.

I nudged Anna. "So you were listening from the bush, I take it?"

"Please don't be mad at me."

"I'm not mad. I actually think it was a pretty grown-up thing you did, talking to your Uncle Tom like that. He really likes you."

"I like him too. Why doesn't he want to visit Grandma?"

"You'll have to ask him that, darlin'."

She leaned against me and I put my arm around her, pulling her close. "I really miss Mommy," she said.

"I know you do."

"When can I see her?"

"March break."

"So in a month?"

"Yes, a month."

"What will I do until then?"

"What you've always done. Go to school, hang out with me on the weekends."

"And visit Gracie and Jenny."

"That too."

"Uncle Tom says he's worried about you."

"He said that, eh? Maybe Uncle Tom should remember that he's speaking to a little girl and not an adult."

She gave me a look that was well beyond her years and said, "He cares about you Daddy, that's all. He said so. He said he was sorry that he never came before but he hoped that it was different now."

I smiled at her. "I hope it is too."

We drove back to town along the unplowed road with a single fish in the cooler. Anna wanted to eat it for dinner and I told her that we could. The sun went down and dusk enveloped us and I kept the lights off as long as I could, knowing that once I turned them on there would be no going back, that the darkness would surround us, swallow us whole. I wanted to ride the daylight out as long as possible because it had been a good day, the best I could remember for a long time. I looked at Tom passed out against the window and thought about what Anna had said. I thought about our childhood and the time since, all the years we were never close. And here was Anna in the middle, bringing us together as though that was her plan all along, as though she saw something in Tom that helped her come to terms with Sarah. Maybe she just wanted to be close to family. That she loved Tom was obvious to me. But like every time in my life when I ride the crest of a wave, the swell rises and peaks and then breaks, and I'm left flailing in the surf, trying to keep my head out of the water so I can catch a single, goddamn breath.

27

I called Jenny on Friday morning and asked her to come for dinner. I told her that my brother was in town, and that Anna was dying to see Gracie. She said she'd love to. She said it would be a relief not to cook.

"What are you going to make?"

"I have no idea. We caught a pickerel, but Anna ate it for dinner yesterday."

"One fish?"

"Pretty pathetic."

"More than I've ever caught on the ice."

"Well then we will have to go sometime, I might be able to get you just one."

She laughed. "I will take you up on that," she said. "I will be very disappointed if dinner isn't good."

"The pressure is on."

"Just a bit."

"No idea at all? You don't have a go-to meal?"

"Nope. I can make fish pretty good, but we've already discussed that. Any requests?"

"Ribs," she said.

"What?"

"I want ribs. I haven't had them in years and suddenly I have a hankering for them."

"You're out of your mind."

"I call it like I see it."

"Alright, ribs it is. I'll see you tonight. And Jenny, don't forget to bring your kids."

I walked through the grocery store looking like the single father that I was. I had a list and wandered around selecting things, looking a bit lost, though over the past few months I'd been improving, and the looks from the cashiers and stock boys had gone from quiet pity to quiet encouragement.

I found some ribs in the meat aisle, and picked up a head of romaine lettuce and some Caesar dressing and fixings. I picked up some baking potatoes too and a shrimp ring and a cheese-cake to tie it all together.

Tom picked up Anna from school while I got things ready. He laughed at how nervous I was, but I told him I wasn't, I just didn't want to screw it up. He said that I was head over heels.

I fumbled in the kitchen, preparing ribs from a recipe on the laptop while Tom drank beer at the kitchen table, and he and Anna had a good laugh at my expense.

"I thought you were barbecuing them?"

"I am, but you need to put them in the oven first."

"That doesn't sound right to me."

"Barbecuing in the winter, Dad?"

"I know you like to stick to what you know, but have you considered that it is minus thirty out there? Do you have propane?"

"I'm glad, Tom, that we are finally reconnecting. Now I need to check if there is propane in the tank."

He nudged Anna and they laughed, and I smiled to myself as I walked outside to get the barbecue going. I took the cover off and checked to see that there was enough propane before I lit it. It was only five-thirty but already dark and I needed the porch light to see what I was doing. I went into the garage and got the fire going in the woodstove.

Tom came outside holding a couple of beer and handed me one. "Plan on staying out here, tonight?"

"Yeah," I said. "I'm giving you my room."

He laughed. "A man's got to have his den. Though I suppose now with Sarah being gone the whole house could be your den."

"I don't see it that way, never have. It's kind of like how the old man would always be gone away somewhere, out in the bush, maybe it was just because he didn't feel comfortable inside his house."

"You don't feel comfortable?"

"Maybe, sometimes. But not really at ease, you know. I like to be out here where I can smell the air and see the stars. I feel too cooped up in the house, the living room, and then all I want to do is drink."

"So then drink," he said, grinning.

"Yeah, well, there's no problem with that now, is there. It's the sitting idle that I can't stand. Need to keep moving, keep the scenery changing otherwise I'm liable to drink too much."

"You and me both, except I don't waste too much time fighting it."

Jenny pulled up in her minivan. The headlights flooded the driveway and the inside of the garage and I thought that Tom and I must look like conspiring criminals. The van idled for a few minutes before she turned it off, and I heard the squeak of a worn-out belt. Jenny stepped out and smiled at us. She had her hair styled differently, up in an intricate bun and her makeup was all done up. Usually when I saw her it was first thing in the morning or after a long day and she looked the way you'd expect a woman to look before and after a long day, but now she was dressed in her fancy clothes and looking fine. I looked at Tom who said, "There's a change of scenery."

I walked over to help her with Maggie, and Gracie came flying out of the minivan and asked where Anna was.

"In the living room, waiting for you," I said. "Go on in and see her."

She ran inside and I went to the back of the van to get the stroller for Maggie.

"Thanks," Jenny said. "She's been talking about Anna all day. Driving me crazy."

"That sounds about right."

Jenny took Maggie from the car seat and put her in the stroller. "I'm really hoping she falls asleep before dinner so we can have a decent time. I haven't been out anywhere in a long time, well anywhere but my sister's, but family doesn't really count now, does it?"

"You look great," I said.

"Ha! I look like hell. I haven't slept and these clothes came from the back of my closet."

"You wouldn't know it."

She kind of laughed and we walked over to the garage where Tom was standing. He was leaning on the frame of the garage door, holding his beer with his arms kind of crossed and a smile on his scruffy face.

"Jenny," he said. "Nice to meet you." He reached out and they shook hands.

"I remember you from high school," Jenny said.

"That doesn't sound promising."

"Don't worry. You're in good company with your brother here."

Tom laughed. "I like her," he said.

"Want a drink, Jenny?"

"Sure, a beer would be great."

"I'll get it," Tom said. "And see if the girls need anything."

He went inside, and I was alone with Jenny. She was just a couple feet from me, in the garage with my tools and workbench, the woodstove crackling and the smell of a barbecue. I wanted to say something to make her like me, to make any lingering doubt disappear, but I was too nervous and just stood there grinning while she looked around the garage summing up my life.

"You like to come out here?"

"Only place I feel at ease."

"Dan was the same way. He'd be out there working on his bike and I'd have to call him in for dinner. Sometimes he'd be outside until midnight or later. When he threatened to put a television in there to watch the game I had to put my foot down."

"We're all the same, aren't we?"

"Possibly. Though I only have one to go on. It seems about right. Especially here, where the garage and what's in it is who you are."

She looked at the barbecue. "Is that thing on? Don't tell me you're making ribs."

"That's what you wanted."

"I was joking. I didn't think you'd actually find them in town in February."

"I was surprised myself. Even more surprised when I found out the only decent way to cook them is to grill them. And so here we are out in the garage, my favourite room in the house. I guess everything happens for a reason."

"It's minus thirty. Let's just bake them. C'mon, let's go inside. I'll help you."

"No way. We're committed now. The meat is on, the fire is crackling. You'll have to deal with a conversation around snow machines and snow shoes and hunting and when Tom gets back—oil fields."

"Lovely. Just keep the garage door open so we don't suffocate, will you."

Tom came back outside with a beer for each of us. "The girls are fine." He looked at Maggie in the stroller. "She warm enough in there?"

"Of course she's warm enough," Jenny said, shooting him a look.

"A little advice, Tom. Never, under any circumstances, question a mother's actions toward her child. They are always right."

Tom took a sip of beer. "I could argue with you on that point."

"Fair enough," I said.

"How long has it been since you've been back?" Jenny said.

"A few years."

"Has it changed?"

"Not really. I went to the hotel bar the night I arrived, just to see if I'd know anyone there and I swear to God it was the same faces I remember from when I was a teenager, sitting in the same chairs."

"Probably the same faces from when we were kids."

"Some new ones, too. It's not something unique to this town, but probably small towns everywhere, and in the city it's just concentrated in neighbourhoods. Why should anything change? Why should people change? In the oil fields you live in a bunkhouse and party like every night is Friday night, and that's just the way it is."

"I told you," I said to Jenny. "Oil fields."

"What about you?"

"I put in my fair share, sure. But it's only because I can. A lot of these guys have families that they see every couple of weeks and they still cut loose like they're bachelors."

"Is the work so hard that they need to blow off steam?"

"No harder than the mine, or the bush. It's just a frat-boy atmosphere. Hard to grow up out there."

"A family changes everything," I said.

"Or at least it should," Jenny said.

I excused myself and went inside to make the Caesar salad, one of my staples since becoming a single dad because it was kind of healthy and didn't take long to make. I checked on the girls playing in Anna's room and they promptly told me to leave them alone, so I knew they were fine.

I put the salad into the fridge, and took the shrimp ring, ribs, and baking potatoes outside. Jenny and Tom were talking about family, why Tom didn't have a family, and for a second, I felt like I was interrupting, and then Jenny smiled and waved me over.

"Maybe I just haven't met the right girl," Tom said.

"How could you meet any girl out there?"

"True. But I'm afraid of what would happen if I did meet a girl and fall in love, and everything that comes with it. My life is not conducive to children, or marriage for that matter."

"But you don't know that," Jenny said. "You don't have a clue how you'll be once you fall in love because you haven't. I think it will change you. It changes people in a way they can't understand until it happens."

"We can go inside," I said.

"But I like it," Jenny said. "We are able to talk like adults when the kids aren't around."

"You see," Tom said. "Everything has to be modified when you have kids. I'm not sure I'm into that. I'm selfish, I can live with being selfish."

"You're right, Tom, everything changes. But it's for the best reason there is. I've seen how you are with Anna; you're a natural. That's all being a father is. Get beyond the food and shelter and all that shit, and all being a parent is, is listening and paying attention to your kids and giving them attention. Engaging with them. Some people can't do that. Many fathers can't do that. I don't have to tell you that. But you have it, I can see that plain as day."

"I have it because I know it's not forever. The idea of forever scares me. If I can't walk away from it, it terrifies me."

I ate a couple of shrimp; they were freezing cold, a bit of ice still on them. Minus one, I thought. I turned the barbecue down low, and put the ribs and potatoes on the grill.

"All it takes is the right woman," I said.

I looked at Jenny and she smiled a little. She told me not to screw the ribs up. She was sitting on the edge of my workbench, with her legs dangling over the side. Her black dress came to her knees and her calves were bare. She was wearing tan Sorels with a black dress and I thought this was exactly why I liked her. She was confident just sitting there, comfortable with herself. She finished her beer and looked at me. Tom said it was his turn to go inside.

"I like your brother," she said.

"I almost forgot how he is."

"Thank you for inviting us."

"Tom wanted to meet you."

"What did you tell him?"

"The truth."

"So he's making sure about me."

"Maybe, something like that."

"I like that you didn't lie about it."

"That's not how I want to be."

"How do you want to be?"

"The same as everyone else."

"You're not everyone else."

"Is that why you came tonight?"

"I came because I wanted to come. And because I haven't had a meal cooked for me in months."

"I'm sorry about that, because mine is not going to impress you."

She laughed. "Those ribs look like the best thing I have seen in a very long time."

Tom came out with the beers and cracked them open. We dug into the shrimp. When the ribs and potatoes were done, we went inside. Jenny called the girls while I set the table and Tom poured the wine. Maggie was asleep in her stroller.

"First time I've been in your house," Jenny said.

Tom gave me a look.

"We didn't want people talking any more than they already are," I said.

"Talking about what?" Anna said.

"Never mind," I said.

"I never get to hear the good stuff."

"You hear plenty."

"It's a nice place," Jenny said.

Anna and Gracie sat beside each other and they were talking and laughing and seemed to have their own little code. I always felt guilty that Anna never had a sibling, but it was never my decision. I had wanted another kid right away; Sarah wanted to wait a while. A while turned into years and eventually I got the picture and stopped asking. I'd watch Anna play alone in the living room and imagine how much different it would be if she had a little brother or little sister. Sometimes she asked why she never had a sibling, why all her friends did and she didn't and I never had an answer for her. Sarah always said she didn't want to go through the hard years again, the years before they start school. I thought: you're not working, what the hell else are you going to do? Turns out there was a lot she could do. The year Anna turned six I asked Sarah a final time if she wanted to have another kid. She just looked at me and laughed, and I knew then that Sarah had seen Anna as a mistake all along, that her view had never changed. Some people have kids early on and they grow into being parents and they find they're good at it. Sarah was good at it, but it's not how she defined herself, not ever. Anna was always the thing that had happened to alter the course of her life forever. She had said that once when she was drunk and I never forgot it. For years I fooled myself into thinking she was happy, and when the end came, maybe, in a sense, I was relieved that we didn't have to live a lie anymore. I was alone and Anna was alone, but at least we had each other and at least it was honest. I didn't have to come home worried anymore about the next breakdown or crazy impulsive decision. I made things stable for Anna, just like Sarah knew I would. Sometimes I think our entire marriage, from the moment Anna was conceived to when Sarah left, she was biding her time, waiting for me to grow up, quit drinking, and become enough of a man to raise our daughter without her. And when that time came, when she was satisfied that I could manage, she waited for a reason to come along that was powerful enough that I might actually believe it. And when I think of her hiding her true self for all those years, concocting some grand plan, waiting me out, I think: thank God I have Anna, because if I didn't there would be no bottom to how far I'd go to ruining my life through whiskey.

I don't know if I'm an addict or not, but I do know there is a point beyond which I can't control it. I know there is a line that I cannot cross, and I've spent most of my life straddling it like a goddamn fool. Maybe what makes an addict is the inability to see the line. And I don't like to judge people, because I don't know what they went through to get them to where they are, but if a person can't straighten out enough to take care of their own kids, well then they aren't parents in my books, just place holders.

Sarah knew I had this hard line in me. She knew me better than I knew myself, that my drinking was less a major problem and more youthful indulgence. She knew that when the chips were down I would do the right thing. She knew how much I resented my father and that I would do anything to keep from becoming him. She used this knowledge against me because she is smarter than me and more manipulative than I could ever have imagined. It occurred to me that not once since Sarah left did I ever worry about her well-being. This was because not only was I too filled with anger to worry about her, but also because I knew she would do just fine without me.

Jenny said she loved the ribs. I thought they were pretty decent, and Tom couldn't get enough. It's the Sweet Baby Ray's, I said. We finished dinner and then the cheesecake, and the girls went to play in Anna's room. Maggie was awake and stirring and Jenny took her to the bedroom for her feeding. It struck me how young Maggie was, a newborn still breast-feeding, still in her father's shadow. It was hard to believe Dan had only been gone a few months. It seemed much longer than that, but when I looked at Maggie in Jenny's arms, it was like he had died yesterday. There is something so innocent and vulnerable about a young mother with a newborn baby, and I felt like I was doing something wrong, violating her family somehow.

Tom said, "I like her. I really do."

"But the timing."

"So you give her all the time she needs. A woman like that, you wait for her. And you don't be a fool about it."

"The girls too."

"Can you be a father for three instead of one? Have you thought of that? Because you'll have three daughters man, three."

I laughed. "Jesus, don't put it like that."

"No other way to put it."

Tom stood up. "I need a drink."

"Let me grab some more beer from the fridge downstairs."

"I was thinking of having a glass of Irish. You have any?"

"Yeah, it's under the workbench in the garage."

"That where you hide it?"

"Yes sir, it is."

"I'll be back in a jiffy."

Jenny came back with Maggie and said she had to get going. She looked a little tired and very beautiful and I told her I was happy that she had come.

"It was nice, Joe. It really was."

"You should get your belt looked at," I said.

"My belt?"

"On your car. It was squeaking when you pulled in. That's not something you want breaking on you when you least expect it."

"Thank you, Joe."

Tom returned from the garage smelling like cigarette smoke as Jenny and her girls were getting ready to leave.

"I didn't know you smoked," I said.

"Once in a while, when I drink."

"Planning on a fun night, boys?" Jenny said with a smile.

"Just a little bit," Tom said. "I haven't seen my brother in so long and by God it appears to be Friday night."

"Well," she said. "Keep him out of trouble, will you? I kind of need the job."

"Ouch," Tom said. "Jenny, it was a real pleasure. I hope we see each other soon."

"Me too, Tom."

I walked her outside. I loaded the stroller loaded into the van. It was freezing, and Jenny was cursing that she hadn't warmed up the car. She started the van and put the girls inside, and we stood there looking at the northern lights, which were moving across the sky in green and blue bands upon a backdrop of brilliant stars.

"Quite a sight," she said.

"I never tire of it."

"It even makes the cold okay."

She put her head on my shoulder and I put my arm around her. She was so slight and small in my arms and she was warm and fit perfectly against me.

She said, "I like you, Joe. But it wouldn't be fair to Dan."

"I know."

"Thanks," she said, but she didn't pull away, not yet. She leaned into me, putting her weight on me, and I felt like I was holding her up, like she wanted to commit to me. She was showing it in the way she stood there, my arms around her, the smell of her hair and her softness enveloping me like the northern lights above. And I knew this would be the last time that I felt her, wouldn't again until she was ready, when the memory of Dan was distant enough to permit it. She was letting us get close now because she wanted me to know that she wanted it too.

I walked back inside the house. The night chill followed me into the kitchen where Tom was sitting at the table with the bottle of whiskey and two glasses.

"Drink?" he said.

"Sure, just the one."

"Don't worry partner, you can get drunk with me and I won't let you get into any trouble."

"Can't leave the house with Anna here."

"Perfect."

"You wouldn't believe how many times I've used that."

He opened the bottle, the lid crackling as the bits of plastic snapped away, and poured two large glasses.

"The Irish," he said. "Grandpa's?"

"The same. Still haven't cleaned out that bunker, but I took a few of these before the snow fell."

"Never goes bad, does it. That's the beauty of hard liquor; it'll never let you down. That gun still in there?"

I nodded.

"I bet you fired a few off, didn't you. Isn't that what you said? You drove out to the cabin after you knocked Terry Pike out cold. You drove out there and got wasted and waited for Officer Fuckstick to come get you? Tell me you didn't pull that forty-five out of the ground and bust a few into the night. You must have. Goddammit I know I would have."

I smiled, not giving him anything.

"That's my brother," he said, grinning. He downed his drink in one go and poured himself another. A look came across his face that I hadn't seen since we were kids, the worried look that Tom always had, like he was hiding a secret, the way I pictured him that final morning when he stood up to my father.

He said, "I have a confession."

He drank some more. His eyes were glassy and his head was rolling around. He was drunk. I realized he'd been putting it back all night because he was drinking with a purpose, preparing for something.

"The morning I left, when me and Dad had it out, and why I never came back, not even to go see Mom, is because I've known something all these years that they wanted me not to know. Not just Dad but Mom too, which is why I can't forgive her, ever, and why I won't be going to see her tomorrow. See, I changed my flight. I have to drive back to Thunder Bay tomorrow to catch my flight. Because I knew once I told you, things would be different, but you need to know."

I sat down and took a drink. I looked at Tom, knowing in my gut already what he was going to say. Part of me didn't want to hear but part of me knew that important things like the truth can never be hidden for long, nor should they, because no matter what damage they do, they always have a balancing effect in the end.

"You see the night I graduated, I considered myself my own man. I knew I was never coming back as long as the old man was alive. I was drunk too, not totally hammered but just sobering up, just sober enough to think clearly. Dad came down the driveway to tell me not to leave, that I had no chance out west on my own where I knew nobody. I looked at him, and called him a murderous son of a bitch because that's what he was."Tom paused, staring at the floor, the memories rushing through his mind. "I remember when he came back. It was the next morning, almost lunch time. You were gone to school but I told Mom I was sick, you remember? I was in my room when he came home. I could tell he wasn't drunk. Funny how much you can figure out through sound alone. I spent most of my childhood hiding in my bedroom whenever I heard that engine rumble up the driveway because I didn't want to face him. So I knew what it sounded like when he came stumbling in, loud, always loud, his boots banging on the floor and his keys thrown onto the kitchen table, always his booming voice. But this time he was quiet, stealthy. He took off his boots and went to the sink to get a glass of water. I heard him talking to Mom, real quiet. So different from normal that I started to wonder what was going on. Then I could hear him mumbling about something, then crying. Not loud, but real reserved like he'd never cried a day in his life and didn't know how to do it, stifling, muffled by her shoulder. I remember the sounds so clearly. I could hear everything, the scratch of her nails on his canvas work jacket, the sound of their embrace, her comforting him. And that was the most startling thing: that they were embracing, that he was weak and she was strong, that he *needed* her. I remember being terrified, thinking something really bad had happened. Because if the old man represented anything, it was strength. And here was weakness, the first time I'd ever seen it. I heard him say: something bad happened, something I couldn't stop. And she was just calming him down, saying: it's okay, it's okay Freddie, what happened, what did you do? He said: He's dead, and I couldn't stop it, there was nothing I could do. Who's dead, she said. And then he said, and I'll never forget it for as long as I live: my father is dead."

I reached across the table and put my hand on Tom's shoulder. He was breathing heavily, nearly hyperventilating. I could see the damage it had done to him after all these years, how keeping it inside had torn him apart. I knew without asking that he had never told another soul, that this was his first confession. The pain of it had never gone away, would never go away. No wonder he hated them so much. He downed his drink and poured another, and I did the same.

"Of course I went out there after I heard that; I was just a kid. And Dad just stared at me. His eyes, the intensity in his eyes scared the shit out of me. I thought he was going to kill me. He knew that I had heard and I was terrified. I had never trusted him less, or trusted him since that day. Since then, it's all been a veneer, a fucking fake. And he just growled at me: go to your room. About an hour later he came in. Again, stone sober, which was so strange because it gave him real purpose. It wasn't just the anger anymore, it was cold, calculating purpose. I was sure he was going to kill me. He said that everything was fine, that nothing bad had happened. He said that if I think I heard something, the best thing to do would be to keep quiet, because if I didn't the cops would come and tear our family apart, and I wouldn't want that now, would I?

"The days that followed, Grandpa's disappearance, the cops at our house, through all of it I kept my mouth shut, not because I was afraid of what would happen to our family, but because I was afraid of what he would do to me. I knew, even at that young age, that we would be better off without him, but there was nothing I could do about it. They questioned me. I told them I was asleep, that I never heard him leave or return, that what the rest of the family said was true. And after a while, you remember, the heat started to wear off and things went back to normal, but things were never the same between me and Dad. Every time he looked at me I knew he was thinking about what I knew. That he was there when Grandpa died, that he knew where the body was, that Grandpa wasn't missing, but dead, that he probably killed him. I watched him lie, both of them, and it was like a switch flipped inside my brain. You think I was messed up before this? It's been inside me, Joe, this whole time, for years now, over a decade. I had to tell you. I'm sorry I told you."

I didn't know what to say. He was near tears, the pain and hurt welling up in his eyes, making his face flush and hot. I could see the toll it had taken on him, how difficult it had been to tell me.

"Do you think he killed him?"

"Why would he hide it if he didn't?"

"Because people wouldn't believe him. Because he didn't want to spend his life in jail."

"And what about her? It was her out, her way to make our family normal, better."

"I'm not sure it would have been better, just emptier. And what if she talked and the cops didn't believe her? What if she talked and he still got away with it? Then what?"

"You're defending her."

"No."

"I'm not going to see her."

"I understand. I'm sorry," I said. "If I could have made it me I would have."

"You were a good brother."

I wanted to say, no I was a terrible brother because I didn't protect you, but I didn't. I said nothing. We finished our drinks, then poured another and went into the garage to have a cigarette. I hadn't smoked since I laid out Terry Pike, and I needed one. Funny how that works.

We didn't say much, just drank and smoked and I hoped there wouldn't be a wall between us. I hoped in telling me, he wouldn't resent me. I hoped that telling me would give him some kind of peace. But sitting there, watching him, I realized how much he looked like our mother. The way his shoulders hunched and how he held his smoke, his eyes focused on some faraway point, something intangible, a point in the past that was lost and he could never get back because not only had our father ruined him, but our mother had abandoned him in the worst possible way, had made him party to a terrible secret, had made him fear for his life. But what choice did she have? This was her husband. A drunk, possibly a killer, but her husband. Where would we have been without his money? Where would we have gone? The last time I saw her, she told me he was an aberration. Now I knew what she meant. But despite Thomas's anger, I felt pity for her. I was sorrier for her than I had ever been. It made sense to me why she was the way she was. This damaged person who chain-smoked and wouldn't change a goddamn thing in the house since my father died. She had been a prisoner to him and his secret for so long she didn't know how to act anymore. It defined her completely. And I know she regretted it because she wasn't an evil person, just a weak one. And just as she couldn't move on, neither could Tom. They were both trapped in this moment, despite each other. He was so much like her and he didn't even see it.

I squeezed his shoulder and looked him in the eye, and said that I was glad he told me. But when he looked back I didn't see the brother who had come from the oil sands, self-assured and cocky, I saw a scared little boy. And I knew why he'd spent his life hiding out there, why he still partied like a kid, why he had never had a serious relationship. Because inside he was still a scared little boy.

"You should stay a bit," I said. "Take some time off. I'm not asking you to see Mom, just maybe be with Anna and me for a bit, be with family."

"I can't Joe, gotta work Monday, you know how it is."

"I know how it is."

"But I'll come back, I promise. I love that little girl of yours, she's something special. You have no idea how much I love her."

"Maybe we can come out there, do a camping trip in the Rockies or something."

"I'd like that.

"Remember at Dad's funeral I told you how Sarah was the wrong one, how I felt it through and through? Well, that Jenny, man, she is the right woman for you."

"I know it."

"So whatever happens, whatever shit Sarah puts you through, people who don't understand what you and Jenny have, you just swallow it down, Joe. You swallow it down. And if you ever need a reason to keep your cool, just think of your lovely daughter and think of Jenny, because from where I'm sitting you're just about the luckiest man in the world."

SPRING

28

Sarah was admitted into the writing program in Victoria just as she said. I wasn't surprised. Nothing about her surprised me. And when March break finally arrived, I kept my promise to her. We spoke on the phone and she sounded like the girl I remembered from high school: confident, self-assured, young. She sounded happy and I have to admit that I was happy for her. I had found some kind of happiness with Jenny, and I couldn't resent Sarah for finding some of her own.

Her writing was getting noticed. There was a teacher who thought she had real talent. She was becoming the Sarah she would have been if I hadn't knocked her up so young. I knew that she secretly blamed me for many things, for Anna, for pressuring her to get married. Of course she never said this, but I could sense it in her newly-found confidence, in the tone of her voice. She talked about her plans, where she saw herself in two, five, and ten years. She had it all mapped out, and the more she talked the more I realized that she saw me as the reason for her failures. I had held her back by convincing her to live a way she knew in her heart was wrong for her. She never said any of this but she implied it in so many other ways, that after several minutes of talking to her I felt the anger welling up in my chest. I wondered how she could leave Anna and expect everything to be okay. I wanted to tell her how good Jenny was to her, how great a mother she was in her absence, but I didn't. I wanted to say hurtful things, but I couldn't. She was the mother of my daughter and I still cared about her. I still rooted for her. I pretended that everything was fine, that I was over it. I didn't tell her about Jenny and she didn't ask. But I'm sure she had her suspicions.

In March the sun is bright, the snow is wet, and the warmth of spring hovers on the periphery. Days get longer as the strangle hold of winter eases its grip. It's not spring yet, not by a long shot, but the hint is there. By March, everyone is sick of winter.

We drove to the airport in Thunder Bay on the Saturday before March break, and Anna boarded the WestJet plane alone. An attendant walked her from the check-in to her seat, and I was assured that an attendant would take her from the plane to her mother. I didn't like watching her go alone, but Sarah couldn't afford to fly to Thunder Bay to pick her up, and Anna was determined and unafraid. It was all she talked about for weeks and I couldn't let her down. Sarah would text me the moment she had Anna so I knew everything was fine. It was the final nail in the coffin for our family. Only broken families send their kids on planes alone.

I headed back to Black River along the north shore stretch of the Trans-Canada Highway. I knew it well. Every rock and cliff face, every side road and house. The drive was long, but I never tired of Lake Superior. The highway hugged the shoreline and the small mountains that plunged into the shore of the Great Lake. Around every turn was a tremendous view across a lake so big it could be an ocean. Rock cuts blasted clear through to build the highway towered on either side of the road. The ice went out about four hundred yards before giving way to open water. Lake Superior almost never froze completely over. Ski-doo tracks tore up and down the ice in straight lines, broken only by the rising rifts and peaks of the constantly evolving sheet of ice. Some ridges were six feet high or more, impossible to see until you're right on them, the end of many a snowmobiler.

As I drove, the sun glistened off the ice and water, and the black ice on the highway. I thought about my daughter on a plane headed to the west coast, and I wondered what her life would be like. We were closer than ever, Anna and I, and I suppose I had Sarah to thank for that. Being a single father made me recognize how absent I was before. I never really listened to her, or spent much time with her. I was quick to anger, I was impatient. I saw her differently now that it was just the two of us. I saw everything differently. I had more patience and compassion, and I felt like it was the two of us against the world. And every time I got upset with her, I remembered that her mom was gone, that it was just us and if I lost my cool she would have no one to turn to. So I never lost it, and I always gave her the benefit of the doubt. I wanted her to know that I would never let her down, that I would never leave.

Still, I worried. In a few years she'd be a teenager, on the edge of womanhood, and that scared me more than anything. I dreaded the change that was like a storm cloud on the horizon. Because I was her father, and wouldn't understand so much of what she'd go through. I held onto the fact that I wasn't the one who had left, that no matter what else Sarah did to make up for it, it was she who had deserted Anna and not me. I would try to understand and support Anna through everything, and I hoped that our closeness would transcend it all.

29

I stood at my mother's door for a long time without knocking. I stood on the porch with the March rain melting the snow, pooling in the driveway. I wanted to leave but I couldn't. I had to see it through. When she came to the door she took one look at me and knew why I was there. She closed her eyes and held the doorframe like I was a ghost from her past.

"Mom," I said.

"Come inside."

I sat down at the kitchen table as she poured a coffee and fumbled for a cigarette. The room was hazy. The stink of smoke permeated everything. The walls and curtains were nicotine-stained, yellow like an old-time photograph. Nothing ever changes.

"Coffee?"

"No, thank you."

"I just made a fresh pot."

"No, Mom."

"I'd offer you a beer but it's nine in the morning. I also don't keep liquor in the house; you know that."

The electric heater hummed beside her, the fan turned on, full bore. It was March and she'd spent the entire winter like this, carrying that thing from room to room.

"It's freezing in here."

"The woodstove is difficult for me."

"The wood is right there beside it, Mom, nice and small. You know how to start a fire."

"It's hard."

"Maybe you just don't want to go downstairs."

"Why wouldn't I?"

"Maybe it's time you got rid of Dad's stuff."

She shrugged.

"Thomas was in town."

"I know."

"Really."

"I still have some friends."

"I didn't think you had any friends."

"It was difficult with your father. He didn't like people very much."

"You don't say."

She frowned. "Why are you here?"

"I wanted Thomas to come but he refused."

She looked at me nervously, lighting the cigarette that was already between her fingers. She was old for her sixty years, ancient, but with the mention of Thomas she looked like a little girl, a trapped animal.

"Is that what this is, then?"

"You tell me."

"He should have come to visit."

"He can't forgive you."

"Forgive me for what?"

I sighed, leaned forward in my chair. I stared at the stack of Chronicle-Journal newspapers on the table. My father had had a subscription for as long as I could remember, and she'd never got around to cancelling it. I don't think she'd read a paper in years.

"I'm giving you a chance to tell me what Thomas already knows, because I want to understand and I want you to be a part of my life."

"I don't know what you're talking about."

"One chance."

She looked at me defiantly. I thought she was going to hold her ground, take it to the grave, but she faltered and her look softened. I knew she was thinking about Anna. She knew I've never bluffed her in my life.

She took a drag, and sipped her crappy black coffee. Always the cheap stuff, whatever's on sale. Never a dime to spend. Her entire life a hand-to-mouth existence, from her childhood to her life with my father, to the old woman she was now. Always counting pennies, always making do. The times I'd offered to help her financially, even in the smallest ways, she'd refused. She was old and stubborn, too far down her path to change. She wouldn't take my help and she wouldn't cut out the smoking so that she could see her granddaughter more often. I wondered if she did this to punish herself for what she couldn't do while our father was alive. Maybe she kept everyone away because she felt she didn't deserve us. Maybe Anna was a reminder of her failures, and it hurt too much to see her.

"Your father's problem was always liquor," she said after a while. "The house you remember, that Thomas remembers, that was our life and it was your father who made it that way. But he wasn't always like that. When I first met him he was a wonderful man: kind, caring, gentle. I never would have married him if he wasn't good. He was the son of a logger, my own father was a miner, just like Sarah's. That's the way it is here, the way it's always been. We were all the same, really. I mean, how different can you be growing up here? How different can you really be? You must have thought that about Sarah, too. You think you know a person and it turns out they only showed you half. You give them everything and in return you get a wall. It's a real fine wake-up call, isn't it, Joe? There's no worse feeling than having to do it all alone. To know you are alone. And I was alone, Joseph. Alone like you are now and scared too.

"He always drank but he had it under control. In the beginning he never let it rule his life. But then one day a switch went off and he just stopped caring. He'd lived in the shadow of his own father for most of his life. Lucas Adler, the great hunter, the great outdoorsman, the survivor. It was your grandfather who built most of the logging roads. It was your grandfather who survived a walk through the wilderness to get to his first logging job in this country. Everyone thought he was this great man. But there was the side of your grandfather that nobody but your father and his family saw, the Lucas Adler who lived in his cabin and never came home and was no kind of father. The Lucas who was short-tempered with his children and even worse with his wife. Your father tried to be a good son but it was never enough. He told me these things when we were young. He told me how he tried so hard to be close to his father but his father didn't want to be close to him. Over time he hardened. A depression settled over him that he never recovered from. He drank more and talked less, and soon he was the man you knew: withdrawn, beaten-down, nasty. The best parts of him, the parts that made me fall in love with him, were gone, and all that was left were our two sons and the shell of a marriage. By the time you were of an age that you could remember, he was an alcoholic, the light in his eyes completely gone. He no longer tried to fix things, he just buried them deeper. I remember thinking one day that his life was already over, that he was just waiting it out. He no longer talked to me, and showed no interest in our family. He shut out all his friends, and spent more time alone in the bush trying to live up to something that he never even understood."

She took a drag and stared across the room at nothing. There were tears in her eyes. Her entire life since my father's death was a path to this moment, this confession. It's what had aged her. My father and the endless cigarettes and the cold winters in the house. The bad memories. The memory she shared with Thomas. And as she began her story, I saw something lighten in her, a load taken off her shoulders, and I swear to God she sat up straighter and looked clear-eyed in a way I hadn't seen in years. She stubbed out the cigarette and looked me in the eye. She crumpled the pack in her hand.

She said, "These things are killing me."

I took her hands in mine and she cried. "I'm so sorry. I'm sorry for everything. I was never the mother you deserved. I should have taken you and Thomas away. I should have had the courage to do the right thing, and you hate me because I didn't, and I hate myself too. I miss Thomas. I miss him so much. He needs me, Joe. He needs me more than you because he isn't as strong as you. Oh Joseph, so many things I regret. I am so sorry."

She cried and I didn't say anything, and when she was done she went to the sink to wipe her eyes and she stared into the morning rain. She stood there for some time before she turned, her eyes wet with tears, flooded with pain and sorrow and history.

"That night he was drinking a lot, even for him. I hadn't seen him in days. A friend called me and told me he was at the bar and so I called your grandfather. He tried to look out for us. He tried his best, but your father never listened. They never listened to each other. He went down there and they argued and it got loud and nasty, and your father stumbled home drunk." She paused, a glimmer of fire in her eyes, aware she was about to say something aloud for the first time. "But he didn't stay home. He went back out. I told the police that he stayed home but he didn't. Nobody saw his truck leave, nobody saw it return. All night and all morning and not one neighbour could say whether or not they had seen his truck, couldn't remember, hadn't thought to look. It was as though God had willed it. He came home in the morning cold and shivering, and he went to the kitchen and he cried. Your father, crying. I approached him, and I didn't know whether he would hug me or scream at me, and then he hugged me and cried in my arms like a baby."

And this is the story, how I remember it, how my mother told it. But you have to consider how many years have passed, how long she kept it inside, how long it has been since I have spoken of it. There is the problem, too, of taking my father at his word, because every word of this story is his and how do you trust a man like that? But it is the story that I have gone with, and forced myself to accept because the alternative would be too much to live with. When I think of it now, all I think of is my father on his deathbed, drunk and angry and bitter. A son of a bitch right to the end. And I think to myself: what right did you have to make everyone around you feel so goddamn fucking low all of the time?

My father came home but couldn't forget what had happened. His own father had called him a drunk and a deadbeat in a bar full of people. He'd grabbed him and embarrassed him. He was mad at my mother for sending Lucas to the bar, but what was she supposed to do? Enough was enough, even in our house. So around midnight, he went back out, and this is what I remember as a boy, the truck leaving again. I had always assumed that my father slept it off in the bush somewhere like he always did. But instead he drove to the camp just like the cops thought he did. He wanted to tell Lucas off once and for all. He wanted to confront him for being a bad father, because he blamed Lucas for everything. He was never one to admit when he was wrong, or when he didn't try hard enough. It was always someone else's fault.

Lucas opened the door, angry because it was the middle of the night and didn't he just tell my father to get his ass home. They yelled. My father was angry, but he was also desperate, pleading with Lucas to admit that he was a terrible father, that he was no role model, that he had a hand to play in how my father turned out. But my grandfather wouldn't budge. That Adler stubbornness I know so well. The same stubbornness that had kept Thomas and me apart for nearly ten years.

You're a drunk, he said, and I'm ashamed to call you my son. Now go home to your family. And with that he pushed my father onto the porch and was about to close the door when my father stepped back inside, with years of built up anger and frustration, anger at his life and how it turned out, anger at his alcoholism, anger at his childhood, anger at his father, anger at the world, anger at himself, and pushed my grandfather into the cabin.

It wasn't a hard push, more of a shove, but Lucas was old and unsteady, and his heel caught something on the floor, a boot or an uneven board, and he twisted and stumbled backward and fell, hitting his head on the cast-iron stove on the way down. My father looked in horror as he lay there not moving. He was face-down on the plywood sheet that he'd put under the stove when he built the cabin. My father knelt down to help him up and saw the blood pooling around Lucas's head, flowing like oil from a can, that's how he described it to my mother: oil flowing from a can. He was a hunter and knew it was too much blood, that this much blood meant death, and for a long time he sat there in shock. He sat on the floor until the blood stopped flowing. He believed that he himself was dead too, that his spirit had left his body, because how could his soul not be damned after what he'd done? I remember the change in him after this, the faraway look he got when he was in the middle of something. The immediate world slipped away and he went to some other place, and now I know where he went. I don't think his soul ever left the cabin.

With the moonlight shining through the window, my father had to make a decision. Who would believe it was an accident? A manslaughter charge if he were lucky, first degree murder if he wasn't, and my father was never lucky. Right then he decided to take control of his fate. He told my mother that he wouldn't leave it to the cops and judges and lawyers whom he despised. He was going to make sure they couldn't bury him over an accident.

What he did next has always haunted me. In a daze, or perhaps as clear-headed as he had ever been (I'm not sure which would be worse), my father took my grandfather's body, wrapped him in an old tarp and loaded him in the back of his truck. He took the canoe from behind the cabin and loaded that as well. Then he drove to a spot that he knew from moose hunting, a spot where he had cut trail and where he was sure no other human being had ever set foot. He put the canoe in the lake and the body in the canoe. He brought a shovel from his truck. In the darkness, he paddled to the end of the lake, which was over a mile long, and then carried the canoe and the body of my grandfather across the trail he'd cut with his own hands, and paddled across the next lake where he went to shore and carried the body into the bush. There were no roads close to this spot, and no plans to cut. It was the remotest place he could think of. No other person had ever been there and there was no reason why there ever should be.

He picked a spot beyond the towering black spruce that lined the edge of the lake, where the land converged in a steep rock face and the alder and poplar were low and not harvestable, and began to dig. Hours, he told my mom, he dug for hours. He used the edge of the shovel to break through the roots that criss-crossed the cold dirt, and flung large rocks out of the hole with the shovel's face. I say this all in great detail because it was how my mother told me, the details not lost even after all those years, buried but not forgotten. He dug until the hole was deep, until he reached bedrock, and he put my grandfather inside and filled it in. He covered the dirt with brush and leaves. He told my mother that he wept and said a prayer. I'm not sure I believe that.

He returned to the cabin and took the only piece of evidence, the sheet of plywood from under the stove, cut it into small pieces, and burned it. He made sure there was no blood and no sign that he'd been there. He put the canoe back in its spot and drove into town along a series of small connecting back roads that led to the far end of town. He knew that if anyone saw him he had no chance. He told my mother that it was the worst drive of his life, that he held his breath at every corner, but he never passed a single truck, like he was meant to get away with it.

"What was I supposed to do?" my mother said. "He came in crying and blubbering like a child, baring his heart to me. And all that he had done, the years of a terrible marriage, all of it came undone when he put his life in my hands. What was I supposed to do? Tell the police it was him? Should an accident—a terrible accident, yes, but an accident none the less—mean the loss of two lives and not one? Would your father being in jail solve anything or bring your grandfather back? What would have happened to us without your father? He was the breadwinner, Joe. You know how it is here. You see it now with the widow you've hired. Where would she be without your kindness, your charity? And who in God's name would have hired me to do anything after your father was sent to prison for murder. What would have happened to you and Thomas? We would have been marked, all of us, and I wasn't going to let that happen. I wasn't going to let your father bring this family down anymore. So I went along with the lie to protect us."

"And Thomas, were you protecting him?"

"It was a mistake, Joe."

"He was terrified. He thought Dad was going to kill him."

"I'm not proud of it. I knew one day you would find out, and I hoped you'd be able to forgive me, to see what I was doing. I had no choice."

"You should've let him burn."

"But I didn't and I have to live with that."

"We all do, Mom. Did he tell you where the body was?"

"No. I didn't want to know."

I looked at her, shook my head. "All a nice perfectly wrapped lie. You lied to me, too. And Thomas, he will never speak to you again and I don't blame him. You have no idea what it's done to him. He lives with it every single day."

"So do I, Joe."

"I have to go."

I got up to leave and she reached for my arm, pulled at the sleeve of my coat. "Joseph, please, don't hate me, don't keep her from me."

"I don't hate you," I said. "I know why you did it. What's worse is how you punish yourself."

"Are you going to tell the police?"

"What good would it do? Better it stays in the bush."

"But Thomas might want to."

"Then you'll have to live with that."

"And Anna, what about her?"

I looked at the pack of cigarettes crumpled up in the corner. "Quit smoking, Mom, that's all I've ever wanted. Quit smoking if you want to have a real relationship with her. The place smells like an ashtray."

30

It was dark outside when Officer Taylor knocked on my door. I flicked on the porch light and he was standing in the doorway and I was sure my mom had broken down and called the cops. But I knew right then that I would never give him anything. I would take it to the grave. Things long dead and buried sometimes ought to stay that way. But Officer Taylor wouldn't understand that. He was as straight-edge as they came. He would dig and turn things over and turn my family on its ear and I couldn't abide that. People only know what you tell them, is one thing the old man taught me.

I opened the door and he looked at me. His expression wasn't one of suspicion but concern, and I knew that something was wrong, just felt it inside, and I immediately thought about Anna and my heart skipped a beat. I told myself that she was safe in her bedroom, that it wasn't about her. Then I thought of Jenny.

He said, "I got a call from Terry Pike's wife. Says he never came home last night." Officer Taylor looked young standing there in the porch light with the darkness surrounding him. "Paul Henri is out of town and Terry's wife didn't know who to call. She was afraid to call you and I don't blame her. She called the station in a fair amount of distress, nearly hysterical. She said in thirty years he's never not come home. Normally we wait twenty-four hours for this sort of thing, but nothing here is normal. Do you have any idea where he could be?"

"He was pulling the final logs out of the cut."

"Alone?"

"He was the last guy in there."

"So he's still out there?"

"Give me a minute."

I went inside and woke up Anna, told her she had to go to Jenny's a little bit early. I called Jenny and she answered after four rings. Of course you can bring her here, she said.

I got dressed and put Anna in the truck, and Officer Taylor followed me to Jenny's. She was waiting in the doorway wearing a hoodie and holding a travel mug of coffee.

"You always look out for me," I said.

"Somebody has to." She looked over my shoulder at the paddy wagon.

"Same old story, cops don't know anything about the bush."

"Think it's serious?"

"Maybe his truck won't start."

"Then why wouldn't he just radio in?"

"I don't know."

"Be careful, Joe."

We drove down the industrial road in the pitch black morning. The gravel road was a mess of ruts and ice and frozen mud from the constant thawing and freezing of late March. My truck thudded and banged in the ruts, and every now and then it fishtailed. I kept an eye on Officer Taylor in my rear-view, careful not to lose him. I cracked my window and the air was moist and cool; it was going to be a warm day.

It was the last week of March and we were making the final push before the road melted under our tires. We had a few weeks before the area was inaccessible. Terry Pike was the last man, skidding out the remaining bundles. There was a log loader but it never moved from the landing area. Only Terry was back in the cut, which is why he could have been left behind if he'd run into trouble. But every truck had a radio. If you got stuck or had mechanical problems, you called in. No cell signal out here so we relied on radio. If Terry's truck was stuck or if the engine was dead the battery should still power the radio, unless his truck battery was dead too, then he'd be shit out of luck.

We turned onto the secondary road and the light was just beginning to show itself in the eastern sky. It was clear, and the moon and stars were visible with the first signs of dull, gray light. The trees were black, the sky a few shades above that. My hi-beams lit up the road and the snow that had melted and then frozen over and formed a hard crust and brilliant sheen that looked something like a skating rink.

We drove into the cut and the winter trees flickered by and I thought of my grandfather buried in the bush, all rags and bones, six feet down in a place that no one would ever find, not even me. The only person that knew the bush better than Lucas was my father, and if my grandfather hadn't been found yet, then chances are he never would be. All those days they scoured the bush and my father at home shaking his head, telling them that they'd never find him, that it had been a monster bear, that one in a hundred that will kill you just because. I knew that people suspected my father, but I never believed it. I never thought he had it in him.

Terry's old Ford was parked beside the log pile at the landing. The log loader was nearby, its clam resting on the ground. I looked inside the truck and saw Terry's lunch was sitting on the seat. Officer Taylor tried the door and said it was locked. I took the keys from the inside the gas tank door and tossed them to him.

"How'd you know he keeps them there?"

"Everyone keeps them there."

He opened the door, and looked inside and lifted Terry's lunch bag, feeling its weight. "Long time to go without any grub. How far away was he working?"

"A little ways," I said.

Officer Taylor took his flashlight from the paddy wagon and we headed into the cut. We were silent. I thought of Dan Lacroix dead in the cut, face under the water, his clothes and hard hat tossed from the cab. Terry didn't come home because he was dead. I knew it but didn't say it. I said it without saying it.

I walked ahead, following the skid trail by the natural light. I could see pretty far and I rarely used a flashlight because it made my world smaller, condensed it to my immediate surroundings. A flashlight makes me feel claustrophobic, and in the open space of the cut the sky was large and wide and I didn't need a light at all. I'd let my eyes adjust and the fuzziness became normal. After a few years, the darkness was second nature. Countless times I've walked out of the bush in the dark. There comes a point when you no longer fear it.

It was quiet and still, and in a few weeks it would smell like spring, the rot and leaves and everything on the ground starting to thaw. But for now, ice and snow covered the skid trail, and with each step my boots crushed a thin, papery layer of ice. The farther we walked the quieter it got, the only sound our footsteps and my breathing and my pulse like a class four river rapids rushing in my ears.

We walked for twenty minutes. The sky was lightening and the ravens were cawing. Officer Taylor shut off his flashlight. It felt like we were heading out on a morning hunt.

"How far is it?"

"A little ways yet. Terry is working at the back. Much quicker with a machine, that's for sure."

"I don't understand how these things can just keep happening."

"Don't give up hope," I said. "He might be okay."

"You know I've been here almost a year now, and I feel like I don't know a goddamn thing."

"That's because you don't."

I saw the skidder across the cut, a green blob in the dull light. It was upright and on its tires, and looked perfectly fine. "Look," I said.

"Thank God."

It was another five minutes across the valley to the machine. The skid trail was churned with snow, bark, and debris. The cut was covered in snow. In the early morning light it was a battlefield, the trees and land blown to bits, the road hammered and abused like it had supported a convoy. In the morning it was no man's land.

We got closer. The green blob became clearer and more defined, its edges and details now visible. There was frost on the windshield. I stood on the step and looked in the cab but Terry wasn't there. "What the hell," I said.

Officer Taylor pointed to the treeline. "Look."

Terry's orange vest was on a pile of logs. I knew it was his because it had a certain pattern that only the old ones had and the reflective tape had long worn away. It was old and faded and barely orange, and he wore it every day. He looked like he was just standing there. He didn't look right. I jumped down from the cab and ran, and the closer I got the more it made sense. He was in a pile of logs, leaning on one. His top half was perfectly upright, but I couldn't see his legs. It looked like he was standing between two logs, just standing there. There was a chainsaw in front of him, out of reach. His head was bowed like he was sleeping standing up. He was pinned between two logs at the waist. He had been cutting and the pile shifted and rolled and he was crushed in between. I couldn't see his legs under the pile, and the logs came so close together there was barely a gap. His pelvis looked crushed. He looked like a head and torso floating over a pile of logs.

I thought he was dead but he turned his head and whispered, "Joe."

For a second I thought I'd imagined him speaking. His face was pale, impossibly pale. Then he blinked and looked at me. My first thought was that he'd been like this all night.

"Terry," I said, trying hard to keep my voice steady. "Hey man, we're going to get you out of here." I stood back because I didn't want to walk on the logs and shift them even more, and have the whole shebang come down on top of him.

Officer Taylor came running up behind me and nearly ran into me. "Jesus Christ," he said.

"He's pinned. We've got to move the logs."

I saw a path to Terry through the logs and walked it. I stayed off the ones that were pinning him and the ones that looked like they might tumble. It was like walking on log piles when I was a kid, on the job sites with my father before the booze had consumed him. I'd climb the log piles to the top and yell: I'm the King of the Castle! He'd always yell at me to come down and I would, but not before I'd made it to the top. I'd come jumping down and he'd grab me by the scruff and say: Those logs can shift! Killed more than a few men out here! Growling because that's how he talked to his boys, because that's how his father had talked to him. Generation after generation of angry men. But angry at what, Sarah asked me once, what the hell are you so angry about that you need to come home and bury your head in six beer? I confessed that I didn't know, that it was just there and needed to be fed, that if I didn't feed it, I might become something less than a man, and certainly less than the wilderness. Like I couldn't be happy with what I had, like I was always looking for something more and was angry that I couldn't find it. My mother once told me that happiness was living in the moment. But without motion, without constant motion, a person can start to reflect on their life and see that they're simply a sum of their parts and nothing more. Booze had always been a way to kill the boredom of being idle, of not being in motion, but all it did was fuel the anger. But since Sarah had left, the anger had begun to fade, because being a father, being a good father, is to be constantly in motion. I realized what a piss-poor father I'd been before.

"It had to be you that come out here," Terry said.

"Ya, I'm sorry about that Terry. Let's call it water under the bridge."

He looked at me. He was paler than a living person should be. I put my hand on his cheek and he was ice cold.

"It don't look too good, Joe."

"You're gonna be alright. We just got to get these logs off you. The officer and I can carry you out. A couple days in the hospital and you'll be good as new."

"I didn't think anyone was going to come. Thought I was going to die first." He nodded at the chainsaw. "Saw a nice big one and wanted to cut a cookie for Deb. She's doing woodwork now. Got the whole garage rearranged for her and everything. Told me to keep an eye out for a nice one. I was going to surprise her. I cut it and doesn't the pile roll on me. Could have cut myself out but I dropped the saw. Tried for hours to reach it, just to get a finger on it. The dumbest thing." He grabbed the sleeve of my coat. "Joe I can't feel anything below my waist."

"It's okay buddy, you just hold on."

I walked back to Officer Taylor and told him I could cut the logs and free him up, but he just shook his head. "We can't do that. His pelvis is crushed. We remove the pressure and there's a chance he could bleed out. We have to get an ambulance out here."

"He's been like that all night."

"We can't risk it. I'll run back and radio for help. Stay with him. Keep him talking." He took a bottle of water from his coat. "Give him this, small sips. Do you have any blankets?"

"There should be an emergency blanket in the skidder."

"Take it, cover him up. He's in shock so you have to keep him talking."

He turned and I grabbed his arm. "Hey," I said. "How bad is it?"

He shook his head. "His hips looked crushed, maybe his spine. But the worst part is if there is major damage to his blood vessels. If the pressure of the logs is blocking the hemorrhaging, he will die as soon as we move the logs. That's why we can't move him until we get a doctor here."

"My God," I said.

"Just try to comfort him. Tell him he will be alright." He turned and started running and soon he had disappeared into the cut.

I got the blanket from the machine, and walked back across the logs to Terry. I draped the blanket around his shoulders, and put the bottle of water to his lips. He took a small sip.

"Where'd that cop run off to?"

"We need to get an ambulance out here before we move those logs, just to make sure it's okay."

"No ambulance is going to make it out here, Joe."

"A doctor, I mean."

He looked at me for what seemed like an eternity, and he seemed to understand something. But his eyes were opening and closing, like he was coming in and out of consciousness, like he was trying to get the gears moving in his head. "The look on that cop's face. Cut the shit, Joe."

"Terry, if I cut those logs away, I might do more damage. You just have to hold on a little while longer. I'm not going anywhere. I'll be right here with you."

"Haven't felt 'em for hours."

"He's getting help. We're gonna help you."

"Thought I would die every damn time I closed my eyes. Know what it's like to fight sleep like that? Worse than any pain."

"Keep those eyes open, Terry. Keep looking at me, keep talking."

He tried to laugh but coughed instead. "Yesterday ... yesterday I would have said just kill me if I knew it would've been you. But today it's nice just to talk to somebody. I miss my wife."

"We're going to get you home to Deb."

He reached out and I took his hand. "I'm sorry for what I said to Jenny. My Deb, she always knows the truth. That's the thing about women, ain't it? They keep you in line. That Jenny, she's a good girl, but I was close to Dan. I was seeing it wrong. Deb told me that too. You tell her I'm sorry."

"You tell her yourself. You're a tough prick, Terry."

His head snapped back and came forward. "I'm so tired."

I squeezed his hand. I put his hands together and rubbed his palms. "You gotta stay awake Terry. Talk to me, you've gotta talk to me."

His eyes opened and he managed a smile. "You gonna write me up?"

"Damn right I will."

"Last night I asked God to let me die."

"You're not going to die."

"Look at me."

"You're just stuck, man, that's all. Like you're caught in quicksand."

"Quicksand."

"Yeah, quicksand. Or those bogs we get. You know, when you step in and your boot gets stuck way down in the mud and you pull your foot out and your boot stays in the mud."

He laughed and exhaled deeply, and slumped forward a bit. I got beside him so he could lean on me. I kept rubbing his hands to keep the circulation going. I was afraid of what was below the logs, of what had become of his body below what I could see. Like his bottom half was caught in the jaws of a great shark that wouldn't finish him off, that took pleasure in torturing him.

The ravens cawed. The sun was rising and the blurry, living darkness was giving way to daylight. I couldn't imagine what he had gone through last night, what it had done to him. He was starting to shiver and I tightened the blanket around him. I got close to keep him warm, put my arms around him.

"I wish you would have brought me a coffee," he said. "You want me to talk. I'm going to talk about your father.

"We were good buddies back in the day, bet you didn't know that. We drank a lot … too much. One day Deb told me she'd had enough and to stop hanging around Freddie Adler, and I did, because I love my wife and would do anything for her, because it's the women who keep us in line. Men like your father and me, and you. Men who don't know how to say no or don't know how to control the rage that burns them from the inside. But your father, Joe, he didn't understand that. I know you understand it because you've found Jenny. I always liked your father, Joe, even when people were saying all that shit about him. I want you to know that stuff between us had nothing to do with him. I was sitting here all night thinking about things, because I knew it was going to be you who found me. I was sitting here waiting to die and wanted to make my peace with you before I did because that's what Deb would have wanted."

I squeezed his hands. "You're going to be fine."

"Sure am."

The sun crested the line of dense, black spruce on the horizon and flooded the cut. The warmth hit me full on the face and Terry closed his eyes. "That's nice," he said.

The ravens were loud. In the stillness, on the edge of the cut. Songbirds always know when winter is over. They announce it on warm spring mornings that smell like earth. But the ravens are ever-present. In the dead of winter, the heart of summer. They are always there, always observing. I sat beside Terry and we watched the cut. We waited for Officer Taylor.

I looked at Terry and knew that life was slipping away from him, like he had held on long enough to see the sun rise one last time. He was slumping over, slipping away, I held him up with my hand on his chest. His breathing became rapid, shallow. I talked to him about life, about how much I loved Jenny, and how I thought about Dan every day. I told him it was my fault that Dan had died. That he shouldn't have been out there alone. That he was right.

"But you got Jenny," he said. "You got what you needed."

He slumped over and I felt his weight on me. His breathing slowed, and his head rested on my shoulder. He gasped a few times and then he was quiet. I didn't move; I didn't want to disturb him. I wanted to give him time to get where he was going.

The cut was a war zone: stumps and slash piles, ice and snow. Broken-down machines at odds with the elements. Men, like soldiers, walking to their posts at the edge of civilization. We took from the land because it was all we knew, all we could do. We lived in the north and we needed to put food on the table. But there were trees, so many trees, more than enough to go around, more than enough for generations if it was managed properly, if they were replanted. We took from the land and every now and then it took from us and in my heart I believed that it was part of the deal, that the land required it. If you let your guard down even for a second the land will punish you. Terry knew it too. He knew he was responsible for his own death. And I thought of all the men I'd known in my life, during my own time and my father's time and my grandfather's time, men whose lives had ended at the hands of some accident, and knew that each one was in its own way a sacrifice, as though their deaths could somehow allow the rest of us to keep harvesting.

I watched Officer Taylor approach from the far end of the cut. A black smudge of uniform crossing the barren no man's land. He carried a heavy blanket under his arm like a football. He was fifty yards away when he saw how Terry was slumped against me, and he knew that he was dead but he kept running anyways, hoping that maybe he was just passed out, that it wasn't too late.

He got closer and looked at me and said, "Goddammit."

My arms were still around Terry. "He held on as long as he could."

He sat down on the end of a log. He was shaking his head. "The death," he said. "I'll never understand this place."

"I don't expect that you ever will."

I stood up and walked across the logs and Officer Taylor reached out to help me down.

"But you stayed with him," he said. "You could have asked me to stay but you did."

"What else would I do?"

"I know people who wouldn't have. People who would have considered it my job, not theirs."

"I don't know those kinds of people."

He nodded and kind of smiled but there were tears in his eyes, emotion for the first time since I'd known him, emotion even though he was on the job. And I knew at the first opportunity he'd be out of this town, off to where the job was more in line with what they'd taught him in school, off to where things made sense.

He walked across the logs to make sure Terry Pike was dead. He checked for a pulse. The sunlight was on Terry's cheek; it was going to be warm day. The winter road was on its last legs.

"They'll be at the landing by now," he said.

"I can't leave him alone out here."

He looked at me. He was fighting back the tears. "Okay Joe. Do what you gotta do."

He walked into the cut, and I was left alone with Terry Pike.

That night I went to Jenny's. I stood in her doorway for a long time without saying a word before she took me by the arm. I thanked her for taking care of Anna and for holding down the fort, and she told me to come inside.

"It's nighttime, Jenny."

"After the night you've had."

"It wouldn't be right."

"Please."

"I think I love you."

She took my head in her hands, looked at me with those beautiful dark eyes and a sadness that was reserved just for me, that put my pain first despite everything she'd gone through, that made me love her even more than I realized. "Love is love, nothing purer than that, Joe. But you're in no state."

"What do you want from me?"

"I want you to be sure before you tell me that you love me. And I want you to stay the night."

"Are you sure?"

"After the day you've had."

"I don't want to confuse the girls."

"You don't think they know what's going on?"

"They're little girls."

"Perceptive little girls. There isn't any other kind."

"What will people say?"

"It doesn't matter."

"If it's what you want."

"It's what I want."

"Jenny, the next time I'll be sure."

"I know you will."

She led me down the hallway past Gracie's room where the girls were already sleeping. We entered Jenny's room, and it was the first time I'd been inside. She went to the bathroom. I looked for a picture of Dan and couldn't find one. The bed was neat and tidy, a thick flower-print duvet. I looked out the window and the street was quiet, my truck parked in the driveway. I sat on the edge of the bed and waited for Jenny. She came out wearing a plaid shirt and her legs were bare and she held a glass of water in her hand. She told me that she wanted to be near me, to feel my heat. She said that what she missed most was human contact, having someone there beside her. I held her for a long time.

That night I thought about Dan Lacroix, how he looked in the cut, how a split-second can change so many people's lives. I felt Jenny's warmth beside me, and hoped that I belonged. I knew that if we were together, we'd have to do things right. We'd have to live under one roof; we'd have to be a family. It was the only way we could do it and keep our pride. We'd have to own it. But like she said: I was in no state. I was living in the moment. Tonight was tonight and we'd worry about tomorrow, tomorrow.

I put my arm around her. It was nice just to hold her, to be near her. It was seven months since Dan died and Sarah left, but it didn't matter. Sometimes a thing is meant to be, and all you need is the circumstance to make it so. You're only given a few chances in this life, so you have to make something of the ones you get, is what I subscribe to.

SUMMER

31

The morning dampness was enough to keep the dust down, which on these industrial roads can be enough to drive you crazy. The way it coats your truck inside and out, how you have to keep your windows up on the hottest days. It glides through windows open just a crack and you can taste it on your tongue, feel it on your skin. You slap the passenger seat and it rises in a cloud, reflecting off the sunlight in a million little flecks, drifting through the cab and coming to rest right where it started.

It was June, and I took the back way to my grandfather's cabin, retracing my father's path. The roads were tight and overgrown, with two gravel tracks and a row of tall grass in the middle that rubbed the axles and undercarriage, and alders that grew across the road. The summer heat had started already and the blackflies were something else. They came through the open window and congregated on the back window of the truck, crawling like ants across the surface, because blackflies never bite indoors.

I drove through the old cut where the replanted jack pine were fifteen years old, and grew in long, straight rows. If it were August it'd be drier than Arizona and the cicadas would be loud and plentiful. But it was still early and in the deepest parts of the bush the ground was wet and cold.

I drove by a pond with a beaver dam that ran alongside the road for a good fifty metres. The dam was built up nice and high and the water level was a few feet above the road and spilled over the side of the dam in places, flowing across the road in little creek beds. On the low side there was a mess of trees flooded from the slow flow of water across the road. The beaver house was on the far side of the pond, which had started to flood out the bush on the other side of the road as well. It was a real mess. More than once I'd destroyed a beaver dam flooding our access road. But all this does is buy you some time. The only way to take out a problem beaver is to shoot it when it leaves the safety of the pond, and I've done that a few times too. But it's nothing like the old days when the problem was dealt with using a stick of dynamite. You've never seen so many sticks and guts and gallons of water in the air at the same time, my grandfather used to say.

I hadn't been to the cabin since the night I knocked Terry Pike out cold. I hadn't touched the whiskey, either. Things were going good and I meant to keep it that way. I came around the corner and the ruins were still there, right where they were supposed to be. I had imagined everything gone, washed away, covered over in soil and grass and in my heart I wished this was the case.

I walked across the burned-out cabin floor where grass grew between the boards. The wood was charred black like the fire had ripped through the day before and the ruins looked like the remains of a forest fire, trees and logs charred and smudged permanently black. A fire rips a terrible hole in the bush, but it always rejuvenates. Old forest needs to make room for the new growth.

I stared at the cast-iron stove, and the ground beneath it. I remembered the plywood that was there, and I remembered it not being there after my grandfather went missing. I suppose if I had been paying attention, I might have made the connection, but I was just a kid and despite it all, deep down, I suppose I had loved my father.

I opened the cellar door and shone in my flashlight and the whiskey bottles shone back. I reached down and pulled them out, their labels faded and worn. One by one, I poured them into the tall grass beside the pickup before I could think too long about it, because I didn't want a reason to come out here again. Because the sad truth was that I'd keep coming as long as that shit was buried in the ground. Things get hard, it's easy to take the drive. It was how my grandfather and father had handled things, and I didn't want to be them anymore. I owed more to Anna, and to Jenny. Whiskey's a tricky thing. It hides in the smallest, deepest places, and it never goes bad. You could dig a bottle out of the ground after fifty years and it would still be as potent as the day you buried it and that is its power. It makes it too easy to take the easy way out.

I took out the ammunition box and looked inside. The gun was right where I'd left it. I put it in my pickup and headed into town, and this time I knew that I was never coming back.

I walked into the police station with the ammunition box under my arm. There was a new cop sitting behind the counter and I asked to see Officer Taylor. He pointed down the hallway to a little office where Officer Taylor was standing at his desk, putting things in a box.

"Joe," he said. "What can I do for you?"

"Looks like you're packing up."

"I'm headed out."

"I thought you had another year to go."

"Seems like they need me somewhere else." He looked at the ammunition box. "What have you got there?"

I put it on his desk and opened it up. "I was out at the cabin today, what's left of it. This was my grandfather's. I didn't know what else to do with it."

"Any papers with it?"

I shook my head.

"A gun without papers, well that can be a tricky situation." He took it out of the box and looked it over. "No lock, either."

He sat down behind his desk and motioned to the chair in front of his desk, and I sat too. "Listen, Joe, I asked to be transferred out."

"Just when you were getting settled."

"I don't think I could ever get settled here. It's just … it's not a good fit."

"Some people are built for this place and some aren't. My wife wasn't, and she lived here all her life."

"It's not just any other town, is it?"

"No," I said. "It's much more than that. I don't hate you, Officer Taylor, I just like my little freedoms that don't hurt anybody."

"And this?" he said, pointing at the gun.

"Truth is, I don't want it in my life anymore. And burying it in the bush isn't going to cut it."

"But it's not hurting anybody, as you say."

"But it's my decision. It's what I want, not what you or anyone else wants. I hated that cabin. Always have."

He put the gun back in the box and set it on his desk. "There's this program they run in Toronto, in the rough neighbourhoods. They take in guns and don't ask questions, because a gun can be a hard thing to get rid of, for a person trying to do the right thing. You understand what I'm saying?"

"I do."

"Take care of yourself, Joe." He reached out and shook my hand.

"Same to you."

I stepped outside and the sun was beating down; it was going to be a hot summer. I drove down the main drag and just about every other house was boarded up. In the abandoned yards grass grew high and gravel driveways were weed-covered. I remember this town as a booming place, when there were three bars and five restaurants and things happened on a Friday night. When I was a kid this town had a heartbeat. The streets were full of children, the kids of miners and loggers. Hard-working families from all over the world, because if you were willing to put in the work, the land had a place for you. The town had a strong sense of identity. There was a brotherhood.

Now it's different. The kids are grown and the ones who stayed either make a killing or make nothing at all. The opportunities that mining and forestry provided in the seventies and eighties are all but gone. You can buy a house for under fifty thousand dollars but it's almost impossible to sell one. More people move to town to exploit cheap rent and welfare checks than move in for steady work. So many people have left that you wonder what the point of staying is. But I'll tell you what it is. It's the landscape that keeps me here. It's the bush, the lakes, and the rivers. It's having all these things in my backyard and the freedom to go wherever the hell I want. It's the endless crown land and the fact that it belongs to all of us, that no matter what a newbie cop tries to tell you, it always will. It's because it's difficult that it's important to stay, because resilience shows your mettle. And the people who grew up here, who stayed here, did because it meant something to them. The little freedoms, the small allowances, all of it. They stayed because the town's a part of them, because if everybody left to make six figures in Alberta then there wouldn't be anybody left. There are old people who need their families, and young people who want an opportunity, a reason to stay. But it's a decision that every person who stays makes, a decision to stay and try to build something out of the ashes. I guess I have the hard-working immigrant spirit that my grandfather had. I guess I see the value in rolling up your sleeves. If there's one thing I know it's that nothing good comes easy. You have to work at it. You have to take heart.

I pulled into Jenny's driveway and she was in the front yard with our girls. They were digging up the garden at the front of the house, laying fresh soil and planting flowers she'd bought at the hardware store. Jenny was manning the trowel while Gracie and Anna were planting the flowers. Maggie was on a blanket in the middle of the yard, playing with one of her toys.

I walked over and Anna ran into my arms like she always did when I got home, nearly tackling me to the ground, yelling, "Daddy!"

Jenny was standing on the lawn with her hands on her hips. There was soil and mud and dirt on her jeans and face. She was smiling with the sun beating down on her, and this is how she looked in the summer.

"So?"

"He took it, not a question asked."

"I told you."

"You were right," I said. "I didn't think he had it in him."

"People can change."

We sat on her front porch while the girls planted flowers. Jenny went inside and came out with a couple of cold ones. I kicked off my work boots.

"Everything set for tomorrow?"

"Truck's gassed up, mostly loaded."

"How long will you be gone?"

"Two weeks out there, less than a week back. We're going to do some camping in the mountains. Maybe I'll bum around Victoria for a day or two. We're in no rush. I'm going to show Anna this country."

"It will be good for you two."

"It will be good for us."

I watched the girls plant the last flowers and bring the hose from around back.

Jenny said, "Not too much water. You don't want to drown them."

"They really are like sisters," I said.

She smiled. "I wouldn't have it any other way."

I put my arm around her and she held my hand. I watched the girls and thought about a life with Jenny, what that would be like. And I knew that it would be exactly like this moment, right now. It would be our house and yard, our girls. It would be this and more. It would be honest.

32

We headed down the highway in the light of early dawn. It was six-thirty and I watched for moose along the shoulder. In the summer, they move by the coolness of night and early morning, and have been the end of many a road trip.

I've always been an early riser. In high school when my friends slept until noon I was up and out, my nose into something or other. Once the sun crested the trees and the birds started chirping I got a move on, afraid that if I didn't the day would get away from me, and that my life would follow. It's how I've lived my life, always in motion, always in the bush. Hunting, fishing, scouting, working, it doesn't much matter; it's really all the same.

I realize now that Sarah and I had nothing in common. We were high school lovers and we should've never been more than that. But isn't that what happens, isn't that the way it goes? And the years we were living together and I was living my dream, she was feeding hers. All that time she was saving it up until she could no longer contain it because that's what true passion is, and I couldn't fault her for that. I never understood Sarah until I understood myself, and for that to happen she had to leave.

We were heading to Victoria because I'd promised Anna she could spend the summer with her mom. So, I'd packed the truck with camping gear, put the maps and road atlases on the passenger seat, and planned to make an adventure of it. I told Anna the mountains would be beautiful, but first there were the prairies which were beautiful in their own way. And even before that, I said, is Lake of the Woods and that area west of

Thunder Bay, which is just about one of my favourite places on earth. Seven hours to Manitoba, four days to British Columbia, because that's how big this country is.

Sarah had suggested we put Anna on a plane again, but I said that wasn't going to happen as long as I could help it. A child needs to be with her parents. A little girl needs her mother. That was something Jenny told me the night that Terry Pike died and I came over on no sleep and messed up and cried like a baby. Cried the way my father did that morning he came home. And I knew she was right. I knew that the best parts of Sarah were the parts that made her leave, and if Anna was going to be strong and fierce and somebody to be reckoned with then she would need those parts. I didn't hate Sarah anymore. I just hated her timing. But there would be summers, and vacations. There would be a relationship.

I loved Jenny and I was sure she loved me, but I had to be sure. I had to be one hundred percent. Because my whole life I'd thought I loved a woman, when maybe I just loved the idea of her. Maybe all that time Sarah was just a warm body, a comfort, a lay. It sounds harsh but how many people have lived their lives the exact same way? Afraid of change because they don't want to lose what they have, afraid that what they have is as good as it will ever get, afraid to take a plunge, afraid that true happiness or true sorrow could somehow be worse than a life of mediocrity. And here was Jenny, and she was beautiful and smart and we clicked in a way I'd never clicked with anyone before and it felt like truth but how the hell did I know what was truth and what was a lie? I'd lived one for years and I didn't even know it. It took Sarah to show me what truth really was. I needed to trust my gut again. I hoped that a few weeks away would give me clarity. I hoped that out there in those mountains I'd find some truth, and that when it came, it would tell me everything I already knew and everything I wanted to hear.

ACKNOWLEDGEMENTS

I would like to thank my beautiful wife for reading the first draft, providing unapologetic insight, and for putting up with my nonsense. My lovely daughter for teaching me the meaning of selflessness, and how to write after seven pm. My father, for his boundless knowledge of the bush, his expertise on grammar, and for being, as always, my first editor. My mother and sister for their support and encouragement. Joan Barfoot, for her valuable input on an early draft. Dan Telegdi, for explaining what happens to the human body under impossible loads. Jesse Castillo, for being a great friend, and for his knowledge on policing. karlson Hunter for taking the time to school me on forestry and fix all my early procedural errors. Robin Philpot, Publisher of Baraka Books, for believing in the story I'm trying to tell. Nick Fonda and David Warriner for their excellent editorial work. The Ontario Arts Council, an agency of the Government of Ontario, for the grant that allowed me to take five months to only write. And my hometown, for a lifetime of memories, because the north is my heart and soul, always has been, always will be.

Notable Fiction from Baraka Books

A Stab at Life, A Mystery Novel by Richard King

Exile Blues by Douglas Gary Freeman

Fog by Rana Bose

The Daughters' Story by Murielle Cyr

Yasmeen Haddad Loves Joanasi Maqaittik by Carolyn Marie Souaid

Vic City Express by Yannis Tsirbas (translated from the Greek by Fred A. Reed)

A Beckoning War by Matt Murphy

The Nickel Range Trilogy by Mick Lowe
 The Raids
 The Insatiable Maw
 Wintersong

And from QC Fiction, an imprint of Baraka Books

Songs for the Cold of Heart by Eric Dupont (translated by Peter McCambridge) 2018 Giller Finalist

The Little Fox of Mayerville by Éric Mathieu (translated by Peter McCambridge)

Prague by Maude Veilleux (translated by Aleshia Jensen & Aimée Wall)

In the End They Told Them All to Get Lost by Laurence Leduc-Primeau (translated by Natalia Hero)

Notable Nonfiction

The Complete Muhammad Ali by Ishmael Reed

A Distinct Alien Race, The Untold Story of Franco-Americans by David Vermette

Through the Mill, Girls and Women in the Quebec Cotton Textile Industry, 1881-1951 by Gail Cuthbert Brandt

The Einstein File, The FBI's Secret War on the World's Most Famous Scientist by Fred Jerome

Montreal, City of Secrets, Confederate Operations in Montreal During the American Civil War by Barry Sheehy

Printed by Imprimerie Gauvin
Gatineau, Québec